Praise for *Before We Were Strangers*

LIVING MAGAZINE "NEW ROMANCE CLASSIC" PICK
LATINA MAGAZINE PICK

"*Before We Were Strangers* is as steamy as it is sweet. With two characters who are meant to be but just can't get the timing right, Renée Carlino has mastered the missed connection. I found myself rooting for Matt and Grace at every turn and aching to crawl into the book to go back to the '90s to join them. Evocative, tender, and satisfying, Carlino has outdone herself."
— Taylor Jenkins Reid, author of *Maybe in Another Life*, *After I Do*, and *Forever Interrupted*

"Powerful and poignant, *Before We Were Strangers* captures the magic and heartache of first love. I couldn't turn the pages fast enough."
— Tracey Garvis-Graves, *New York Times* bestselling author of *On the Island* and *Covet*

"I loved every single thing about this book! Nostalgia, first love, the echo of heartbreak, the rocky road to where you were always meant to be — this book has everything and then some. You can't help but be transported."
— Jay Crownover, *New York Times* bestselling author of *Better When He's Bad*

"Sometimes we need a reminder that love is worth fighting for. *Before We Were Strangers* is a beautiful, real, heartfelt reminder."
— Kim Holden, author of *Gus* and *Bright Side*

"I felt like I found a piece of my soul in this book. I've highlighted so many lines to use as a reference for daily inspiration. I was that moved."
— Kim Jones, author of *Red*

"This is one of the most romantic, heartfelt and consuming books I've ever read. To say that I'm in love with it would feel like the biggest understatement, ever . . . I'm blessed, so insanely lucky, to have found a story that I finished reading with tears in my eyes and a more beautiful outlook on life, love and believing in second chances."

—*Book Baristas*

"Exquisitely written. . . . I highly recommend this if you're in the mood for a really great, heartfelt journey, loaded in angst and healing, all in the name of true love."

—*Maryse's Book Blog*

Praise for *After the Rain*

"Renée Carlino's writing is deeply emotional and full of quiet power. You won't be disappointed."

—Joanna Wylde, *New York Times* bestselling author

"*After the Rain* tore me up in the best way possible. Sexy, sweet, and sad, all woven together with an overwhelming undercurrent of hope, Nate and Avelina's story is one that goes straight to my list of all-time favorites."

—Amy Jackson, *New York Times* bestselling author

Praise for *Nowhere but Here*

"There is a certain 'magic' or 'spark' or whatever you want to call it that really makes a book come to life as you read it. As a reader, I'm on a constant search for that special spark and I absolutely found it here. *Nowhere but Here* was a unique and beautifully written love story. I laughed, I swooned, I wiped happy tears away, and I fell in love. This book warmed my heart and left me with the most wonderful feeling. I highly recommend it for all fans of romance!"

—*Aestas Book Blog*

"The kind of romance that gives you butterflies in your stomach, that tingly feeling all over, and a huge smile on your face. . . . If you are looking for something emotional, where you can truly experience what the characters are feeling through the beautifully written words of an amazing author, complete with a wonderful epilogue that will give you a sense of completeness, then look no further."

—*Shh Mom's Reading*

Praise for *Sweet Thing*

"Sassy and sweet, *Sweet Thing* melts in your mouth and goes straight to your heart!"

—Katy Evans, *New York Times* bestselling author of *Real*

"Surprisingly, this is Renée's debut novel because she writes like a pro with words flowing effortlessly and beautifully, totally hooking me from the beginning. There was something intangibly real and special about this book, which kept me reading until I finished it . . . one of my favorite stories of the year."

—*Vilma's Book Blog*

ALSO BY RENÉE CARLINO

SWEAR ON THIS LIFE

A Novel

RENÉE CARLINO

ATRIA PAPERBACK
New York London Toronto Sydney New Delhi

ATRIA PATERBACK
An Imprint of Simon & Schuster, Inc.
1230 Avenue of the Americas
New York, NY 10020

First Atria Paperback edition August 2016

ATRIA PAPERBACK and colophon are trademarks of Simon & Schuster, Inc.

For information about special discounts for bulk purchases, please contact Simon & Schuster Special Sales at 1-866-506-1949 or business@simonandschuster.com.

The Simon & Schuster Speakers Bureau can bring authors to your live event. For more information or to book an event contact the Simon & Schuster Speakers Bureau at 1-866-248-3049 or visit our website at www.simonspeakers.com.

10 9 8 7 6 5 4 3 2

Library of Congress Cataloging-in-Publication Data has been applied for.

ISBN 978-1-5011-0579-1
ISBN 978-1-5011-0580-7 (ebook)

To Anthony, you're always the just one person

SWEAR ON THIS LIFE

1. He Found Me

In class we say *That's too on the nose* when someone has written a story or a scene where exactly what you think *should* happen *does* happen. Or when the events are too perfect or precise. But in real life we have a hard time recognizing serendipitous moments because we're not making the story up as we go along. It's not a lie—it's really happening to us, and we have no idea how it will end. Some of us will look back on our lives and recall events that were a bit too perfect, but until you know the whole story, it's impossible to see the universe at work, or even admit that there is something bigger than us, making sure everything that *should* happen *does* happen. If you can surrender to the idea that there might be a plan, instead of reducing every magical moment to a coincidence, then love will find you. He found me.

"WOW, THE SEAGULLS are going crazy. I think there's a tsunami headed this way," I said, staring out the window of my second-story apartment as I watched the marine layer thicken over La Jolla Cove. The fog was moving fast toward my building as the storm clouds swirled in the distance.

Trevor laughed. "Such a San Diegan, overreacting to the weather." He was sitting on the floor with his back against the overpriced leather couch that my aunts Cyndi and Sharon had bought for me when I first moved in.

"Do you think we need sandbags?"

"No, you're being crazy," he said.

"Crazy or cautious?"

"More like neurotic. It's drizzling. California is still technically in a drought."

I noticed that Trevor had put down the short story I had written so he could continue playing Angry Birds on his phone.

"Trevor . . ." I warned.

"Emiline . . ." he teased back without looking up.

I plopped onto his lap and threw my arms around his neck. "I really want you to read it."

"I did. I read it fast."

"What's it about, then?"

"It's about a girl who discovers an ancient formula for cold fusion."

"So you got the gist. But did you actually like it?"

"Emi . . ." He paused. His eyes darted around the room. When he focused on me again, I saw pity in his face. "I liked it a lot," he said.

"But . . . ?"

"I think you should write what you know. You're a good writer, but this"—he held up the paper—"seems a little silly."

"Silly? Why?" I could feel anger boiling over inside of me. Trevor was honest—it was one of the reasons I liked him—but sometimes he was blunt to the point of belittling.

"For one, it's unrealistic."

"It's science fiction," I shot back.

"It needs more character development." He shrugged as if his statement were obvious.

"Trevor, please don't start spewing that Writing 101 crap at me. I get enough of that in the program. I want to practice what I preach. I'm constantly telling the undergrads to forget the rules and write intuitively. Now I'm asking you for realistic feedback, from a reader's point of view, not an instructor's."

"I'm trying to. I thought that's what I was doing. You know how hard it is for me to critique your work. You can't handle it. I didn't connect with the characters, so I wasn't interested in reading the rest of the story. So there. I'm just being honest."

"There's a nice way to be honest," I muttered.

"I still finished the story, and now I'm trying to help you, but you're not being receptive to it. Just tell me what you want me to say."

I crossed my arms over my chest. "Are you serious right now?"

"Yes." He got up abruptly and I toppled over onto the floor.

"You're not a reader. I shouldn't have asked you to read it. Are we actually fighting over this?"

"We're always fighting over this," he said. "And I resent you for saying that I'm not a reader, as if I'm some kind of illiterate Neanderthal."

I had been dating Trevor since our senior year at Berkeley, so I knew exactly where this insecurity was coming from. Seven years—that's a long time in anyone's book. When we met, he was a superstar quarterback destined for the NFL, and I was a bookworm trying to be a wordsmith. He was Tom Brady handsome, and for so long I wondered why he was into me at all. Yet for some reason, in the beginning, it just felt right. We got along beautifully, and our relationship went on like a fairy tale—until he injured his throwing arm in the last game of the season. His professional football career was over before it even began.

He graduated unglamorously and then took an assistant offensive coaching job at San Diego State so he could be closer to me while I worked on my MFA at UC San Diego. It was a major show of dedication, but I couldn't help but feel like a little light had gone off inside of him. He was there in San Diego with me, but sometimes I felt like he wanted to be somewhere else.

The dynamics of any long-term relationship tend to shift in subtle ways, but for us, the change was more abrupt: the moment he got injured, I wasn't the nerdy bookworm infatuated with the star quarterback anymore. And while that never bothered me, it definitely bothered him. Even after he followed me to San Diego, we continued to live separately, and neither one of us pressed the issue, even after I finished my MFA. I told myself I was waiting for him to make the move, to own the decision, but honestly I didn't know if I wanted to move in with him either.

So I kept living with my roommate, Cara, a fellow graduate from the UCSD writing program. She was saving money and teaching a couple of writing courses while she worked on her first novel, and I was trying to do the same. Her longtime boyfriend, Henry, was a surgical resident in New York, and she planned to move at the end of the school year to be with him. I knew I had to figure something out by then, but arguments like this made me think Trevor and I still weren't ready to take the next step.

"I'm going for a run," I said to Trevor as I hurried toward my bedroom to get dressed.

"What? One minute you're worried about a tsunami and the next you want to go for a run? What the hell?" He followed behind me. "Emi, you're going to have to deal with your shit at some point."

"*My* shit? What about *your* shit?" I said flatly as I sat on the floor, tying my shoes. I wasn't even looking at him. I got up and tried to move past him to leave the room. I might have been carrying around some baggage, but so was Trevor.

"You have to stop running every time I want to have a bigger conversation with you."

"Later," I said.

"No, now," he said firmly.

I shimmied between his body and my bedroom door and headed toward the kitchen. I busied myself filling up a water bottle.

"We've been together since we were twenty, Emi."

"Jesus, I just asked you to read a fucking story."

"It's not about the story."

"What is it about, then?" I asked sharply.

He looked frustrated and defeated, which was rare for him. I felt a twinge of guilt and softened.

"Trevor, I don't know if you can tell, but I'm having

a hard time with my writing right now. I don't want to be an adjunct creative writing professor forever. Do you get that?"

"You're already a writer, Emi." He seemed sincere, but it wasn't exactly what I wanted to hear.

"All of the other adjuncts have been published in some right, except for me."

"Cara's been published?"

"Twice," I said under my breath.

He hesitated before continuing. "You want to know what I think? It's not a lack of talent, Emi. I just don't think you're writing what you know. Why don't you try writing about yourself? Explore everything you went through when you were a kid?"

I felt myself getting mad again. He knew my childhood was off-limits. "I don't want to talk about it, and besides, you're totally missing the point."

Pulling my hoodie up over my hair, I pushed the door open and jogged down the stairs toward the walkway as the rain pelted my face. I heard Trevor slam the door and jog down the steps behind me. I stopped on the sidewalk, turned, and looked up at him. "What are you doing?"

"I'm going home," he said.

"Great."

"We still need to talk."

I nodded. "Later." He turned on his heel and walked away. I stood for a moment before turning in the opposite direction . . . and then I was running.

I was convinced that the years of therapy my aunt Cyndi and her partner, Sharon, had paid for guaranteed my past would always be just that. Still, I knew in the back of my mind that I hadn't quite dealt with what happened on that long dirt road in Ohio, all those years before I came to live with Cyndi and Sharon. I was guarded and withdrawn, hiding in my relationship with Trevor, in my job as an adjunct professor, in my writing. I knew all of this, but I wasn't sure how to get out of the rut.

After a few miles, I found myself jogging through the parking lot at UCSD, getting thoroughly soaked by massive raindrops.

"Emi!" I heard Cara call from behind me. "Wait up!"

I turned and tightened the strings on my hoodie. "Hurry, I'm getting drenched!"

Cara's straight blonde hair clung to her cheeks, making her look even thinner than she was, as she jogged toward me. She was the opposite of me—tall, lanky, with light hair and light eyes. I had frizzy, dark hair that flew everywhere, all the time.

We took cover beneath the overhang of the building that housed the creative writing department. "Jeez, Emi, your hair." Cara tried unsuccessfully to pat it down as we walked into the building and shook the water off our clothes. Before I could retort, we caught sight of Professor James as he was locking up his office.

"Professor!" Cara called.

He fit every possible stereotype of a college professor. He was plump, had a thick beard, and always dressed in herringbone or argyle. It was easy to imagine a pipe dangling from the side of his mouth as he talked.

"Do you have those notes on my story for me?" Cara asked.

"As a matter of fact, I do." He shuffled through his

distressed leather briefcase and handed Cara a stack of papers. "I've written them in the margins."

Cara craved constructive criticism, but I never found the professor's notes all that helpful, even when I was in the program. After I graduated, I stopped letting him read my work.

As she scanned his marginalia, Professor James looked me over. "What are you working on, Emiline?"

"Just doing scene exercises." I looked away, avoiding his stare.

"I didn't mean with your students. I meant with your personal projects."

I thought idly that the only personal project I wanted to work on was plucking my eyebrows and shaving my legs. "Oh, just some short stories."

"If you ever want some feedback, feel free to drop your work off in my office."

I shifted uncomfortably. "Thanks, I'll consider it."

I glanced at Cara's story and noticed, in bold red writing, at the top of the page, the note *BRILLIANT!!*

Professor James nodded good-bye and walked away. I turned to Cara. "Two exclamation points? He's never said anything that nice about my work."

Cara frowned. "You know what I think about that, Emi."

"Oh man, here we go."

"I know you don't like to hear it, but it's true. Maybe you're writing about the wrong stuff."

First Trevor, now Cara? "I'm really good at baking—does that mean I should be a baker?"

"You know that's not what I mean," she said.

"I know." I looked down at my thrashed Nikes. "I'm just

tired of missing the mark on these short stories. Trevor basically panned my last one." I looked up and nodded toward the end of the hall. "Come on, let's walk."

We headed toward the staff room to check our mailboxes in silence.

"Maybe you could work on a memoir? Even if you don't finish it, you might figure out what you want to explore in your short fiction. Something that's more personal to you?"

"No, thanks," I said, hoping that my tone conveyed how much I wanted her to drop it. She seemed to have gotten the hint and abruptly changed the subject.

"So, have you heard of this new writer that everyone's talking about? J. Colby?"

I shuffled through papers from my staff mailbox, tossing the junk mail in the trash. "No, who's that?"

"Columbia grad. He's around our age. I can't believe he's already published. Everyone's raving about his novel."

"Good for him," I said bitterly.

"Well, I'm going to read it, see what it's all about," she said as she jammed a sheaf of mail into her tote bag. "It's called *All the Roads Between*. Don't you love that title?"

"It's all right, I guess. Kind of reminds me of *The Bridges of Madison County* or something." I turned to her. "Okay, well, I'm done here. I'm gonna head home. You coming with?"

"I'll see you back there—just have to run a few errands. But, hey, you know what we should do since it's so rainy out? We should stay in, get takeout, watch trash TV, and drink until we pass out. That'll cheer you up, right?"

"I guess. Yeah . . . that sounds good. Great, actually. Let's do it." Never mind that I'd told Trevor I'd watch football with him and talk. What I needed was a night in with my best friend. "I'll pick up the wine, you get the Chinese?"

"Deal. See you at home."

THE SUN WAS going down behind the storm clouds as I sat on the window ledge and watched the waves crash against the rocks of the cove. I thought about the story I could write. I knew I had more than pages' worth of material. I had books' worth. I just didn't know if I could ever put the words to paper.

Cara came barreling through the door with a Barnes and Noble bag.

"They have Chinese food at Barnes and Noble now?" I joked.

"Our date is off! I went and got that book we were talking about, read twenty pages in the store, and could not put it down. I have to know what happens. Emiline, I'm in love with this author. I'm going to find him and make him marry me."

"How will Henry feel about that?" I teased.

She threw the bag on the counter and poured herself a glass of wine as I watched her from the window ledge. "He'll understand," she said, giggling.

"So you're bailing on me to read in your room?"

"You know how I am when I get into a book. I can't be stopped."

I understood exactly how she felt—I was the same way. "Fine, you're off the hook. But you owe me."

"Maybe Trevor can swing by with Chinese?"

I laughed. "You're ditching me but you want my boyfriend to bring us food?"

She leaned over the couch and smiled. "Are you mad?"

"No, I'm kidding. Go, read, enjoy!"

An hour later, when Trevor showed up with Chinese, Cara came out, got a plate, and darted back into her room.

"What's her deal?" he asked.

"She's really into her new book."

"Well, I guess it gives us time to talk." We sat down side by side at the breakfast bar, opening cartons silently, waiting for someone to go first.

After a few bites, I put my chopsticks down. "You want to talk? Fine? Why don't you ever tell me you love me?"

"I've told you I love you before," he said, astonished. "And this isn't what I wanted to talk about."

"Well, I do. You *have* said it but you don't say it often. Don't you feel like you can say it to me?"

"You never say it to me either."

Fair point. "I don't think we even know what it means," I said through a mouthful of sesame chicken.

"Whatever it is you're going through has nothing to do with me," he said. Trevor had this way of shifting responsibility away from himself in every argument. It drove me crazy.

"People are in relationships so they can share things with each other."

"This, coming from you? Emi, after seven years, I still barely know you. I only know what you share with me, which doesn't include anything from your past."

I could feel myself getting defensive. "Since we're playing the blame game, you haven't made much of an effort to get to know me, or to commit to me in any real way."

Trevor's face fell, and I could tell I'd struck a nerve.

"Are you serious? You keep saying you don't know where you'll end up a year from now. What does that even mean? How do you think that makes me feel?"

"Then why are you here?" I asked, simply. I didn't want to sound callous, but I could tell that I'd gone too far. That I was cutting him too deep.

"I moved down here for you, Emi. I built my life around our relationship." He got up from his stool. "We're not kids anymore. I can't deal with your fickle shit and listen to you say I won't make a commitment to you. You're the one who won't commit to me."

I felt all kinds of retorts bubbling inside of me. *The only job offer you got was at San Diego State. You didn't move here for me. I'm just the girl you're passing time with. We both know it. Why else would you have a hard time saying I love you? Why else can't I see our future?*

I got up and headed toward my room, and Trevor followed right behind me. I turned around to face him and rested my hand on the door for a moment as he waited silently in the doorway. And then I pulled him toward me and kissed him, pressing my body against his. I didn't want to talk anymore.

THE NEXT MORNING, as I drank coffee at the breakfast bar, Cara came skipping by. "What's eating you?" she asked. I didn't know how she could tell these things just by looking at the back of my head, but she could intuit moods like no one else. She poured herself a mug of coffee and leaned against the counter, facing me, waiting for my response.

"Trevor."

"Trevor eating you?" She smirked.

"Not in a good way, pervert." I rolled my eyes.

"Are you guys fighting again? Sounds like you made up last night."

"We're always fighting. Even when we're making up."

She straightened, as if something had just occurred to her, and then rushed off. "I'll be right back. Don't go anywhere."

When she came back into the kitchen, she set a book down in front of me. I glanced at the jacket. *All the Roads Between.* "You're finished already?" I asked.

"Stayed up all night. I loved it. You said I owed you one for bailing on you last night, and this is my repayment. I think you could use the escape."

"Oh yeah?" I ran my hand over the cover. It was a faint image of two kids holding hands on a road. There was something familiar about the scene, but I couldn't put my finger on it.

"Maybe you can escape your own slightly flawed love story for a bit and get lost in something more satisfying—even if it is fiction."

I sighed and picked it up. Maybe she was right. I grabbed my mug of coffee with my other hand and headed toward my bedroom. "Thanks, Care Bear," I called back.

"Anytime."

Once inside, I plopped down on my bed and cracked open the book to the first page. From the moment I read the second line in the first paragraph, my heart rate tripled. Instantly, I was sweating. By the end of the first page, I was almost hysterical.

From *All the Roads Between*

By the time our school bus would get to El Monte Road, Jax and I would be the only kids left. We'd bounce along past the open fields, past Carter's egg ranch, past a whole lot of run-down houses, dust clouds, and weeds. We lived right off El Monte, at the five–point-five-mile marker, at the end of a long, rutted, dirt road, our houses preceded by two battered mail-boxes askew on their dilapidated wood posts. It was a bone-shaking journey by car and almost impossible by bus, so Ms. Beels would pick us up and drop us off at the mailboxes every school day, rain or shine. Those mailboxes were where Jax and I would start and end our long journey.

Ms. Beels, a short, plump woman who wore mismatched socks and silly sweaters, was our bus driver from the time we were in first grade all the way until high school. She was the only constant and reliable person in my life. That is, be-sides Jax.

Every morning she would greet me with a smile and ev-ery afternoon, just before closing the doors and pulling away, she'd say, "Get on home, kids, and eat your veggies," as if our parents could afford such luxuries. Her life was exactly the same, day in and day out, but she still put a smile on and did her job well.

When your family is reduced to nothing, you look at people like Ms. Beels with envy. Even though driving a bus in a rural, crackpot town isn't exactly reaching for the stars, at the age of ten I still looked up to her. She had more than most people I knew back then. She had a job.

We lived in Neeble, Ohio, population eight thousand on a good day, home to ex-employees of the American Paper Mill factory, based in New Clayton. Most of the workers moved out of New Clayton just after the factory closed and brought their families to the rural, less populated towns where rent was cheap and the odd job less scarce.

My family had always lived in Neeble. My dad had grown up there, and his dad too. They would commute to New Clayton together when the factory was still running, starting and ending their days together the same as Jax and me. They were good friends and good men—at least that's how I remember them. And we had a nice life for a while. My father called what we had at the end of that road a little slice of heaven. And it was . . . for a long time. But if there's a real heaven here on earth, then there has to be a hell too. Jax and I learned that the hard way.

He and I weren't always friends. In the beginning he was just a smelly boy with dirty fingernails and shaggy hair covering his eyes. In the early years, I barely heard him utter a word except for "yes, ma'am" and "no, ma'am." He'd shuffle behind me all the way down that dusty road to where Ms. Beels would greet us. We'd climb onto the yellow Fern County school bus and hunker down for the long hour-and-a-half drive to school. I always sat in the very first seat, and he'd walk straight to the back.

As we passed through town, we'd pick up a whole bunch of kids, at least thirty of all ages, but the two I remember well, besides Jax, were world-class assholes. I was convinced that Mikey McDonald, with his blond crew cut and baggy pants, wanted to make my life hell.

"Emerson? What kind of name is that? Isn't that a boy's name?"

I would roll my eyes and try to ignore him. I never got a

chance to ask my parents what kind of crack they were smoking when they named me.

By the third grade, Mikey had a crony: Alex Duncan. Whatever I was carrying, they would walk by and try to slap it out of my hands, and then they would sit in the seat behind me on the bus and torture me all the way home. "Maybe you can marry a book someday, Emerson Booknerd. Haha, Booknerd. That could be your last name."

Alex had a big birthmark right on the end of his nose, like he had been sniffing shit. For so long I kept my insults to myself, but everything changed in the fourth grade. The factory had been closed for almost a year, the money was running out, and my father wasn't doing anything but drinking and listening to talk radio. Rush Limbaugh's Oxy-laced voice was more familiar to me than my own father's. He was shutting down. He had stopped talking. He got mean and so . . . my mom left. She left me alone with him, without even a brother or sister to help shoulder the burden.

Everything changes when a man can't afford to put food on the table. Some men rise to the occasion and find a way to make ends meet, no matter what it takes. Other men have too much pride to see that their life is crumbling down around them. My dad was a third-generation American Paper Mill worker, and Jax's dad was the same. It was all they knew.

After years of torment from Mikey and Alex, I hit my breaking point when quiet, reserved Jax decided to join in on their juvenile idiocy.

I always took care to make sure my clothes were clean and my face washed. After my mom left, my dad started hanging around with Susan, a woman who worked as a maid at a nearby motel. She didn't dress like a maid, but she always brought us those little soaps from the motel bathroom, so I guessed she was probably a maid. I had to use cheap motel soap for everything, including washing my hair, so naturally, after a few weeks of that, my bouncy brown curls became a frizzy mess. The kids on the bus called me Medusa. If only I had been that scary.

On a typically humid day in June, Jax followed me down the road and took his usual seat at the back. Halfway through the route, Mikey and Alex called Jax to come up and sit with them. They started giggling behind me.

"What, did you stick your finger in a light socket, Medusa?" Alex said.

"If I touch it, will it bite me?" Mikey taunted.

"Yeah, cool hair," Jax said.

I turned and shot daggers into his eyes. "Oh, nice one, Fisher. Real original. You better watch it or I'll tell your father." I didn't care about the other boys, but I wasn't about to take that shit from the neighbor kid. He didn't respond—he just stared right at me and then squinted slightly. He didn't come back with another insult; it even seemed like he felt bad. He wouldn't take his eyes off of mine, which was quite the statement for a fourth grader.

"Take a picture; it'll last longer," I said. He blushed and then looked away.

I heard Mikey say to Jax, "Will she really tell your father?"

Jax shrugged. "I don't care."

Alex turned his attention back to me. "We're so scared— Poodle Head is going to tattle on us. Ruff, ruff."

The boys continued their taunting without Jax's help. He just kept his head down and waited until it was just the two of us on the bus and we were speeding past the mile markers on

El Monte once again. I wasn't sure if Jax was frightened of my threat or if he realized what a bunch of twerps they were being, so I turned in my seat and peered over the bus bench at him. He was looking out the window. "I wasn't kidding, Jackson Fisher, I *will* tell your father."

"That might be kind of hard, Emerson. My dad's gone. He left." It was the first time I had ever heard him speak my name. He enunciated it so clearly, like an adult would do.

"Where'd he go?"

"Who knows? Where'd your mom go?"

I didn't think he even knew about my mom—I thought it was the big family secret. But then again, there's no such thing in a small town.

"They're not . . . you don't think . . ." I hesitated, embarrassed. *Jesus, did my mother take off with Jackson's dad?*

"No, they're not together. I just meant they went to the same place: away from us." He looked back out the window and stared straight ahead.

I felt sad and confused. I wanted to pinch his nose and tug on his ears for making fun of me, but I also wanted to hug him. I knew what he was feeling, and it hurt so bad it made my teeth ache. At least Jax had an older brother at home. I had no one but my books.

We didn't talk for the rest of the ride, but we did walk shoulder to shoulder in our amiable silence down the long dirt road. Something felt different, like a truce had been made. At the end of the road, I went into my dark house and he into his. I walked past my snoring father on the couch, clutching a bottle of Jack Daniel's. I went into my room, found a pair of scissors, plopped down in front of the mirror, and slowly and methodically cut off all of my hair. I dozed off without eating dinner and woke up at three a.m. to the sound of my father's drunken babbling. He was crashing into walls and cursing at no one. I cowered under the covers until he came stumbling through my bedroom door, my dark room filling with light from the hallway. I was terrified.

"What are you doing, Emerson?"

"I was sleeping. It's late, Dad. I have school tomorrow." I tried to make my voice sound small and penitent. He had food bits stuck in his mustache, and I wondered what he'd been eating. My fear was strong, but I was hungry enough in that moment to zero in on that detail.

His eyes narrowed as they adjusted to the darkness. "What in the hell did you do to your hair?"

"Nothing . . ." I reached up automatically to twirl my hair, but there wasn't much left of it. I cursed myself for destroying the one thing I used as a coping mechanism.

"Nothing?" he screamed. "Doesn't look like nothing!" He towered over me like a cartoonish, belligerent giant. I stood up weakly in his shadow and combed my fingers through my boyish cut. "I . . . I . . ."

"Shut up, you stupid, stupid girl. You're just like your stupid mother." He shook his head with such disappointment and disgust. "Get to bed."

I didn't know what version of my father I would get from one day to the next. At that age, it was hard for me to understand what he had gone through, losing the only job he knew how to do, and then his wife, all in rapid succession. Still, his alcoholism and rage couldn't be justified by his bad luck.

Curling up in a pile of blankets on the floor, I closed my eyes and prayed that one of us would disappear. Him or me—it didn't matter. When I heard him in the kitchen pouring another drink, I relaxed. He would drink until he passed out, I knew that. It was his routine, and I sure as hell didn't want to be there when he woke up with the mother of all hangovers. I stayed awake for a while longer and listened to make sure he wasn't coming back. Before I dozed off, I put a hardcover copy of *The Lion, the Witch and the Wardrobe* in the back of my pajama pants and fell asleep with my face buried in a pillow. Sometimes he would come in to spank me in the middle of the night, oftentimes for no reason. I wondered if all parents did that. I was ten, after all. I didn't exactly go around asking people these things.

By morning, I was so tired that my bones felt dense and my brain hazy. I didn't know how I would get through a whole school day. But the fear was too much to keep me home. School was my refuge, and books were my friends, so I got ready and headed toward the door. I tiptoed out of the house and went to sit on the short, brown fence in the front yard until Jax came out. I cried as I waited, sad that I didn't have a mother and that I didn't have any friends.

He came up behind me and flicked my hair. "We were joking. You shouldn't have cut it all off." I looked up at Jax and watched as understanding spread over his face. He knew I had been crying. That moment of sympathy was the exact moment that Jackson Fisher became my one and only friend.

"What's wrong, Emerson?"

"I got in trouble for cutting my hair. My dad was really mean about it."

"So you're crying because of your dad, not what I said to you, right?"

I nodded. "I don't want to cry anymore." My voice was hoarse.

"I'm really sorry." He said the words like he meant it:

pained, remorseful . . . gentle. His eyes were sincere. There was unfeigned honesty in his expression, even at that age. It was a look I would never forget. "It's not your fault your dad's an asshole," he said. He dug into his backpack and pulled out a Pop-Tart package. He took one pastry out for himself and then held out the other one toward me. "Hungry?" I grabbed at it like a feral animal and began chomping away. "Geez, slow down, Emerson. You're going to make yourself sick."

"I know, I know."

"Come on, we better get going."

Once we boarded the bus, Jax took the seat right behind me. When Mikey got on board, Jax said to him, "Sorry, this seat's taken. Find somewhere else to sit."

Ms. Williams, our fourth-grade teacher, could barely see past the first row of kids, let alone to me in the back of the classroom, so no one ever asked why I didn't have a lunch to carry out when the bell rang. We didn't ever have much food at home. My dad would give me a dollar here or there, and I would buy the cafeteria lunch, but most days I would just find stuff other kids threw out. That day, Jackson found me in the library as I was coming out at the end of our lunch period. He didn't say anything, just handed me half of a peanut butter and jelly sandwich. I said, "Thank you," went into the bathroom, and devoured it before the bell rang.

Later that afternoon, before we parted ways at the end of the road, Jax said, "Meet me behind the shed in an hour?"

The shed housed a bunch of old tools that no one used anymore, and it was just beyond a small patch of trees where our property line met the Fishers'. You couldn't see the shed from either one of our houses.

"Why?"

"Just do it."

"No, you're scaring me."

He shook his head. "Don't be scared. I cleaned it out. I go back there all the time."

My eyes widened. "I'm not scared of the shed . . ."

"You're scared of me?" He put his hand to his chest. "I'm trying to help you."

"Why?" I said.

"I don't know."

"How are you helping me?"

"I was going to bring you a plate of food. My mom leaves us casserole on the nights she has to work. I just didn't want Brian to know."

Brian was Jax's older brother by ten years. Whenever their mom had to work, Brian was in charge. He was in a band and would play his guitar in the garage at all hours of the night. My dad called him a druggie. Back then I didn't understand what that meant.

"Oh."

"Never mind, geez."

"No, I appreciate it, Jax. I just don't want you to get in trouble."

"I won't get in trouble. Meet me out there in an hour. If it's dark, there's a lantern right inside of the door on the left. Take a flashlight."

"Thank you."

He walked away toward his house, so I went inside mine. My father was sitting at the kitchen table, smoking a cigarette, holding a glass of brown liquid. The beige curtains were blowing delicately over the kitchen sink.

"It's windy today." I walked to the window and shut it. "It'll get all dusty in here if we leave the windows open."

He didn't respond. I walked to the refrigerator, opened the door, and scanned the contents. There was a jar of pickle relish, some expired salad dressing, and an open aluminum can of olives. I took the can and went to the trash to dump them out. My father glared at me as I crossed the kitchen. He waited until I dropped them in the trash can, and then he stood abruptly, scraping the chair legs over the dirty linoleum floor. Two long strides were all it took before he was towering over me.

"You got money to replace those?"

"You're not supposed to store food in an open aluminum can."

"Says who?"

"Mom said it can make you sick."

"Your mother's dead. And what I say goes." He seethed, a drop of saliva springing onto my cheek.

I wiped it away slowly and then felt my eyes well up. "What do you mean she's dead?"

"She's dead to us now." His eyes were molten, full of anger and rage, and he was gripping the refrigerator door so hard I thought it would break apart inside of his hand.

"Okay, Dad." Very timidly I said, "Is it okay if I go next door for casserole?"

"Do whatever you want." He slammed the refrigerator and walked away.

I went to my room and grabbed a sweatshirt and then headed out into the fading light of dusk. The shed was about a football field's length away, and I had to walk through knee-high weeds to get there. Sticker bushes clung to my socks and pant legs, but it was worth it for a warm meal. As I walked, I thought about where my mother had gone. She was dead to my father but to me she was still alive somewhere living a better life. I didn't hate her. I didn't understand her, but I didn't hate her. I just wished she would've taken me with her.

When I got to the shed, the narrow wooden door swung open. "Come in, hurry!" Jax whispered.

He wasn't lying; he'd cleaned the shed out and made it into quite the pleasant little fort. There was a small table with two chairs and an old camping cot in the corner. Jax reached behind me and lifted a butane lamp onto the table. He turned the dial, opening the valve, and pressed a button to click the flint until the lamp was on. There was one window that looked out of the back of the shed to the tree line in the distance. The sky was getting dark fast.

Jax sat down and pushed a tinfoil-covered plate toward me. "There's a fork in there too."

I removed the tinfoil to reveal a giant mound of slop. "What . . . . is this?"

"It's tuna and noodles and soup and stuff. There's, like, potato chips on the top. It doesn't look good, but it is. Go ahead, before it gets cold."

My mouth was already watering from the smell. He was right; it was delicious. In just the few months since my mom had left, I had already forgotten what homemade food tasted like. I had been living on cereal and the occasional McDonald's cheeseburger. When my dad would bring one home for me, usually after he went to cash his unemployment check and see Susan, he would act like he'd had to battle dragons for it. Every first Wednesday of the month he would come home drunk, with a paper bag full of hotel soaps in one hand and a

McDonald's cheeseburger in the other. He'd throw them on the table and say, "Look what your dad brought you! Look how lucky you are." If I didn't indulge him with enthusiastic prostrations of gratitude, he would call me a selfish, spoiled little bitch.

I was more grateful for the day-old casserole inside of Jax's tiny toolshed than a cold cheeseburger and harsh soap from the whiskey monster. It was only the beginning, though. Over the next couple of years, Jax continued walking with me to the bus stop, sitting in the seat behind me, finding me at lunch, and sharing his food. Occasionally, he'd sneak out to the shed to bring me a plate of whatever had been reheated for him and his brother. I yearned to go inside of their house but didn't for a long time. Not until Brian's accident. That's when things on the long dirt road changed once again.

2. I Wasn't Looking

When I finally stopped reading, I realized that I had been weeping the entire time. I felt like a gutted fish. I got up and went into the living room, making my way past Cara as she sat on the couch, typing on her laptop.

I turned toward her with red, puffy eyes. Her own eyes widened with concern, and she froze as she watched me walk into the kitchen, like she was waiting for me to crumple onto the floor and shatter into pieces.

"I'm fine," I said. "It's an emotional book. I'm just getting a glass of water." I reached for the tequila.

She got up and followed me into the kitchen. "That's not water."

"And?"

"It's ten a.m."

"And?"

"You look like you've been crying for an hour straight . . . and you're hitting the hard stuff at—and I repeat—ten a.m."

"Cara, you have the most amazing powers of perception."

I looked at the bottle in one hand and the glass in the other, shrugged, set the glass down, and headed back to my room with the bottle only.

"I'm worried about you," Cara called out as I walked away.

"I'm fine. Just gonna sit in here, read, and have myself a little mental health day." I turned and smiled and then locked myself in my room.

"Mental health days don't usually involve tequila at ten a.m.!" she yelled through the door.

"I'm fine!"

I heard her mumbling something, but I was too eager to get to the hard-core Facebooking and internet stalking I needed to do.

I examined the book jacket and copyright page of *All the Roads Between* carefully. No author photo or bio, just a website and publicity contact at the publisher. I was looking for some clue to the author's identity, but I didn't really need any. I knew exactly who had written this book. The only mystery to me was where the author had been for the last twelve years.

From the first line of *All the Roads Between*, I saw myself in J. Colby's story. That's because I *was* in his story. The long dirt road, the hour-and-a-half-long bus ride to school, the alcoholic dad, the mom who vanished, the secret lunches and meals in the shed . . . These were the details of my own life. Emerson was none other than me. And Jax? He was most definitely Jason Colbertson, the boy next door who had once been my everything . . . my first. The same person I hadn't talked to or seen in over a decade.

I was having a mild coronary, to say the least.

Some girls might be flattered to be the source of inspiration for the protagonist of a bestselling novel, but I was too busy planning out Jase's murder in detail. Through my homicidal haze, a million questions rose to the surface. *Why did Jase write this book? Why is he telling it from my perspective? Was he hoping I would read this? Or was he hoping I wouldn't—and just wanted to use my story for his own bestseller?* I needed to find him to get the answers to these questions . . . or at least give him a piece of my mind.

I searched for "J. Colby" on Facebook, Instagram, and Twitter—I already knew "Jason Colbertson" wouldn't be on any of these platforms because I'd looked before. Nothing came up; apparently both of his identities eschewed social media. Then I googled his pseudonym and clicked on "Images."

I'm fairly certain that my heart stopped. I took a swig from the bottle. No chaser, no lime, no salt—just tequila and my angry fingers clicking on every hyperlink.

His picture was pretty much the same on every listed hit. He had grown even better-looking in the twelve years since I'd seen him. More distinguished, more chiseled. But still, there was something boyish and arrogant in his smirk. That fucker.

I knew he would do it. I knew he'd write a book before me. He was brilliant at the age of ten. Why wouldn't he be at twenty-seven?

Another swig from the bottle, then I read a snippet about him embedded in an interview.

> After graduating from Columbia University, J. Colby
> switched coasts and made his home just outside of Los
> Angeles. His short stories have been published in the

New Yorker and *Ploughshares*. His highly anticipated debut novel, *All the Roads Between*, has been criticized for being soft compared to his earlier work, but Colby himself has been quoted as saying, "It's the grittiest and most real piece of fiction I'll ever write." He says his novel is a complete work of fiction but credits his childhood in rural Ohio for being his biggest inspiration.

I started laughing and crying at the same time. I typed in his website URL from the book jacket, which brought me to a clean, spare site with a form box where I could submit a message to "J. Colby."

Sweet. I would get to tell him directly what a fucking prick he was.

Dear Jason,

You fraud. I wanted to personally email you even though I haven't heard from you in twelve long years. Not since that day when you did what you did—remember that? Well, no sense in rehashing that right now. Let's talk about how you stole my life story and got it published. You're a despicable human being. Why didn't you ever contact me? You said you would find me and you didn't. I spent an entire year looking for you, wondering what happened, where you went, why you hadn't come looking for me yet. Don't you feel guilty for what happened? And now you're benefiting from my horror, my pain? You opportunistic piece of shit. I cannot believe that I ever loved you and trusted you. I cannot believe what you did to me . . .

Emiline

P.S. You're a shitty writer.

I stopped typing, deleted everything, cried, and then took another swig and began again.

Dear Jason,
I don't understand anything. What happened to us? Where have you been? What have you been doing? Are you married?
Emiline

P.S. You're a terrible writer.

I deleted and took another swig.

Dear Jase,
Why?

I deleted, took another drink, and then cracked the book open again.

From *All the Roads Between*

When we were in sixth grade, the winter brought a deluge of rain, which sucked for me and Jax. He'd carry an umbrella for the both of us as we walked to and from the bus stop, but it usually wasn't enough. The worst part about rain when you live on a dirt road is the mud—and there was mud everywhere. I'd even find it inside of my socks and between my toes and up the backs of my pant legs. There was just no stopping the mud, but we dealt with it the best way we knew how. We even played in it; we'd cake it on our faces, act like zombies, and try to scare Brian as he practiced with his band in the garage.

My hair had grown out a bit straighter ever since the hair-cutting incident, thank you Jesus. Being twelve is awkward enough without a rat's nest on the top of your head. Jax was starting to look a little goofier, his skin a little oilier, but I never said anything to him about it. I barely understood the changes our bodies were going through.

We hung out a lot, and pretty soon the kids at school got used to seeing us together.

Everyone said we were boyfriend and girlfriend, but we didn't care. We liked each other, so if they wanted to say those things about us, then so be it.

When we played together, we'd pretend like we were explorers on a big ship in the middle of the ocean. I'd never even seen the ocean in real life, but I saw it in my dreams. I would say to Jax, "Someday I'll have a house on the ocean, and dolphins will swim right up to my back porch and I'll feed them grapes."

"Dolphins don't eat grapes, dummy. They eat fish, and

they're better at catching it than you are, so you don't need to worry about feeding them."

"Where'd you learn that?"

"Discovery Channel."

I wished we had cable, but we didn't. My dad would always say, "That costs money. Last time I checked, you weren't making any."

The urge to say, "Neither are you," was so strong in me, I literally had to cup my hand over my mouth to stop it from slipping out.

This was all during Jax's Melville phase. He'd stand on the top of our wooden fence in the pouring rain and point and yell, "There she blows, a hump like a snow hill, it's Moby Dick!" I would laugh and roll my eyes, but I'd still call him Captain Ahab when he was feeling down, and that would lift his spirits.

We were each other's only friends. That year Jax's mother, Leila, was working two jobs and his brother was always busy doing whatever to pass the time. Jax had to quit baseball since no one could pick him up after practice, which pretty much ruined his chances of ever making male friends. He was alienated, isolated, just like me. We were outcasts in every sense of the word, but as time went on, I cared less and less what everyone else thought. All that mattered was us.

We both got into books. Even at twelve, we were determined to read all of the classics. They were probably way over our heads, but we challenged ourselves anyway. Our only escape was that back toolshed among the weeds and out of earshot of my father's drunken rages. There, we could make our own fictional world. We could be English royalty in the sixteenth century, or wizards or dragon slayers. We weren't poor, hungry, abandoned kids at the end of a desolate road. We were superheroes and magicians and presidents of our own country.

When spring finally came, we were ready to be outside and explore again. There was a creek about half a mile behind our houses, past the tree line. Because of all the rain that year, it had become more of a river, with the strongest currents right behind where we lived. Every adult warned us to be careful; even my deadbeat dad would say, "You better use that big brain of yours and stay out of the creek. You want to go swimming, you can go to the pool in town." But the community pool was a seven-mile bike ride away, and it cost three dollars to get in. There was no way I was going unless Leila gave us a ride, and even then, I would have to borrow the money to get in. Frankly, going to the town pool was a pipe dream. It became a myth to us, a fantasy, like Disneyland or Europe. Jax and I would try to imagine what it was like to go there.

"I bet they sell Popsicles and popcorn, and they probably have clowns too," I said as we lay spread out in the weeds on an old sleeping bag I had found in my garage, enjoying a makeshift picnic. Jax had brought a jar of applesauce, and I had brought Fun Dip that my dad had bought for me at the 7-Eleven. We mixed the Fun Dip into the jar and took turns eating spoonfuls.

"Community pools don't have clowns, genius."

"How do you know?" I said.

"Because I just do."

"I bet there's a high dive, like fifty feet in the air."

"Do you know how high fifty feet is? You would die hitting the water. The impact would kill you."

"You're such a know-it-all, Jackson. Why can't you let a girl dream? We're never going to that pool because no one will ever take us. Plus, it costs money, and last time I checked you weren't making any."

He lay back on the blanket, propped his hands behind his head, and closed his eyes. "I'm not a know-it-all—I just have cable. And as soon as I turn sixteen, I'm getting a job. I'll pay for us to go to the pool. You'll see. It's just a big hole with water in it."

I took the time to inspect every inch of him as he lay there, his eyes still closed. I was so curious about his body. My own body was changing, and I was terrified of it. Jax was getting taller, and I was certain he was going to be as tall as his father, but he looked more like his mother in his coloring and features. Jax's mom was French, and they both had this creamy skin that looked sun-kissed year-round. His brown hair and brown eyes had strands of gold running throughout them. He was letting his hair grow longer because he'd been watching some show on TV that took place in California. He said everyone in California had long hair.

I was trying to grow out my own unruly brown locks. I didn't know why since I always wore them in a braid. Maybe a part of me thought I would go to California with Jax one day, and I wanted to look the part. We both yearned for more than weeds and corn. All the books we read gave us silly ideas, filled our heads with things that might never be.

I lay down beside him and stared directly into the sun. He turned on his side and propped his head on his elbow.

"You'll go blind doing that," he said in a low voice.

"Leave me alone."

"Why are you in such a bad mood? You PMSing?"

"What do you know about it?"

"A lot."

"I doubt that, and even if I were, it's beyond rude to talk to me about it." I hadn't started my period yet, but I wasn't going to tell him that.

In the distance, we could hear Leila calling Jax. "Shit. I better go," he said. He grabbed the jar of applesauce and disappeared into the weeds. I lay back, closed my eyes, and fell asleep. I woke up just before dusk and realized I had been eaten alive by mosquitos. My stomach was in knots, and my head ached. When I stood, I felt a warmth between my legs. I tried desperately to clamp my legs together as I rolled up my sleeping bag.

By the time I got to my front door, I knew there was blood all the way down the back of my jeans. I closed the door as quietly as I could and tiptoed past the kitchen table into the hall.

"Emerson? Where in hell have you been?"

I tiptoed toward the kitchen, where I could see my father sitting at the table. "I was outside. I accidentally fell asleep."

His eyes went first to the rolled-up sleeping bag and then to the crotch of my pants. He stood so fast that the force knocked his chair over. "Dad, no."

Before I could do anything, he grabbed a handful of hair at the base of my neck and forced my head back so we were looking each other in the eyes.

"Emerson!" This time my name was like thunder in his chest. "What in god's name were you doing?"

"D-Dad . . ." I could feel blood running down my leg at the same pace the tears were flowing. It was going to be a bad day. "I'm having my period."

He blinked. His mouth dropped open then closed, then he blinked again, let go of my hair, and took a step back. His eyebrows furrowed. He brushed his hand down his mustache a couple of times while he stared off into space. "Go clean yourself up," he muttered to the floor.

I ran to the bathroom, slammed the door, and turned the shower on. With my hand under the stream of water, I waited and waited and waited. *Goddammit, why now?* My father hadn't paid the gas bill, so there was no hot water. Susan, my dad's weird friend from the motel, told me a month earlier just to take a whore bath if I ever needed to. A whore bath is where you wet a towel and clean yourself with it. By that age, I was aware of why Susan knew those things. A whore bath is what I needed.

An hour later, the bathroom looked like a crime scene. My mother hadn't even left one maxi pad on the off chance that the prepubescent daughter she had abandoned would start her period while she was at home alone with the whiskey monster.

I was sitting on the toilet in silence, wrapped up in a blood-stained towel, adding up the days in my head until I would be an adult, until I could leave this godforsaken town. Two thousand and seven days, fourteen hours, and twelve minutes until I was eighteen.

"Knock, knock." A female's voice came from the other side of the door. "Who is it?"

"It's Leila Fisher. Your dad asked me to come over."

Figures. That fucking coward.

I opened the door very slowly and scanned the hallway. She was standing a safe distance away with her arms crossed. Leila was a thin, naturally beautiful woman with plump lips and long, straight hair. Even though her husband had left her to raise two boys on her own, she still had hope in her eyes. I envied her for that.

"Are you going to help me?" I asked as I twirled my hair nervously.

"Yes."

I opened the door wider to let her in. "I have a change of clothes." I held up a pair of tattered underwear. "But these won't last long if I don't get a pad or something."

"I have nothing at the house. I wish I would have known."

"Yeah, me too," I said. I could feel the blood flowing again, so I sat back down on the toilet.

"No, I wish I would have known your mother hadn't left anything. I would have given you some pads to keep here, just in case."

"Well, she didn't."

"All right, well . . ." She stood for a moment, as if she were trying to figure out what to do, then she walked toward me and pulled out several lengths of toilet paper from the roll, winding them around and around her hand. "Put this in your under-wear, get dressed, and come with me. I'll take you to the store. Your father gave me a few dollars."

"He did?" I was shocked.

She laughed. "Of course. He's not a monster."

"He kind of is," I whispered.

"Yeah, but he loves you, Emerson. He's still here, isn't he?"

"He doesn't love me. Look at me." I crossed my eyes and stuck out my tongue. She laughed. The mood felt lighter. "You're a silly girl. No wonder Jax is so fond of you."

There was silence for a few seconds. "Fond of me?" The words came out like a breath. I knew Jax and I were friends, but the way she said those words made me feel like maybe my deepest feelings, the ones I didn't even consciously acknowl-edge, meant something. Everything felt lighter, like the planet had been catapulted into the cosmos and we were spinning freely through space and time. My cramps were killing me, I had blood running down my leg, but it didn't matter: I was floating on a cloud, all because Jax was *fond of me*. Even though I knew it myself, to hear someone else say it validated everything for me.

"Does he know?"

"What, honey?"

"About my, um . . . um . . ." I pointed to my crotch.

"He was there when your dad came in. He was worried because your dad was in a panic."

I was mortified. "So he knows?"

"Don't worry. Just get dressed and meet me outside."

I did as she asked, walking by my father as he sat at the kitchen table staring out the window.

"Be right back, Dad."

He didn't answer, but that wasn't unusual. Sometimes my dad would have a human moment, like he did when he went to Leila's. I imagined what he looked like, out of breath and asking for help. It still wasn't enough to make me feel completely loved *by* him, but it was enough to make me feel some kind of love *for* him. Or maybe it was pity. When you're twelve, it's hard to know the difference.

Inside Leila's Camaro, she blasted Guns N' Roses. She didn't turn it down or make an attempt to talk to me the whole way to the store.

Once we were inside the store, she threw a package of pads in the basket, along with some granola bars and Fruit Roll-Ups. "You keep these hidden from your dad, okay? Keep them in your room in case you get hungry."

I hesitated for a moment. "You know that Jax gives me half his lunch, right?"

"I know. I've known for a long time. And it's okay with me. Your dad's just not functional. He's in a bad way. It's just too bad he can't go back to that functioning alcoholic we all knew and loved."

I paused. "You mean my dad has always been an alcoholic?"

"He wasn't an asshole, but he was always a drinker." She held up a chocolate bar. "I bet you're craving one of these right about now."

"Oh god, I would die for one."

"I thought so." She threw it in the basket.

"What else did Jax tell you?"

"It's not my business. I've got enough to worry about myself." Instantly, the fantasy I'd been harboring of Leila Fisher ever adopting me went poof! I thought she was perfect, that she was the kind of person who could never live with herself knowing that I was next door, neglected and starving because of my drunk father. But I realized she knew about everything—the lunches, the meals in the shed . . . and yet she had never stepped in to talk to my dad about what was going on.

Having a bunch of shitty adults constantly letting you down really kills a kid's view of the world.

Leila grabbed a twelve-pack of Budweiser and carried our stuff to the checkout. "Pack of Camel Lights," she said to the clerk, and then paid him in singles.

On the way back, she turned the music down. "Now that you're a woman, you can get pregnant. You know that, right?"

"Yes. We learned it in sex ed."

"Okay, well, you and Jax better keep your paws off each other." The way she said that made me nauseous.

"We're just friends."

"You were friends 'cause you were just kids." She glanced over at me. "You're not kids anymore."

Time to change the subject.

"Are you sad that Jax and Brian's dad left?"

She popped her gum. "It's been long enough. I don't think about it anymore. Anyway, Brian and Jax don't have the same dad. You didn't know that?"

"No, how would I?"

"Jax never told you? Well, Brian's dad passed away when Brian was two. Car accident." She looked off into the distance. "He was a good man. Brian's just like him." She seemed choked up.

"Is Jax like his dad?"

"Jackson's dad left, the fucking coward." She turned and glanced at me, still chomping on her gum. "Sorry, sweetie, that was harsh. Let's hope Jax is nothing like his dad. Some men can be real assholes when they want to be. It'd be wise of you to learn that now. I do think Brian is going to make a woman very happy someday."

I was already getting stars in my eyes over Brian—what twelve-year-old girl wouldn't? When I'd see him drive up in his old car, I'd run outside and sit on the fence. He'd always walk past me, carrying his guitar, and say, "Hey, cutie." I was way too shy around him to respond. But I also felt sad for how Leila dismissed Jackson's sweetness just because his father had left. My mother had left too. Did that make me just like her?

When we got to the end of the road, I noticed Susan's car was parked in front of our house.

"That your dad's girlfriend?"

"Yeah." It was dark and no lights were on.

"I'm not working tonight. Come over. I'll teach you how to use tampons for when you're older."

I hesitated. "I don't want Jax to . . ."

"Oh, don't worry. He won't pay attention—he's glued to the TV."

I was nervous. In the two years that Jax and I had been friends, I'd never once been invited into his house. We either played outside or hung out in the shed. As I walked in behind Leila, I realized that Jax's house was almost an exact replica of my own, except everything was on the opposite side, as if the houses were mirror images. It was dark, and only the light from the TV in the living room lit our path. The brown, outdated carpet was worn thin, and the whole house smelled of stale cigarettes and something else I couldn't figure out.

All this time, I'd had this idea of Jax's house as some pristine image from a Martha Stewart magazine. Now I could see that, despite the warm casseroles his mom made, his life wasn't all that different from mine.

We walked through the living room, where Jax was watching TV on the couch with his back to us. As we passed, he turned and looked up at me. He shot me a sympathetic smile and then turned back to the TV.

Inside Leila's messy bedroom, I sat at the end of her unmade bed. I picked up a small article of clothing that looked like a leather tube top and stared at it.

"It's a skirt," Leila said.

"This?" I held it up.

"For my work. I've been dancing. Didn't Jax tell you?"

"No." He was probably ashamed. I knew what she meant by "dancing," but I wasn't about to say anything.

She walked over to me and placed her hands on my thighs. She leaned in. "I take my clothes off for money because I got knocked up with Brian when I was sixteen. Ever since then, my life has been a shit show."

I jerked back. "I'm sorry."

"I take my clothes off for money, Emerson. How sad is that?" She stared into my eyes as she continued to work the same piece of gum she'd been chewing the whole night.

"Um . . . sad, I guess . . . but at least people want to see you naked?" I was always trying to be the silver-lining girl. In the months before my mom left, I'd trained myself to find a positive angle to every situation. I thought if I could be the happy-go-lucky girl, it would rub off on them. No such luck.

Leila wasn't looking for acceptance, anyway. She was trying to teach me a lesson.

She stood up and crossed her arms. "Men will pay to see anything naked."

"I don't know about that."

"It's true."

"Well, at least you stuck around. At least you're here with Brian and Jax." Leila didn't deserve accolades for good parenting, but at least she hadn't abandoned her kids.

Tears slipped from her eyes. I felt my own throat tighten at the thought of my mother living on some beach somewhere in paradise. Leila sat next to me on the bed without making a sound, but I knew she was crying.

"I could never leave these boys. They're so precious to me."

"You're a good mom, even if you have to wear shit like this." I held up the leather skirt.

THAT NIGHT, LEILA read to me from the back of the maxi pad package. She taught me how to use a tampon, which was weird, and she reminded me over and over again how hard it was to be a young mother. She talked about Brian and his musical gifts. She said he would be famous, a legend. He was ahead of his time and a natural genius on the guitar. She said he was going to save them all, travel the world, make lots of money, and rescue the family from the pits of Neeble.

Occasionally, Leila would go into the bathroom alone and say she was blowing her nose, but I knew otherwise. At about eleven p.m., we heard a knock on her bedroom door, and Brian walked in. There was a glow that followed Jax's older brother, like he really was heaven-sent. He had longish hair and a superstar smile. I was smitten. I had been from the first time I saw Brian plucking his guitar in the garage.

"Mom? Mom?"

Leila seemed a little out of it as she sat at her tiny vanity stool, staring at her reflection. Brian gave me a small smile as he walked toward his mom, making my stomach do somersaults.

"Brian, I'm fine," Leila said.

"You should call it a night, Mom. You have to work a double tomorrow. Emerson, I think it's time to go." He said it nicely, but it still made me feel embarrassed.

"Of course."

"No, Emerson, stay. Brian, let her stay. She can read to me and then she can go."

He looked at me first, as if to ask if this was okay with me. I nodded then he turned back to his mom. "Okay." He headed toward the door, but as he came toward me he bent down and whispered in my ear. "Don't let her keep you up."

I shivered, little tingles shooting down my arms just from his breath on my neck.

"Yes . . . sir."

He laughed. "You don't have to call me 'sir.'"

My heart bounced around inside of my chest. "Okay."

After he left, Leila got under the covers. "Come sit here next to me." I scooted up to the head of the bed, and she handed me a *National Enquirer*. "Read that, will you?"

"Okay."

"I always wished I had a daughter," she said, and it made me feel good. There were actually people in the world who wished they had daughters.

I read her an article about a boozy Hillary Clinton being shipped off to rehab. "This can't be true," I said.

"I knew Hilary was an alkie," Leila slurred.

"I think this is fake." I thumbed through the rest of the magazine, past the Jesus sightings and UFO reports. By the time I finished reading all the main articles aloud, Leila was sound asleep. I crawled off the bed and headed down the hallway. I spotted Brian in his room as he smoked something out of a pipe—pot, I assumed. He threw a hand up in a motionless wave as I walked by, so I did the same.

"Hey!" he whispered.

I backed up to his doorway. "Hi," I said timidly.

He put the pipe down. "Come in here."

I waved smoke out of my face and walked up to where he was sitting on the bed. "What's up?" I looked around. There were posters of rock bands on his walls, along with a calendar with mostly naked women on it.

"I'm working on a song. You want to hear it?"

"I'd love to."

I sat on the bed next to him while he pulled an acoustic guitar onto his lap. "Promise you won't laugh?"

It struck me that Brian was nervous, and I wondered if he

saw me differently. I'd grown up overnight; I wasn't his little brother's playmate anymore.

"I would never laugh . . . I think . . . I think you're amazing." My voice was shaking with nerves.

He chuckled and then pulled his long hair into a ponytail at the back of his neck. I had the stray thought that Jax would be taller and better-looking than Brian when he grew up, but I banished the thought from my mind. I'd had a crush on Brian for years, and he was about to serenade me.

He strummed the guitar and then plucked out a complicated melody. I thought he was going to sing, but he didn't.

"What did you think?" he asked nervously.

"It was good, but what about the lyrics?"

He laughed again and then reached out and messed up my hair like he was petting a freakin' Labrador. "Such a goofball. I'm the guitarist in my band. I don't write the lyrics."

"Oh, sheesh, what do I know? Well, anyway, it was really cool." My face was getting redder by the millisecond.

"Thanks for listening. Hey, it's getting pretty late. You better scram, kid."

"Okay." I put an extra bounce in my step as I left the room, hoping Brian wouldn't see how totally heartbroken I was that he didn't try to kiss me. I guess that would have been pretty wrong for a guy his age.

In the living room, Jax was asleep on the couch. I put a blanket over him, and he stirred.

"What are you doing?" he murmured.

"I'm leaving. I just wanted to put a blanket over you," I said.

He popped up to his feet, suddenly awake. "I'll walk you."

"Next door, doofus? You don't have to walk me."

"I want to."

He yawned about five times on our thirty-yard trek. At the doorstep, he shoved his hands into his pockets.

"Tomorrow's Saturday."

"Yeah?" I said.

"You wanna play explorers out on the rocks?"

"That's kind of a kids' game, don't you think, Jax?"

"Oh, right," he said. "Well, you wanna go read by the river? My mom picked up some new books from the library for me."

"Maybe. I have to see how I feel."

"Of course," he said through a yawn.

"I better go." I searched his eyes for a sign.

He just smiled, unaware. Jax wasn't where I was emotionally or physically, and I was too young for Brian. *Damn.* "Night, Em."

"Night, Jax."

My house was dark, and my father and Susan were passed out in their underwear on the living room floor. I had a bag of granola bars, some Fruit Roll-Ups, a package of maxi pads, and a worn-out copy of *Tuck Everlasting*. I went into my bedroom and stared at myself in the mirror behind my door.

For the first time, I noticed that my hips were wider and my breasts were finally larger than peanuts. I was a woman. That was the moment I started hating my mother. Even though it had been a couple of years since she'd left, the pain of her absence was searing. I had never felt her abandonment as sharply as I did the day I became a woman. Maybe it was Leila's flawed attempt at kindness that made me miss the tenderness of a mother. My own had been kind and gentle when she was around, but she couldn't handle the life she'd been given. Burned bread in the oven would send her into a fit of tears. I didn't know where she'd gone, and I didn't know any of her extended family or if she even had family. She had just vanished one day, and there was little impression of her left in our home . . . almost like she had never existed.

3. I'm Running

By one p.m., I had to stop reading. Frankly, I was drunk, emotional, and torn.

It was strange how Jase knew how I had felt toward my mother. Then again, he had been my best friend. I had told him everything. And he'd used all of that to create an emotional landscape that was strangely true to everything I remembered. The only difference was that Emerson was introspective at a young age, and I wasn't so much. Things were happening to me back then, but only now, after reading a few chapters of Jase's book, did I realize how I had really felt as a kid. He must have been so tuned in to me to realize I had a crush on his brother. He'd just sat there watching, taking it all in.

If I felt a tiny bit of forgiveness toward Jase, it vanished the moment I remembered that here he was making money off this story. *My* story. He had beaten me to the punch.

I curled up on my bed, too emotionally drained to do anything else, and fell asleep.

———

I WOKE UP later that evening to the sounds of Trevor and Cara making small talk in the kitchen. I put on my running gear, left my bedroom, and headed for the front door, ignoring Trevor as he stared me down from behind the kitchen counter.

"Where are you going?" he asked.

"For a run," I replied. "Want to join?"

I noticed Cara sneak off to her bedroom behind me without saying a word. Trevor and I had fallen into the habit of making people around us feel uncomfortable. I knew we were giving off weird vibes.

"I just had PT and my arm is killing me," he said.

"You don't use your arms to run." I stood near the door with my hand on the knob.

"Yeah, actually, you do. Hey, will you turn around and look at me?"

I turned and leaned against the door. "What, Trevor?"

"What's going on?"

"Nothing is going on. I just want to go for a run."

He laughed drily. "You have no idea how typical this is of you."

"Do you want to start tossing insults at each other the moment we're in a room together? Didn't you just get here? I didn't even know you were coming over." He shook his head as if I were an awful person. I took a deep breath and softened my voice. "Isn't there a game on? I'll go for a run and get takeout and be back in a bit. You can hang out here. When I get back, we can eat and watch the game together. How does that sound?" Was it weird that I had never told him I didn't enjoy watching football, even when he was the quarterback?

"That's fine," he said. He plopped down on the couch and turned the TV on.

I ran to the cove. The children's pool, as they called it, was formed by a wall that was originally built to break the waves and create a safe swimming environment for small children. But it was roped off halfway up the beach because about two hundred seals had made it their home. I sat on the steps going down to the pool, letting the cold breeze whip through my hair. There were no people here, only seals loafing on the sand. It was exactly what I needed.

I typed Jase's website into my phone and scanned it for details once again.

J. Colby lived in L.A., but he was currently on a book tour. There was a menu page for his tour dates and cities. I clicked the page link, and lo and behold, I discovered he was going to be in San Diego the day after tomorrow. "Are you fucking kidding me?" I said out loud. One of the seals looked up and barked at me. "Sorry!"

This was all too coincidental.

I stood up, jogged up the stairs, and took off running. By the time I was out of fuel, it was dark and I was sweating profusely in the cold air, breathing so hard I knew I had to stop. I walked to a taco shop, picked up food, and headed back to my apartment, where I was grateful to see Trevor asleep on the couch with some football game blaring in the background.

I knocked lightly on Cara's bedroom door. "Come in," she said.

She was sitting at her desk, typing away on her laptop, as per usual. She was nothing if not a dedicated writer. I stood in the doorway and kept my voice down so as not to wake up Trevor. "How's it going?" I asked.

She smiled. "Good. I wrote a lot today. What about you? How are you? You seemed a bit loony this morning."

"I'm okay. Sorry about that thing with Trevor earlier."

"No biggie. Are you still reading that book?"

I nodded.

"That fucking author's hot," she said. "I've been internet stalking him."

I laughed. "Yeah, he is."

"You googled him too?" she said, smiling.

"Uh, yep. Uh-huh."

"He's going to be in San Diego the day after tomorrow."

"I saw that," I said.

"Let's go meet him and get the book signed." Her face turned bright red.

"I don't know. You can go." *Time to change the subject.* "Hey, I left some tacos on the counter. I think I'm going to bed. I don't feel great."

"Oh, okay. Should I just leave Trevor out there?"

"He's fine," I said, and then I went into my room, shut the door, and cracked the book open again.

From *All the Roads Between*

At the kitchen table the next morning, I watched as my dad poured whiskey into his coffee. "Did Susan leave?" I asked.

"Who wants to know?"

"I was just wondering."

"Yeah, she left."

"Is she your girlfriend?"

"Mind your business, Emerson."

I was feeling bold that morning. Maybe because I was a woman now and I felt like I needed answers. "Where'd Mom go?"

He sat down next to me and took a deep breath. For a moment I thought we were going to have a heart-to-heart. I stared at a large brown stain on his white T-shirt as I waited for his answer.

"Your mother's a fucking whore."

I glanced down at my fidgeting hands underneath the table. He grabbed the whiskey bottle, poured a healthier dose into his coffee, and then slammed it on the table. "Did you hear me?! I said your mother's a fucking whore!"

"I heard you!" I yelled. I stood and kicked my chair out. He gripped my arm so hard that it forced me to sit back down.

"I'm not done," he seethed through gritted teeth.

"Dad, please."

"She's Satan."

"You're being irrational."

"Big word for a twelve-year-old." I couldn't take my eyes off the disgusting wad of spittle forming in the corner of his mouth.

"I'm thirteen."

"Since when?"

"Since today. Today is my birthday, Dad." He let go of my arm. There was nothing he could say to me because he didn't know how to be a human anymore. He couldn't be kind because it hurt him more than it hurt me. I could see confusion and guilt in his eyes. *Good, feel like shit, you bastard. You deserve it.*

I slithered away quietly and went into my room and cried. The tears turned hot with anger, and soon I found myself packing a bag. I would ask Leila if she'd take me in. She'd said she'd always wanted a daughter. I could go live with them and cook and clean and help her take care of Jax and Brian.

I took extra time to make my hair look nice. I found light pink lipstick and blush in an old box of random things I had tried to preserve of my mother's. I painted my face with her cheap shit. I cursed her in the mirror. I studied my big brown eyes, so like hers, and wondered if I would fail at life the way she had. I put on the flowered dress she had bought at a resale shop over two years ago, just before she left. She called it my "church" dress, even though there was no sign of god in any of our lives. It finally fit me right. I had breasts, albeit small ones, but enough to fill it out. I had secretly started shaving my legs with my dad's razor, so when I looked in the mirror that day, I saw no sign of the little girl I once was. I would end my nightmare right there because I knew Brian would fall in love with me the moment he saw me. I was convinced. He would marry me and take me all over the world on tour with him. We would buy a house for Jax and Leila to live in, and we would visit them all the time. We would be rich and everything would be fine. My nightmare would be over because I would become a Fisher and leave this hell behind.

My father was in the bathroom when I snuck out the side door. Jax was sitting on the fence in my front yard.

I strutted up to him. "Is your mom home?"

Jax wrinkled his nose. "Why are you dressed like that, and why do you have that stuff on your face?"

I shrugged. "None of your business. What are you doing over here?"

"Forget it. You're clearly still in a bad mood." He picked something up off the ground and started to walk away.

"Wait. What is that?"

"Nothing!"

"Come here, hold on," I pleaded.

He turned around abruptly and held up a package wrapped in brown paper. "It's for you, for your birthday."

"I'm sorry, Jax. I didn't know."

"Whatever. You should be nicer to me." He handed the present over but kept his eyes glued to the ground as he mumbled, "Happy Birthday, Em."

With my index finger under his chin, I forced him to look at me. I smiled and he smiled back. "Jackson Fisher, how'd you get so great?"

"I thought I was the most obnoxious boy in the world? That's what you told me last week."

"I know, and I'm sorry. It's just that I'm a woman now, Jax. I have emotions, okay? You're not obnoxious today." I unwrapped the package to reveal a hardcover edition of *Anne of Green Gables*, my favorite book of all time. "Today, you're freaking awesome." I hugged him quickly and awkwardly. "Where did you get this?"

"I won it in the book fair drawing at school."

"And you're giving it to me?"

"I want you to have it."

"Thank you." I ran my hand over the cover and thought idly that it was the only gift I had been given in over a year, aside from hotel soap and cheeseburgers.

"What's the bag for?"

"I was gonna see if I could stay with you guys for a while."

"Oh . . . okay," he said. "Let's go talk to my mom."

"Is Brian home?" I asked.

"His car is here. He's probably in his room. Why do you ask?"

"Just wondering. Let's go talk to your mom." We went into the house, and I set my bag down in their kitchen and followed Jax down the hall. Brian's door was cracked, so I pushed it open gently, hoping it would look like an accident. I wanted Brian to see me, but his room was empty. Walking behind Jax, I said, "Your brother's not in there."

He backed up and peeked in. "Bri!" he yelled. No answer.

"Keep it down!" Leila yelled from her bedroom.

"I don't know where he is," Jax said.

We went to Leila's room, where she was curled up on her side at the foot of the bed.

I stood behind Jackson. "You okay, Mom?"

"Fine," she said groggily.

"Can Em stay here for a while? Her dad's being kind of a jerk."

I hadn't even told him that, but he knew.

Leila squinted and then sat up and glared at me. "You're twelve years old."

"Thirteen," Jax answered for me.

"You can stay here today. Eat what you want, but you have to go home tonight. You'll get over it with your dad," she said, before lying back down.

"Okay, thank you." It would be good enough for now.

We left her room. "Let's find your brother. Maybe he can teach us how to play the guitar."

"I know how to play a little, Em," Jax said in a clipped tone. I followed him into Brian's room, but the guitar was gone. "It's not in here. He's probably down at the river with his girlfriend."

I tried not to think about Brian's girlfriend as a rule. "Blah," I said out loud.

"Let's go play outside," Jax said. "I mean . . . hang out," he corrected himself.

"'Kay."

We meandered our way toward the river, mostly silent until we got to the shore. Neither of us was in a particularly playful mood.

"Hey, there's your brother's guitar," I said, pointing to his acoustic guitar lying on the ground. My heart raced with the anticipation of seeing Brian.

We walked toward it, and I noticed Jackson stiffen up. "Bri!" he yelled. "Where the fuck is he? he mumbled. "Brian!" he yelled again.

"Brian!" I shouted.

We ran up and down the shore. I wasn't sure what was making Jax panic, but the longer we shouted, the more I realized that something was wrong. Why would Brian's guitar be lying there on the ground all alone? He loved that thing; he wouldn't just leave it unattended. He would at least be nearby. And yet he wasn't answering our shouts . . .

I followed Jax as he ran through the trees to get to the footbridge, where we could cross. The whole time we were running, Jackson was shouting Brian's name. As soon as we got to the clearing that led to the footbridge, we climbed down a little ravine where the mud met the water.

That's where we were struck by the most horrifying sight— an image that will never, ever leave my mind.

"No!" Jackson's cry was unprocessed, unfiltered, like a child's. "No!" he screamed again.

"Oh god, oh god, oh god," I repeated over and over, but there was no god to help save Brian. His bloated body was facedown, floating near the shore.

"No! No! No!" Jax kept shouting as he moved closer to Brian's body, reaching his arms out to grab him.

"Don't touch him," I said. "You can't help him."

He turned to me instantly and fell into my arms. I held him as we cried together. "That's my brother." Jackson sobbed. "That's my brother, isn't it? He's dead, isn't he?"

We didn't need to flip his body over to see his face. We recognized the hair, the clothes. We had seen the guitar on the ground. "Yes," I choked out.

"What happened?" Jax screamed into my chest.

I tried not to look at Brian floating behind Jax. I held him as he sobbed and sobbed. I was doing nothing, but I was doing everything at the same time, and I could feel it in how fervently he held me back.

I knew we had to get up to the house and tell Leila and call the police. I led Jackson back to the house while he continued to cry, nonstop. I went into his kitchen and dialed 911.

The emergency operator picked up. "Nine-one-one, what's your emergency?"

"My friend's brother is dead in the creek," I said flatly.

The rest of the conversation was a blur. Jackson was still crying audibly next to me. When I hung up the phone, we both turned around and saw Leila standing at the end of the hallway. She hadn't made a noise. She had heard the conversation, but she was clearly in shock.

She looked at me and then back at Jax a few times before starting to cry. "Is it true?" she squeaked out.

"Yes," Jax whimpered.

"The ambulance will be here as soon as they can," I said quietly.

Leila dropped to her knees and pounded her fists on the floor. "No!" She made a bloodcurdling sound and then fell into a pile, screaming, crying, and writhing like she was being burned alive. That's how I imagined losing a child would feel . . . maybe even worse.

Jax and I held each other again as he continued sobbing.

My mother had taken off, and his father had done the same, but neither one of us had ever faced the reality of death in this way. At that age, you don't have a full grasp on mortality until you see the body of a healthy man you spoke to mere hours ago floating in the water, facedown, tethered by a broken branch to the shore, like a dead animal.

Jackson's full-throated sobs evened out into painful whimpers. My shirt was drenched with tears and snot, but I didn't care. In the smallest voice he said, "You're all I have left. You're holding my whole world together, Em."

"But you have your mom. She loves you a lot," I whispered.

"My mom is a shell, and she'll be even less than that now that her golden boy is dead."

"That's not true, Jax," I said, but I wasn't sure I believed my own reassurances.

———

LATER ON, AFTER the EMTs, police, and coroner arrived, Jax and I sat side by side on the fence, as we'd done so many times before. Jax was sniffling, but he had calmed down a bit. We were watching Leila, who was wrapped in a blanket and sitting on a bench on their porch, speaking to an investigator.

"When she looks at me, all she sees is my dad, and she hates him. She loved Brian more than me. She'll wish that was me in the river."

"Stop it, Jackson Fisher. You stop that right now. You've been reading too much. Don't ever talk like that," I said.

"I guess now you can't marry him."

I hopped off the fence, turned, and looked at him pointedly, but I had no words. He got down too. We were face-to-face. I felt crushed, and Jackson looked tormented. I started crying again. "Don't, Jax. Don't do that."

He started to cry again too, and then he hugged me and buried his head in my shoulder. "I'm sorry," he said. "He's gone. I can't believe he's gone."

That moment was followed by days of grieving. Jax and his mom sat inside of that dark, dank house, now further tainted with loss and tragedy. When the investigation was over and foul play was ruled out, Leila had Brian cremated. We all went into town for a short service at the funeral home. The cause of death was never once mentioned.

We sat in the front row while a stranger spoke from notes that Leila had written about Brian, detailing his musical achievements and how kindhearted he was. His girlfriend, who we later found out was a street kid, sobbed in the row behind us. Other than that, there were only a few people he worked with and went to high school with in attendance. The whole event made Brian seem so insignificant. I wondered how long it would take for the dirt road to end Jax or me. How long it would be before any chance at a legacy would be robbed from us.

Jackson was dressed in slacks that I knew he'd had since he was a kid because they were high-waters on him. He wore one of his brother's black Led Zeppelin T-shirts and the wallet chain Brian had handed down to him a year before.

Leila looked like she had aged ten years. On the car ride home, she just kept mumbling, "It's not natural."

From the passenger seat, Jax said, "What's not natural, Mom?"

"To bury a child."

Later that night, Jax told me that Leila got high and drunk and said that she wished it had been him who'd drowned. We both knew it was coming. He didn't cry like I thought he would. He said, "She's pathetic, Em. I can't hate her because I pity her too much."

"You're the smartest person I know, Jackson," I told him, and it was true. The comment earned me one of his cute smiles. Even though he tried to act tough, I knew Leila had wounded him. I vowed never to hurt him in that way.

That week, I went home each night to my despondent father, who said little about Brian's death except that the kid was a druggie. I thought that it was sad that my father judged Brian based on Leila's actions. Beyond pot, Brian wasn't a druggie at all. He was just a guy who'd lost his father young and grown up in a shit-hole town with an addict for a mother. Who knew what he could have become.

Jax and I weren't surprised when the autopsy came back with the result that Brian had simply drowned. He was likely pulled under by the strong current created by a season of rainstorms.

No one knew what frame of mind Brian was in the night he died, or why on earth he would go swimming in the middle of the night, fully clothed, with his damn boots on. We just knew that he was gone forever, and things would never be the same for any of us.

4. Things I've Put Away

I was crying when Trevor came into my room in the middle
of the night. He was groggy and squinting. "What's wrong,
Emi?"

I closed the book and pushed it to the side. "I'm just
confused about some things."

He flipped off the light and got into my bed. I scooted
under the covers and let him spoon me.

"Talk to me," he said gently. His voice was soothing next
to my ear.

I buried my face in his arm. "On my thirteenth birthday,
I found my neighbor dead, floating in the river behind my
house." Jeff was his real name and he *was* magical. In what
felt like a single breath he was gone. His death affected Jase
deeply, as well as myself.

Trevor paused for a moment, absorbing my words. "Oh
Jesus, Emi. I'm so sorry. That must have been horrible for
you. Is that why you never want to celebrate your birthday?"

I nodded in the darkness and told him the whole story.

He just listened and held me tighter, his silence a comfort after all the fighting we'd been doing. It wasn't long before I fell asleep in his arms.

Telling Trevor what happened didn't heal me, but reliving that day did in some way. Jason's insights in the book and his view of me, and what I was going through in that moment, gave me a sense of closure. His brother's death had to have been much more traumatic for him, but he was still aware that I was experiencing the horror along with him. He was always so perceptive and compassionate.

Too bad I was so pissed off at him.

WHEN I WOKE up the next morning, Trevor was gone, but the memory of the night before lingered. I turned to his pillow to see he had left me a note. I had finally shared something from my past with him, something he'd been asking me to do for years. I wondered if the moment had meant as much to him as it did to me.

The note simply said he'd had to go to PT. Nothing else but an "xo, T" at the end.

I felt hollow, but that empty feeling was too much to confront. So I went back to the book.

From *All the Roads Between*

For a few years, I was the tallest kid in school, but by the summer going into ninth grade, everyone was catching up and passing me by, including Jax. His voice was changing, and he was getting hair on his face. He still acted like a five-year-old every now and then, but despite the fact that he was living with a junkie, had lost his brother a couple of years before, and had no father, Jax somehow managed to keep getting sweeter and sweeter.

I knew he was dealing with a lot, but he held it together and focused on his schoolwork. When Leila wasn't working, she was comatose on the couch. When she'd clean up her act a little and go to work, there'd be an endless stream of sleazy men hanging around the house for days.

Jax and I spent more and more time in the shed. We both found things we could steal to make the place more habitable, like it was our own house.

"What have you been writing in that journal?" I asked. Jax was lying on the cot in the corner and scribbling notes in a black leather-bound notebook.

"I'm just outlining my novel."

I was sitting in one of the wooden chairs with my arms wrapped around my legs, staring out the window at the swaying trees.

"The one about the ant family?"

"No, I ditched that. I'm writing about a boy and girl who become superheroes and save the world."

"*The Adventures of Jax and Em*?"

"Something like that."

"You want to go swim in the creek?" The water in the creek had settled down for the season, and one of Leila's short-lived boyfriends had built a deck and rope swing for us. We had carved our names, along with Brian's, in the wood. It was our memorial to him. Jackson would go down there alone a lot; I knew he was talking to his brother.

"I'm kind of busy," he said. I got up and yanked the journal out of his hands. "No, Em. I'm serious, give it back."

"I want to read it," I whined.

"Please don't." His voice cracked, and his face was red. He wasn't playing around.

"Why won't you let me? You let me read the ant story."

"Because this is different. It's not done yet. You can read it when it's done."

I handed the journal back. "I'm bored. I just want to find something to do."

"Fine, let's go swimming."

I went home and got my swimsuit. It was a purple, tattered one-piece that I had bought at the Goodwill for two dollars, but it did the job. By then we were on welfare and food stamps, so it felt like I was living the life. We had cereal and cheese and milk and juice all the time. My father would give me twenty dollars every month to buy the things he had too much fucking pride to buy, like tampons and dish soap.

No wonder my sad excuse for a mom had left, but why couldn't she have taken me with her? Besides the fact that my dad was a bigot and a belligerent alcoholic, I was especially saddened when I realized I was being raised by a misogynist. Jax had taught me that word. He basically called every man Leila brought home a misogynistic creep.

"Where are you going in that?" My father spoke from the hallway as I stood facing the bathroom mirror. I didn't make eye contact with him as I wrapped my hair in a ponytail.

"I'm going swimming with Jax."

"Look at me when I'm talking to you."

I turned and faced him. His beard and hair had grown thick, and there was always a yellowish tint clouding his eyes. Was it terrible that I wished his liver would finally call it quits once and for all?

"Put a shirt over that."

"It's a one-piece, Dad. It doesn't show that much."

Smack! He slammed his hand on the wall. "Are you talking back to me?"

"No, sir," I said, stiffening.

"I said put a shirt on. I don't want you slutting yourself around with that boy. Why don't you have any girlfriends? Why are you always with Jackson?"

"I don't know." My father knew exactly why, but he liked to make me feel bad about my life anyway. I would never bring anyone to my house, even if I did have other friends. I would never subject some poor kid to the kind of crap that went on here at the end of the dirt road. But besides that, I liked Jax more than anyone else. Our friendship was easy and we cared about each other. Even though we didn't have the words back then, he was the only person I trusted.

"Out of the bathroom. I need to shave," he said, finally dismissing me. But I lingered in the hall, confused. "Why are you shaving your beard off?"

"Your dad got a job, kid."

"Really?"

"You didn't think we were gonna live on food stamps forever, did you? We're better than that." He lathered up from an old can of shaving cream and pressed the razor to his face. Honestly, I *had* thought we'd be on food stamps forever, and I was kind of okay with it, but I had noticed that my dad was trying to pull things together lately. He was still a mean drunk, but it wasn't as bad as it was right after my mom left, and he'd mellowed some with time. "Where'd you get a job?"

"Doing maintenance at the motel."

"Did Susan get you that job?"

"No, I got me the job."

I'd wounded his ego, so I had to flee. "Okay, I'll be home later. I'll put a shirt on." As I walked away I said, "I'm glad you got a job, Dad."

I got to the shed before Jax. When I lay down on the cot, I felt a lump under the blanket. I pulled it out from under me and saw that it was his journal. My stomach did a little flip. *Just a little peek wouldn't hurt anyone.*

> *She sat there holding her smooth legs to her chest, staring out the window, popping her gum, bored, and saying inconsequential things. But still . . . she was the center of the universe. She could make the whole world go around without even breaking a sweat.*

The wooden door swung open. I closed the journal and looked up to see Jax in the doorway, scowling at me.

"What the hell is the matter with you? Have you no respect for my privacy?" He marched up to me and tore the journal out of my hands.

"I didn't read any of it."

"Liar. I can tell you read it. Your face is beet red."

"I only read one line."

"It's not about you."

It's totally about me, I thought.

He turned and headed back out the door.

"Who's it about then?" I called after him.

"Not you. I'm going home."

I ran after him and yanked his shoulder back and spun him around in the field of weeds. "Talk to me, Jax."

"It's about Desiree Banks. She's my girlfriend. Go home, Emerson, and mind your own business."

"We're not little kids anymore, Jackson," I said to his back.

"Yeah, exactly! I don't have time for your kid games."

My kid games? "You can tell me how you feel about me. I'm here. I'm listening."

He said nothing, so I followed him until he went inside of his house and slammed the door. I turned around and dragged my feet home, regretting what I had done. My dad had already left to go to his new job, so I was alone, left to think about the passage Jax had written.

IN THE MORNING, I waited fifteen minutes for him to come outside, but he didn't, so I had to run all the way down the road to catch the bus. The white Converse I had bought with my own money from my new weekend job were covered in dirt. I was pissed. When I got to the mailboxes, Jax was already there, waiting for Ms. Beels.

"Why didn't you wait for me?"

He looked up from his book and then looked back down and said, "I don't have to do everything with you."

"These shoes were five Saturdays at Carter's, and now they're all dirty." Jax and I had been doing odd jobs around Carter's egg ranch on Saturdays for three dollars an hour. We were grossly underpaid, and we had to walk two miles to get there, but at least it was a job.

"That's what you get for spending all your money on shoes."

I stomped my foot. "Ugh! You're not being fair."

Still staring at his book, he said, "I'm not doing anything to you."

"I said I was sorry. You left your dumb journal in our fort, almost like you wanted me to find it."

"I'm not fighting with you because I don't care, Em. I told you ten minutes earlier not to read it. You can't even apologize the right way."

"Sorry I'm not perfect like you."

"Oh, and by the way, it's not a journal, it's a novel, and it's going to kick ass when I'm done with it. And the fort is mine, Emerson, not ours. It's on my property."

I turned my back to him and stared down the road, fuming silently. When the bus pulled up, I took our normal seat at the front. Jax passed me and went all the way to the back.

"Real mature, Fisher," I called out. We were acting like our ten-year-old selves, but we weren't ten anymore.

The freshmen at Neeble High had their own hall, so it would be impossible for Jax to avoid me all day. And avoid me, he didn't. Coming out of English class, I saw that he was standing in the spot he always stood to walk with me to math, except he wasn't alone. He was leaning against a row of old lockers no one used anymore with his arm around Desiree Banks.

STUPID BOY.

"Grow up," I muttered as I passed him. Desiree shot me her best stink eye, which made her look constipated.

Jackson could get any girl he wanted, and he knew it. He

was the only boy at that age with perfect skin, strong arms, and the beginnings of a six-pack. And he was tall. He had grown fast. He'd outgrown all the goofiness of his preteen years by the beginning of our ninth-grade year—or maybe I just didn't see it anymore. I had developed early too. Not that I had nice breasts—they were barely there, but by the end of ninth grade, I was done growing in every direction. Unfortunately, the same could be said for Desiree, who had grown in certain ways that I never would.

I sat in the library at lunch and talked to Ms. Lilly, the librarian.

"Where's Jax today?" she asked. Even the teachers knew we were inseparable.

"I don't know. He has a girlfriend now."

The small gray-haired woman in her sixties looked surprised. "A girlfriend? I thought *you* were his girlfriend."

"When we were kids people used to say that. It was just dumb kid stuff."

"Oh."

I held up a copy of She's Come Undone. "Thanks for getting this for me."

"It's not exactly on the reading list, Emerson. Keep it hush-hush."

"Always, Ms. Lilly. Thank you." I went to a table to read, but I was distracted. I wondered why, in all of the time that Jax and I had spent together, he hadn't tried to kiss me. He never even brought it up. I wasn't the prettiest girl in school—no butt, no boobs, just a beanpole with a mop of dark hair—but I had nice skin and he'd told me once that I had pretty eyes. Actually, he'd said they were weird and so big, he felt like he could dive in and swim around in them. So maybe "pretty" wasn't the right word . . .

Maybe he really *was* writing about Desiree. Maybe I was just his buddy from childhood that he used to play in the mud with.

On the bus on the way home, he was sitting in the front seat. "Hey, Em!"

He looked far too chipper for Jackson. As I took the seat beside him, I peered closer at his neck. "What in god's name . . . Is that a . . . oh, gross." It was a big, purplish-brown hickey. "I didn't take you for a boob guy, Jack-son."

"Whatever do you mean, Emer-son?"

I held my hands up to mimic big boobs. "Desiree, you idiot."

He smirked in that shit-eating kind of way. "Oh. Yeah, hmm. I hadn't really noticed."

I huffed and then scurried to the back of the bus, thinking two could play this game. I ran home and threw my backpack down in the entryway. Racing past the kitchen, I glanced in and saw my father sitting at the table, reading the paper and drinking coffee. I stopped abruptly and backed up to the doorway. He looked up and smiled. "How was your day, honey?"

Honey? His eyes looked clearer than I had ever seen them. *My day was horrible.* "Good. How was yours?"

"Good. I made a meat loaf for you to heat up after I leave for work."

Who is this man? "Thank you, Dad."

He stood from the table. "Well, I better go get ready for work." When he left the room I walked to his coffee mug and sniffed it. There was a very detectable amount of whiskey in his coffee, but the fact that he wasn't sitting on the couch in his underwear, drinking it straight from the bottle and cursing at the TV, was an improvement.

Before he left, he peeked into my room, where I was lying on the bed, staring at the ceiling, thinking about Jackson's stupid hickey. "If you want to take the meat loaf over to the Fishers', that's fine by me. You don't have to eat alone."

"That's okay." I was used to it. "Jax and I aren't really hanging out much. He has a girlfriend."

He looked moderately relieved. I would've loved to think it was because he didn't want anyone hurting his daughter, but I had been told so many times before not to get knocked up that it had to be more for that reason. "Okay. I'll be home in the morning," he said, and he was gone.

AT SCHOOL THE next day, I found Hunter "The Hoover" Stevens, who was known far and wide as the make-out king of our school. I think I was the only girl he hadn't defiled behind the bleachers of the football field. I knew he was an easy target because he had been dropping me sly hints over the last few months. Like, "Hey, Emerson. You want to go study for the math test under the bleachers?"

Up until that point, I had ignored his pathetic attempts, but Hunter, Jackson, and I all had math together, so I took the opportunity to exact my revenge. I sauntered past Jax and leaned against Hunter's desk. "I don't really get this algebra stuff. I heard you're, like, a pro."

His eyes shot open and then dropped to my boobs. "You heard right."

"How 'bout at lunch?" I said.

"Okay, meet me behind the bleachers on the football field."

"I'll be there." I looked to the seat behind Hunter, where Jackson sat. He was slouching in his chair with his long legs spread out in front of him, in the cool-guy pose, pretending not to pay attention.

At lunch, I went into the bathroom and stared at myself in the mirror. I ate a breath mint and put on some lip gloss and thought about being kissed for the first time. All the other girls were way ahead of me in that department. Ruthie Brennerman came in and tapped me on the shoulder. "So, you and Hunter, huh?" She rolled her eyes. "Everyone thought you and Jax were together."

"Nope, we're just friends."

"Oh."

She put lipstick on and made kissy lips in the mirror. "Have fun with Hunter."

I thought about how everyone used to call her "Toothy Ruthie" until she got braces. We were all growing up. I felt sad. I looked in the mirror again and saw my younger self with the wild hair and bushy eyebrows, and then I saw Jackson's younger face, his sweet smile, and his kind eyes. I started to cry. I wanted him to be my first kiss. I wanted to be his.

I ran out of the bathroom and smack into Jax's chest. "Get out of my way."

"Em, are you crying?"

"Don't call me that," I yelled as I ran away.

I met Hunter by the football field. His hands were bracing my neck before I was able to even get a word out. He pressed his lips to mine and then his tongue was in my mouth. It was weird, warm, slobbery, and gross, but I kissed him back anyway. Hunter was short with buzzed hair and no real standout features, but he wasn't terrible-looking either. He just wasn't Jax.

The whole time I thought, *Why am I doing this?* Hunter was pressing himself against me with enthusiasm. It wasn't exactly romantic. I could feel that he was turned on. Not surprising for a fifteen-year-old boy. About a month before, Jax and I had been lying on the cot, reading to each other, and I'd noticed something growing in his pants. I'd laughed and he'd gotten embarrassed and then left the shed, cursing at me. I wished I hadn't laughed. I wished I would have pretended not to see it. That's what he would have done.

Hunter tried to put his hand up my shirt as we made out against the chain-link fence that ran behind the bleachers. That's when I heard someone say, "Em?"

I broke away from the kiss to see Jax standing a safe distance away, near the bleacher post. He had his black hoodie on, and it shadowed his face so I couldn't see his expression. His hands were shoved deep into the pockets of his jeans. He looked different . . . dejected. No more Tough Jax.

"Yeah, what's up, Jackson?"

"You okay?" His voice was low, timid.

I looked back at Hunter. "You know what, I'm . . ."

"What does he want?" Hunter asked.

"I have to go," I said.

"But we're kissing," Hunter said. He really was a bright one.

"I know. I have to go, I'm sorry." But I wasn't. The only thing I was sorry for was kissing him.

As I approached Jax, he looked up from his shoes. His eyes were bloodshot. We stood there facing each other in silence.

The corners of his mouth turned up, but it wasn't a cocky smile. His eyes were downcast. It was a sad smile.

"Are you into him?"

"No. Not really."

"What does that mean? Were you just trying to get back at me?"

"Listen . . . I . . ."

"It *was* about you . . . what I wrote. It was all about you." His bottom lip began to quiver.

"I know," I said, my voice shaky. I started to cry then. There was no holding back. "I loved it, every word. It was so beautiful."

He reached his thumb out and wiped tears from my cheek. "Em, can we please go back to the way things were?"

"Yes . . . definitely."

He pulled me into his chest. "I mean, Hunter Stevens? Really? That guy's such a slimeball."

I wiped my tears and laughed into his shirt. "Come on, Desiree Banks? She's a slut and everyone knows it . . . and those boobs, my god."

"For the record, I'm not really a boob guy. Well, I mean . . ."

"I get it, dork! I can't believe she was your first kiss."

He pushed my shoulders back to look at me. "Desiree wasn't my first kiss."

"She wasn't?"

"No. I kissed Katy Brown in the seventh grade. We made out in the reading room in the back of the library." He scratched his chin. "And then there was Chastity Williams, and then Lizzy Peters, and . . ."

"Okay, okay, geez, I guess Desiree's not the slut here."

"Was that your first kiss, Em? With Hunter?"

I was beginning to feel like a total fool. "Yeah, kinda." I said it so quietly I could barely hear myself.

His piteous smile was back.

"Don't look at me like that, Jax. So what? Who cares?"

"No, it's not a big deal. I just figured . . . You always seemed so, I don't know, I just figured . . ."

"You figured what? What Jackson? That my first kiss would be with you?"

He shrugged. "Maybe."

"That's not an answer."

He sighed. "You're special."

"Oh, I'm special? That makes me sound retarded."

"I hate that word, Emerson."

"Well, what do you mean?" My voice was getting higher and my cheeks were getting pinker.

"I mean, I wanted to practice for you. I wanted our first kiss with each other to be perfect."

"Really?" I leaned up on my toes, trying to physically absorb his words.

"I swear. I've always wanted to kiss you. You have to have known that."

I blinked a couple of times before reaching up and craning my neck toward him. *Hmm, that clean Jackson smell.* Around eighth grade, he started remembering to put on deodorant, thank god. "I guess I kind of knew."

I leaned in closer.

"Well, I'm not gonna kiss you now, with Hunter's slobber all over you. We have to disinfect you big-time. Soap in the mouth and everything."

"Oh, shut it, you." I punched him in the chest.

He grabbed my hand and pulled me along. "Come on, we're late for biology."

5. Still Not Talking

"You still reading that book?" Cara asked as she walked by me while I folded laundry on the couch.

"Yeah," I said, and then followed her into the kitchen. I sat down at the bar while she took out ingredients for a smoothie. It was noon, and I knew she had a class to teach in an hour.

"You haven't really been eating, Emi."

"No, I have been. I'm fine. Hey, do you want to make Bloody Marys instead?" I asked.

She laughed. "Are you becoming an alcoholic?"

"I have something to tell you," I said, abruptly. She stared at me and her smile faded.

"Do I need to cancel my class?" she asked.

"You know that, uh . . . book? You know. The one by J. Colby?"

"Uhh, of course I do. I just read it. You're reading it now. I just asked you about it literally thirty seconds ago."

"Yeah, well . . ." I wanted to tell her the truth, but I

couldn't bring myself to do it. "I just wanted to say thanks for passing it on to me."

She smiled. "That's it?"

I nodded.

"You still want me to make you a Bloody Mary?"

"No, you should get to class," I told her.

"Aren't you going in?" she asked.

"No, I canceled mine. I have a bad headache. I think I'm going to go for a run and maybe try to get some words on paper."

"Good girl." She hustled to the door with her bag and then called back, "Oh, you're welcome for the book, but you should thank whoever stuck that *New Yorker* article in my box at school. That's how I found out about it to begin with."

I stared at the closed door after she left. Someone had left her an article about J. Colby?

I RAN FOUR miles, came back to the apartment, and sat at my computer. Writing would be impossible, so I went back to his website and stared at his picture, navigated to the form box, and began a new message to him:

Jase, Why bring it all back up? Why? Why? Why?

Oh, and your writing sucks.

I deleted it then opened the book once again.

From *All the Roads Between*

Mr. Williams, our tall, brainy-looking biology teacher, stood at the whiteboard and lectured, occasionally asking questions of the class, but I didn't hear anything he said. I was thinking about Jax, who was sitting right behind me. As I twirled my hair through my fingers, I imagined what kissing him would be like.

His body was too long for our classroom desks, so he had to sit kind of low with his legs spread out in front of him. I could just make out the length of his legs in my peripheral vision. I was starting to notice all these feelings that I hadn't really thought about before, and I could feel his warmth emanating from behind me.

Mr. Williams cleared his throat and said loudly, "These are cells that lack a membrane-bound nucleus. Who knows what they're called?"

No one raised a hand.

"Fisher!" Mr. Williams barked out.

"Prokaryotes?" Jackson said, like he wasn't sure, but I knew he was.

"That's right," Mr. Williams said. "Emerson, are you paying attention?"

I sat up straight in my seat. "Yes, sir."

"Okay," Mr. Williams said. "Then tell us, the system we've been talking about this whole class period is called what?"

My heart was racing, and the room started spinning. I hated being called on. I had no idea what the answer was, but then Jackson whispered, "Binomial nomenclature."

It was like he had said, *I want to make love to you.* That's how Jackson saying "binomial nomenclature" sounded to me.

Mr. Williams was still glaring at me. I pointed my finger to the ceiling and announced, "Binomial nomenclature!"

"So you *are* paying attention, Emerson. Good, " Mr. Williams said.

On the bus ride home, Jax said, "It's really hard to pay attention in class when you're always playing with your hair in front of me." He squeezed my hand and smiled. Something about the way he was touching me felt different from all the other times.

"You don't seem to have a problem getting all the answers right."

"I'm just saying. I wanted to lick the back of your neck today."

"Jackson," I said in a low, conspiratorial whisper. "That's gross!" But I could feel my neck tingling with anticipation.

"Seriously, I want to lick your mouth, but I keep thinking about Hunter's tongue down your throat."

"He did stick his tongue down my throat." I shuddered, and Jackson laughed some more, so I elbowed him. I could barely deal with our flirty banter.

"It looked bad, Em."

"Well, I've never kissed anyone before. Stop teasing me."

"I'm not teasing you. It's just there's a certain finesse to it, you know? I'll teach you later." He winked.

"Geez, you really are so full of yourself sometimes."

"You love me."

"I have no choice," I said.

We jumped off the stairs of the bus one after the other. "'Bye, Ms. Beels," Jackson yelled from the mailboxes. "See you tomorrow."

"Is your mom working tonight?" I asked him.

"Yeah, what about your dad?"

"I think so."

"Okay, you want to come over? We can watch TV at my house. And I can undo everything Hunter taught you," he deadpanned.

"Jackson Fisher, will you stop that right now?!"

"I'm kidding, I want you to come over and hang out. No pressure."

"All right, I'm gonna do homework first and then I'll be over."

He put his arm around my shoulder. "You can do mine if you want."

"No, you can do your own, Casanova."

He laughed. "You're right. I have a higher percentage than you in biology and math."

"You know what, you sure have let all this attention from girls go to your head. I'm not sure you deserve me."

"Well, I don't care about any of the other girls. Only you."

The air was full of anticipation. We talked and laughed all the way home. We didn't know it at the time, but we were lovesick. Our innocence was beautiful, impossible to capture again, impossible to re-create. Sometimes on the bus, when it was just Jax and me passing the mile markers, I would daydream that Ms. Beels would turn around and drive us all out of Neeble. The three of us would live together in that bus, somewhere, anywhere where there were no brothers drowning in the creek, no drug-addicted mothers, no whiskey monsters lurking.

My smile faded when I noticed my dad's beat-up Toyota truck parked oddly in front of our house. "See you in a bit," I said absently.

Jax kissed the top of my head. "I can't wait."

Just before I reached my front door and he reached his, we both turned around. He kissed his hand and waved. I did the same.

The moment I opened my front door, I knew. The house was dark. The musty smell of booze and BO hit me as I walked through the entryway. On my way to my room, I glanced over to see my dad passed out on the couch, the TV blaring and an empty bottle lying on its side next to him.

As quietly as I could, I closed the door to my room and started on my homework. He was supposed to leave for work around four p.m., so at a quarter till, I went into the living room and tried to wake him.

"Dad?" I shook his shoulder, but he slapped my hand away. "You're gonna be late for work."

"Fuck that job. I'm not going back," he mumbled into a cushion. The whiskey monster was back. I hadn't seen him like this in a while.

"Dad? Come on."

"I said leave me alone, Emerson! Don't you listen?"

"Okay, I'm sorry." I went back into my room to finish studying for the biology test the following day.

A short while later, I heard him lumbering down the hallway. He swung my bedroom door open, staggered to my dresser, and started rummaging through the drawers.

"Where is it?"

"Where is what, Dad?"

"Your money from the egg ranch." His chest was pumping in and out. I stood up and went to a small purse I had hanging on my bedpost. I reached in and took out the wad of money, mostly ones and fives—about thirty-eight dollars. I had been saving it for so long to buy a dress for the end-of-the-year dance.

He snatched it out of my hand. "Dad, that's for my . . ."

"I don't give a shit what it's for. Haven't I been good to you?"

"Um . . ."

"Haven't I?!" he screamed.

"Yes, sir."

Sweat was forming on his brow. "I'll get another job, okay, you little cunt?" The word stung and made me feel physically sick. I noticed that I had torn out a chunk of my hair from twirling it so violently from nervousness.

He stormed out of my room, and a minute later I heard his truck start. I went to the window and watched him fly down the road. Instead of sulking about the money, I tried desperately to focus on thoughts of Jax.

I took my time washing up and changing into sweats. I grabbed a package of microwave popcorn and walked over to Jax's. He opened the door shirtless, barefoot, and wearing a huge grin. He had on my favorite pair of jeans. I smiled, but he could see the sadness in my eyes. "What's wrong?" He held the door open but stood in front of me and wouldn't let me pass. He pointed to my house. "What did he do to you?"

"Nothing. It's not a big deal. He's gone now."

"Come here." We hugged for longer than normal. His chest was hard against my cheek. I could feel the indentions on the sides of his narrow hips. Jackson was a man and I was a woman, and when we were pressed against each other like that, the whole world made sense.

I pulled away reluctantly and held up the popcorn. "Can I pop this here?"

"I'll do it."

I followed him into the kitchen. "What do you want to watch tonight?"

"I'll let you pick. Lady's choice. But first, why don't you tell me what happened?"

"Nothing that unusual." I hopped up on the counter next to the old yellow refrigerator. "My dad was drunk. He didn't go to work."

Jax started the microwave, came over, and stood between my legs. He pressed his palms to my thighs and rubbed them up and down. "I like these."

"My sweats?"

"Yeah. I like it when it's just you and me like this. Comfortable."

My heart was racing. "Now you're all words and feelings. What's gotten into you, Fisher?"

"It was hard to see you with Hunter."

I cocked my head to the side. "It was hard to stare at this for two days." I pointed to the fading hickey on his neck.

"I know."

"He called me a cunt."

"Who?"

"My dad. He's never called me that before."

Jax closed his eyes in disgust and shook his head. "I'll kill him," he whispered. That wasn't the first time Jax had said something like this, but we always knew it was just talk. "God, Em. You don't deserve that."

I started tearing up. "I don't want to cry any more today."

He tilted my chin up so we were eye to eye, and then he ran his index finger down my jawline. He studied my face, looking from my eyes to my mouth. There was reverence in his expression.

"What?" I said, and then his lips were on mine. He kissed me slowly, sweetly. He gently braced my neck with both hands and deepened the kiss. I anchored my hands on the outsides of his biceps. He felt bigger to me. He felt safe, warm, familiar. When he broke away, he opened his eyes and smiled for a moment. I smiled back, and then he kissed me again. I moved my hands to his ribs and pulled him closer. He trailed kisses up my jawline and to my ear. My breath was quickening. Near my ear, in a low voice, he said. "I have wanted to do that for so long."

"Was it okay?" I said nervously.

"Shhh, it was perfect."

He bit my earlobe gently. I whimpered.

"Take your hands off her." My father's slurred voice traveled down the dark hallway.

Jax pulled back but kept his hands on my neck and his eyes focused on mine. I was frozen.

"I said take your fucking hands off her."

Jackson's eyes started to water and then he squeezed them shut like he was trying to make us disappear. He shook his head and whispered, "This is not happening."

"It's okay, Jax. Let me go. It'll be okay."

He let go of my neck finally and just mouthed the words, *I'm sorry.*

"It's not your fault."

"Get your ass home, Emerson." My father's voice shook the walls around us.

"Okay, Dad." I hopped off the counter and walked toward him. "Let's go," I said to him, and pointed to the door.

"I'm gonna have a word with this degenerate first."

"Dad, I kissed him. Nothing else happened. That's the first

time we ever kissed." I looked back at Jackson, whose eyes were now wide with panic.

"Shut up! Get your ass home now!"

I pleaded one last time, "Please, don't hurt him."

I stood just outside of the front door and listened. All I heard him say was, "Touch her again and I'll kill you. I got a loaded shotgun waiting for you at my house."

When I heard him coming toward the front, I ran home, into my bedroom, and shut the door.

He didn't come in right away. I think he had to drink some of that nice bottle he'd bought with my egg ranch money before he was ready to scream in my face. For a while, I thought he might leave me alone, but that wouldn't be his style.

Forty-five minutes later, my door swung open. "Stand up, you lying little bitch."

For the first time ever, I held my head high and walked toward him. I looked him right in the eye and was rewarded with a *smack!* I stared at him in shock. He'd slapped me. He had never hit me like that in the face. He'd grabbed me roughly before and shoved me around when things got really bad, but he'd never struck me with such purpose and force. I gathered myself, straightened my shoulders, and lifted my face to him again. I was scared and shaking.

"Do you want to be a liar and a slut?"

"No, sir."

Smack! "You little bitch." *Smack.* "You lied to me, Diana!" *Smack.*

Why was he calling me my mother's name?

"It's Emerson, Dad!" *Smack.* I started to sob. "I'm sorry, Dad." *Smack.*

"I didn't even have to touch that little pussy Jackson. He practically pissed himself right there on the kitchen floor."

Something changed within me all of a sudden. I felt like my father could say anything to me and anything about my mother, he could talk about all the people in the world he despised, all the sluts and druggies and degenerates, but in my book, he wasn't allowed to touch Jax. He wasn't even allowed to breathe his name. I wouldn't let him without a fight.

In a strangely resigned voice, I said, "Fuck you." My father stood there, glaring at me, motionless, stunned. "I said fuck you, you mean bastard. You have no right."

With an open-fisted smack, he shoved me to the ground and kicked me in the head. I blacked out and came to seconds later. He was beating me on my back and butt with the buckle end of his belt. I started screaming from the pain and begged him to stop. I tried to scurry away on my hands and knees, but he stepped on my back and then swung me around by my hair. He punched me in the face and I blacked out again. I was hovering somewhere on the brink of consciousness, and I could feel my body getting pummeled as he struck me over and over again.

When my bedroom door creaked open, I saw Jackson's black hoodie and sneakers coming toward us.

I tried to yell, "No, Jax!" but my voice was gone. I was afraid my father would kill him. In one motion, Jax lifted my father's weight from me and threw him down, against my wood dresser. I was trying desperately to stay conscious. There was blood on my face and in my eyes, but through it all, I could still see Jackson straddling my father, punching him, one blow after another in fast succession.

"You piece of shit!" He was screaming and crying as he hit

him over and over again. When it looked like my father had either passed out or had been knocked out, I watched Jackson get up and come over to me with wide, scared eyes. He lifted me effortlessly. His tears fell onto my face, but I couldn't feel anything anymore. "Oh god. Oh god." He kept saying over and over again. "Don't die. Please, Em, don't leave me."

I thought idly that I must look really bad, and then I lost consciousness again. When I came to, I was lying across the front seat of my dad's truck. My head was on Jackson's lap. He talked continuously as he drove, "Try to stay awake, Em." My clothes were sticking to me from the cuts. I started to feel the stinging and ache everywhere on my body. Jackson had his learner's permit. He would be sixteen in another month and would have his license. *Maybe then we can leave Neeble behind*, I thought.

"Emerson, I love you. Please try to keep your eyes open." But I couldn't anymore because I just wanted to dream about Jackson and me, in some other life, loving each other.

Jax wouldn't leave my side at the hospital. Even after police and social workers from Child Protective Services told him I would be fine, he wouldn't leave. I had a concussion, blackened and swollen eyes, a split lip, some minor lacerations from the belt buckle, and a lot of bruises, but otherwise I was okay. When we got word that my father had been arrested without much resistance, Jackson relaxed a little, but he still wouldn't leave. Not that I wanted him to.

We became something of a media sensation over the two days we were there. A story was written about Jax and me in the paper. The fifteen-year-old boy who saved his girlfriend's life, drove her fifteen miles to the hospital, and then carried her weak body into the ER. We both got a lot of special treatment.

The nurses fed him, fixed up his hand, and let him sleep in my room. But our happiness was short-lived.

"You're going into foster care," he said the morning I was discharged.

"I know. They're sending me to New Clayton. It's not that far. We can see each other on the weekends." I was devastated and so was he, but I wanted him to understand that we could still be together. "You're my best friend," I said to him.

"I'm so in love with you." His eyes were pleading. He was starting to look pretty rough after two days without a shower, and his worry made him seem older than fifteen. His longish brown hair was going every which way, and his eyes were bloodshot.

"I'm going to be okay, Jax. We're going to be okay, and I love you too. When you get your license, you can come and see me."

Near my hospital bed, he put his hand on my cheek. I winced. "I can't believe he did this to you. Why was it so different this time?"

"I don't know. Don't worry about me, okay? I'm gonna be good . . . better. Only a couple of years and we can go to California. We'll be together and we can go to college and you can finish writing your book and we'll get a cat."

He laughed. "I like dogs."

"We'll get a cat and a dog."

"You swear?"

"I promise you, Jackson. That means more than swearing."

"I'm gonna hold you to it. I'll come and find you and make you keep your word."

"You won't have to," I told him.

Paula, my social worker from CPS, came into the room. "Hi, Emerson. Hi, Jax. Before we leave, Emerson, you'll need to sit down with the detective from the police department. I can be in there as your advocate. They'll need a brief statement from you. Your father has pleaded guilty, so you won't have to testify, but you do have to give a statement."

"Okay."

After I met with members of the police department, Jax and I went to the front, where his mom was waiting in her old car. She only waved at me; she didn't even bother getting out. I wondered why.

"What's with your mom?"

"I don't know. Don't worry about her."

"Did she say anything to you when you called her this morning?" He shook his head. "Tell me, Jackson, please."

He sighed. "She was worried that being involved with this stuff with your dad was gonna get me into trouble—jeopardize college and stuff. You know how she's banking on me to take care of her, right?" He rolled his eyes.

"You did an amazing thing. Please do not let her make you feel bad about it. You're a hero."

He reached down and ran his thumb over my bottom lip. "I think you're the hero, Em. You're so strong . . . fearless."

"I'm a huge wimp. Remember when you found that big brown spider in the shed?"

"You're right. You're a huge wimp, but only when it comes to spiders."

Paula pulled up in her car and waited for Jax and me to say good-bye.

"I am so grateful to have you in my life, Jackson. You keep saving me over and over."

He smiled, his eyes watery. "Being on that stupid road without you is gonna suck."

"Keep telling yourself that it won't be for very long."

"You'll call me every day, right?"

"I'm gonna try. It's only New Clayton. It's not even that far. Think she'll let you use the car when you get your license?"

He glanced over to Leila. "Come on, Jax, I gotta get to work!" she yelled.

"Probably not. God, I'm so frustrated, Em. I don't want to leave you."

"Don't stress, okay? We'll figure it out. Maybe Paula will help. She really likes you."

I ran my palm down his cheek. There was pain in his sweet, tender eyes. "I love you, Jackson, and you love me. That's all that matters."

He nodded and then leaned down and pressed his lips to mine. When I closed my eyes, I felt a tear hit my cheek, and then he was gone. Right before his mother pulled away, he looked up through the passenger window, kissed his hand, and waved. I did the same.

6. It Was All True

I closed the book and took a deep breath. So far, almost everything Jase had written was accurate. Unbelievably, he had nailed every moment of that fateful night, right down to my complicated feelings. There were only a few subtle differences. My father was more of a sloppy drunk than an angry one, and "the whiskey monster" was Jase's name for him, not mine. My dad was verbally abusive and neglectful, but he was rarely physically violent, with the exception of the few times he lost control. But nothing compared to that last night I lived under his roof.

That night changed my whole life, and it was the main reason I refused to look backward. But whenever I had been forced to talk about it during therapy sessions, I always got lost in my own memories and feelings. I never really thought about how Jase had felt in that situation, how that night might've impacted him deep down inside. But clearly, it had. It *did*. I wondered if writing those scenes was somehow cathartic for him.

Leila, whose name was actually Lisa, obviously had been a heroin addict, though the book tried to make her addiction seem harmless and less urgent. I wondered if Jase was trying to protect her by lightly skimming over the facts. She had tried to provide for her sons, but by the time they were teenagers, she was pretty far gone. Her arms were covered in track marks, and she spent most of her money on drugs. There had been a lot of unsavory characters in and out of Jase's house—we could only imagine what for.

Reading Jase's book was like reading the story I would've written myself if I ever followed Cara's advice to start a memoir. The entire experience was strange. It was like my memories had come to life, complete with every sensory detail. Each page transported me back to that ugly place in Ohio where Jase and I had been stuck for our entire childhoods.

Yet the idea of the book still made me angry, not grateful. I kept going back to the opening pages before the text, looking for a dedication, but there was nothing. He was going to drag me all the way through my painful past, steal my story, and not even dedicate the damn book to me.

Later that night, Trevor came over with a pizza. We sat at the breakfast bar and ate in awkward silence as I waited for him to bring up our conversation from the night before. He had been begging me to share a part of my past with him for so long, and finally I had opened up to him. But nothing had really changed between us, and now I felt further away from him than I had before.

"So . . . what did you do today?" I asked through a mouthful of food.

"Just PT, then I grabbed some beers with the other assistant coaches. You?"

"Nothing much. Laundry."

Trevor laid a greasy slice down on his plate and paused. "Emi, are you still feeling emotional about that thing you told me last night?"

That thing? "I opened up to you about some very traumatic things and you've barely acknowledged that. You know I hate revisiting my past, and this book I'm reading isn't helping. So yeah, I'm feeling pretty shitty."

"What book?" he asked, totally missing the point.

I felt something snap inside of me, and before I knew it, the words were tumbling from my mouth. "I'm reading a book about me, Trevor. My first love wrote a whole book about our childhood, from my perspective, and it's a huge hit. And now he's a bestselling author. And you know what? I'm more than just upset about it; I'm fucking devastated and confused because I don't want to relive those awful memories, and I certainly don't want anyone else profiting from them."

He was looking right at me now, his eyes wide with shock. "What the . . . Where the hell did you get this book? Let me see it." No apology for his insensitivity. No sympathy for what I was going through. Typical Trevor.

"No way."

"Why?"

"Because it's mostly about my relationship with another guy."

"If he was from your childhood, weren't you guys just kids?"

"I mean, I haven't seen him in twelve years, but our connection was very . . ." I swallowed nervously. "Intense."

He crossed his arms and gave me a skeptical look. "I'm

not going to be jealous of your juvenile relationship, Emi. I just want to know what he wrote about you."

Suddenly, I regretted telling him about Jase and the book. "Just let me finish reading it. It's personal, that's all."

"The whole world can read it, but your boyfriend can't?" He rolled his eyes. "That's bullshit."

I didn't respond, and he didn't push. He wasn't wrong exactly, but I didn't need to justify myself. It *was* personal. If he wanted a copy, he'd have to buy it himself.

We sat in silence as we finished our dinner, then we moved to the couch so Trevor could watch football while I curled up into a ball and continued reading. He assumed his standard position as he slouched against the cushions, his feet kicked up on the coffee table, his hands clasped together behind his head. It struck me that there was something wrong about his casualness. We had just had a fight, yet his body language suggested that nothing had happened. Like he had moved on.

To the untrained eye, we looked like the picture of intimacy, but there was nothing intimate here. Our relationship was lazy. He should have been rubbing my feet, and I should have been practicing full disclosure, but instead we were as far apart as we could be in every sense of the word. It was easier that way.

From *All The Roads Between*

On the way to the foster home in New Clayton, Paula gave me all the pertinent details of my new life. Mr. and Mrs. Keller were in their sixties and had been foster parents for over thirty years. I would be the oldest of five foster kids in their home, which sounded kind of great to me—I loved the idea of having little kids around to play with. By the time we pulled up to the old, yellow, three-story Victorian, I had stars in my eyes. It looked like a dollhouse.

Paula thought the Kellers would be a great match for me, and I couldn't agree more. I was so excited to meet my new family.

The door opened, revealing a stout woman with heavy frown lines at the corners of her mouth and gray hair permed and styled into a short crop. Mrs. Keller opened the door and then immediately turned around and yelled, "Sophia, up to your room!" Her thunderous voice made me step backward off the porch step. "Leaving already? You just got here."

"I . . . I . . ."

Paula spoke for me. "Hi, Mrs. Keller. This is Emerson. She's fifteen and loves to read."

"What happened to your face, child?"

"My—my . . ."

"She was just removed from the home she shared with her abusive father," Paula answered for me.

"I know all that. I heard the story. I want to hear her speak. In this house you can speak, Emerson, as long as it's with respect. You understand?"

"Yes."

"He was one of those paper mill boys, wasn't he? None of

them are worth a damn, are they? Well, come on in—what are you waiting for?"

Paula put her arm around my shoulder and walked me into the house. "Mrs. Keller," Paula said, "can I see where Emerson will be sleeping?"

"Sure can. Follow me."

The house smelled of citrus wood cleaner. It was tidy and quiet for a house with four children. I held on to the freshly polished wooden banister as I made my way up the stairs behind Mrs. Keller and Paula.

Paula, a thin, fit woman in her thirties, was out of breath by the time we got to the third story, yet Mrs. Keller, with her rotund body, barely even broke a sweat. Once we reached the landing, Mrs. Keller led us to a small room in the attic space beneath the pitched roof. It was immaculate. You could see the vacuum passes in the carpet, and the single bed under the window was draped with a pristine pink chiffon and lace comforter.

"Fit for a princess," Paula said.

"Yes," I agreed. "This is amazing."

"You'll be expected to keep this space tidy," Mrs. Keller said.

Paula turned to me. "Why don't you get your suitcase? I'm going to ask Mrs. Keller a few questions in the meantime."

"Okay."

On my way downstairs, I spotted a little girl peeking at us from around the corner.

"Hi," I called out to her. To my surprise, she came out and stood before me. "Hi, I'm Sophia." She had long, perfectly combed blonde hair that framed her angelic face.

"I'm Emerson." I held my hand out. "It's nice to meet you."

"Likewise."

I had never heard a child talk that way. "How old are you?"

"I'm eight. How old are you?"

"I'm fifteen. I'll be sixteen in July."

"Only three months away. Lucky you."

"Yep. Do you like it here?"

"Yeah, I love it."

"How old are the other kids?" I asked.

Out of the corner of my eye, I saw a few pairs of feet. Then I heard the sound of pitter-pattering, coupled with the glorious sound of children giggling. "Come out, you guys," Sophia called out before turning back to me. "They're really excited to meet you."

From behind the stairs came three little boys, all around the same age. "The twins are Brandon and Daniel. They're five. Thomas is six."

"Hi, Emerson," they said, almost in unison.

"Hi, guys."

They ran up to me and hugged my legs.

Sophia smiled. "They're really sweet, but they can be a pain in the butt too. And they eat a lot."

"I think I'm gonna like it here. How are the Kellers?"

"They're great. You just have to follow their rules."

"Of course," I said. *That sounds totally reasonable.*

"I mean they have a zero-tolerance policy. They're very good to the children they foster, but they don't get attached. A lot of the older kids don't last long here because they get into trouble."

I wondered what these rules entailed, but just then, Mr. Keller appeared in the hallway. "Emerson, I'm Mr. Keller." He shook my hand. He was wearing a plaid Pendleton shirt and

Dockers with a perfect crease down the front of each leg. He had a well-groomed beard and a kind face.

"Hello," I said.

"Kids, go finish your chores and let me have a word with Emerson."

Three pairs of feet scurried away, but Sophia kept looking back at me as she walked up the stairs.

"We run a good home here, Emerson, but you should know we don't take a lot of teenagers because we don't like putting up with the drama. Okay?"

"I understand."

He didn't waste any time before laying out the expectations. "Your social worker said you'd focus on schoolwork, do your chores, and follow the rules. Can we count on you to do that?"

"I will, I promise. But what are the rules exactly?"

"Only school- and church-affiliated extracurricular activities. Homework and chores must be done before dinner. You're expected to attend church and Bible study on Sundays. And respect for all members of the house is required. We don't tolerate any talking back."

"So . . . no social life?"

He blinked at me for ten uncomfortably long seconds. "Is that all you got out of that?" Before I could answer, he said, "Judging by the look of your face, you're in need of a safe place to live. Am I right?"

"Yes."

"Follow the rules and you'll get that here," he said, and then he walked away.

I wondered if they would let me call Jackson. I thought he qualified as a non-school-related extracurricular activity.

Paula was coming down the stairs as I headed up. "I think you'll be comfortable here. It's a nice place and these are good people," she said.

"Am I going to be able to see Jackson?"

"You'll have to ask Mrs. Keller. But, Emerson, it's very hard to find good foster care these days. Please respect their rules."

"I have to be able to see him, Paula. He's the only person I have. He saved my life."

"You'll have Sophia and the three boys and Mr. and Mrs. Keller. They're very involved in the community church. I'm sure you'll meet new friends here in New Clayton."

"Sophia and the boys? They're little kids." My head started pounding and my hands felt clammy. We were facing each other on the second-story landing. I set my suitcase down and braced myself against the banister. "I have to be able to see him. I have to be able to talk to him. Paula, you don't understand."

"I understand. I was fifteen once."

"No!" I raised my voice and then noticed Mrs. Keller standing at the top of the stairs, wearing a skeptical look.

"Don't mess this up," Paula whispered, and then she brushed past me and headed toward the door, calling back over her shoulder, "I'll call tomorrow to check in."

I was dizzy. I took small, deliberate breaths and then buckled over and dry-heaved.

"Don't go spilling your guts all over the carpet, missy," Mrs. Keller's voice said as she hovered above me.

I fell to my knees, dry-heaved again, and then passed out.

Mr. Keller was carrying me up the stairs when I came to. He never looked down at my face; he just set me on the bed and left the room. Mrs. Keller came in a moment later with a cold washcloth and a glass of water.

"Don't drink too fast or you'll heave it right back up. You're likely still dealing with the concussion your father gave you. We'll watch you close. You're gonna be fine."

"I'll be sick without him," I said, my voice pained. "I'll die without him."

"You don't need that sad excuse for a father. You're safe here. You'll get used to it, I promise," she said as she dabbed antibiotic ointment on my lip and forehead.

"Not my father—my friend."

"You'll make friends here." Neither Mr. nor Mrs. Keller had made eye contact with me since they'd carried me up the stairs.

"Will you at least let me call him?"

"We'll see, Emerson. It's important that you focus on fitting in here first. For now, just get some rest."

I slept for almost ten hours straight.

It was dark in my attic room when I woke up, but I could see a mop of bright blonde hair sitting in a small chair in the corner. "Sophia?"

"Yep, it's me."

I was groggy and had a hard time focusing. "What are you doing sitting here in the dark?"

"It's my watch. We were all taking half-hour turns, but Mrs. Keller said the dark would make your head feel better. I was going to read to you, but I couldn't find my book light."

"Do you like to read?"

"It's pretty much my whole life." I loved her enthusiasm.

"When I'm feeling better we'll have to go to the library and pick out some books I think you'd like."

"I would love that."

"So . . ." I said.

"So . . . can I turn on the light now?"

"Sure."

She hopped off the chair and turned on a dim floor lamp in the corner. "You look a lot better, Emmy," she said as she scanned my face. "I hope you don't mind the nickname. I just love it."

"It's nice, Sophia, thank you."

"You can call me Sophie." She laughed. "Brandon calls me 'Soapy' 'cause he still can't make the f sound."

"That's funny."

"Yeah." She looked around. "You hungry?"

"I'm starving."

"Well, come on, then."

"Wait, Sophie, do you know how I could make a phone call?"

"Hmm. Umm. I guess you'll have to ask Mrs. Keller. I've never called anyone before."

"How long have you been here?"

"Since I was two," she responded immediately.

"Oh." I tried to hide my surprise. Sophia and the Kellers seemed too cordial to have been living together for seven years. "What happened . . . when you were two?"

"What do you mean?" She tilted her head and smiled.

"Why did you come here?"

She pinned her shoulders to her ears and laughed. "I guess nobody wanted me."

"That can't be true."

"Why are you here?" Her eyes focused on my stitched lip.

How was I supposed to tell an eight-year-old the truth? "Well, we don't get to choose our parents, Sophie. All we can do is remember that sometimes their actions have nothing to do with us."

"I guess, but if they loved me, wouldn't they have come back for me by now?"

"Maybe they're lost. People get lost all the time, especially grown-ups. My dad is lost. That's why he did this to me." She looked confused. "Most of the time people who are lost don't ever find their way back."

"That's really sad, Emmy."

"Yeah. Such is life, my friend."

Poor Sophia. I could tell she hadn't ever experienced love. Not with her parents, not while living in the big yellow house with a revolving door of teenagers and children, and certainly not with the Kellers and their "rules." They projected an illusion of warmth with their home cooking and hand-stitched quilts, yet underneath the façade was an institutional rigidity, as if they were running an orphanage where children would be fed and cared for but never loved. Love was such a key ingredient in molding humans, yet it was inaccessible to kids inside of the system.

I followed Sophia down the stairs and into the kitchen, where the three boys were helping Mrs. Keller make biscuits. "Emerson, so glad to see you feeling better," Mrs. Keller said as she wiped her flour-covered hands on her apron. "Sophia, why don't you show Emerson how to set the table."

"Mrs. Keller, before I do that, I was wondering if I could use the phone to call my friend."

She went to the sink and began rinsing the dishes. With her back to me, she said, "Haven't we discussed this already? Go with Sophia and set the table."

I did as she said, and then I ate chicken and dumplings and biscuits around the big oval table with the rest of the children. Mr. and Mrs. Keller ate at a separate, smaller table.

There was a healthy amount of chatter among the children, but the adults kept quiet. All I could think about was Jackson. How I was eating a delicious homemade meal while he was probably eating cereal for the third time that day. I was scared to press the issue of calling him, but I was more scared of losing him.

In the middle of the night, I snuck down to the kitchen, took the phone from the charger, and went back up to my bedroom. I was the only one on the third floor, so I actually had privacy. I dialed Jackson's house number. It was two in the morning, but he picked up on the first ring.

"Hello?" he said.

"Hi."

"Emerson? Why are you whispering?"

"It's two in the morning, and the Kellers don't want me to call you." My voice started to crack.

"Why?"

"They're really strict," I said.

"Can't be any worse than your dad."

"No, it's different. They're good people, they just have rules."

"What kind of rules?"

"I'll try and call you every night, but I don't think we'll be able to see each other until I settle in here and earn some trust."

"Are they nice to you?"

"Yes, I'm totally safe. There are healthy, happy little kids here. The little girl is adorable."

"Okay."

"Okay, what?"

"As long as you're safe. Paula called me and told me she dropped you off in New Clayton."

"Why?"

"She wanted me to know that she found you a really good home. She asked me to keep my distance."

"Keep your distance?!" I whisper-shouted.

"Shhh, Em. Don't get yourself into trouble just to call me."

"What are you saying, Jax?"

"Nothing at all. I just want you to be safe. You could be farther away, living with assholes. It could be worse."

"It's only been a day, and I'm already sick of people telling me to stay out of trouble. I've done nothing. Talking to you doesn't make me a bad kid. That's just ridiculous. I'm going to find a way to call you no matter what."

There was a long silence. "Fuck, I miss you so bad," he said.

"I miss you too. Don't worry, I'm going to call you and I'm going to see you again soon."

"I keep thinking about our kiss . . ."

"Yeah?"

"How sweet you tasted." I sucked in a sharp breath. No one had ever talked to me like that before. "The sounds you made when I kissed your neck." His voice was rough, strained.

"Jackson, what are you doing?"

"Thinking about how badly I want to kiss you . . . and touch you." His voice was low.

My heart was pounding. "You're sleepy."

"Nope, not sleepy at all. Em, do you touch yourself when you think about me?"

I was overwhelmed with embarrassment. Jackson and I hadn't ever talked about this kind of stuff. "Um . . ."

He laughed quietly. "You don't have to be embarrassed. We've known each other our whole lives."

"That's why I'm embarrassed." It's unusual for kids at that age, especially a boy and a girl, to talk openly about these things. We were learning about ourselves together. We didn't have any grown-ups in our lives to guide us. Jax and I were raising each other.

It wasn't about what he was doing or what he was curious about. It was the fact that he could say it to me, the person he was fantasizing about, and he knew it would be okay. It made me love him more.

"I just hope you think about me. I miss you, that's all," he said.

"You're basically all I think about, dork."

"Ha! There's my girl. So, you start at your new school tomorrow, right?"

"Yeah."

"Okay. Please stay away from the Hunter Hoovers of the world."

"I'll call you tomorrow," I said.

"Okay."

There were a few seconds of silence before I whispered, "Good night."

"Night, Em."

We hung up. I fell asleep with my hands splayed across my belly, imagining that I was lying next to Jax and he was holding me.

THE NEXT MORNING, I woke up to the smell of French toast and bacon. Before even opening my eyes, I was already smiling.

"What are you smiling about? You almost got busted. I saved your butt."

I opened my eyes to find a serious Sophia. "What? What are you talking about?"

"Mrs. Keller and I came in here this morning with your laundry, and I found the phone sticking out from under your bed. I hid it in my shirt and put it back, but it was a close call."

I sat up and put my hand to my chest. "Oh shit."

"Watch your mouth," she whispered. "Mr. Keller has no tolerance for bad language."

"It seems like Mr. and Mrs. Keller have no tolerance for anything."

"Look, this place is all I've ever known." She leaned in conspiratorially. "But I've heard a lot of stories from the kids who have been through here, and I don't want to know what's out there, okay? Mr. and Mrs. Keller are strict, but they're not mean, and I think they care about me. I don't want to mess this up. What's the saying . . . you know, about the devil?"

"Better the devil you know?"

"Yeah, that's it."

"You've been here a long time, so I can see why you'd feel that way. Thanks for covering for me—you didn't have to do that."

"It's fine. I didn't want you kicked out the first week. You're the only one who wants to hit the library with me."

I slid out of bed and pulled on a pair of jeans from a folded pile on the dresser. "What time do we leave?"

Sophia looked at the clock. "Seven fifty sharp. Mr. Keller will drop you off first, then me."

"What about the boys?"

"Mrs. Keller homeschools them."

"How come?"

"Thomas is autistic, and the twins are really behind because they were neglected."

"Oh." Aside from their insane rules, Mr. and Mrs. Keller seemed like angels. What they were doing was good. And I was sure they had good reasons for their rules. But for me, I just couldn't imagine not having Jackson in my life. They didn't know how much we needed each other.

As I brushed my hair in the dresser mirror, I noticed Sophia behind me, watching with curiosity. "What?"

"Who did you call? Last night?" Her voice was soft, hesitant.

I turned around to face her. "My boyfriend."

"You have a boyfriend?" Her face flushed. She moved to my bed and plopped down, wearing a giddy smile. "What's he like? What's his name? Oh my god, do you kiss him?"

I went toward her with the brush. She was dressed and ready for school, but she still had a swirly nest of bedhead just above the back of her neck. As I brushed out her hair I told her all about Jax like we were long-lost sisters. "He's tall, with nice muscles." I giggled. "He's a really good swimmer, and he's a great writer. He has golden-y brown hair and eyes, and his skin always has this glow to it. He's very handsome."

"And the kissing? Tell me about it, please. I'm dying. Oh my god, I'm dying to know what it's like."

"Girls!" Mrs. Keller's voice boomed from the bottom of the stairs.

Sophia popped up and darted for the door. "Breakfast!" She turned in the doorway. "We gotta get down there. Promise you'll tell me after school?"

"Promise."

At the bottom of the stairs was a brand-new backpack and

sweater. "Will that do?" Mr. Keller asked from where he was standing statue-like near the front door.

"Yes, it's great, thank you."

He nodded. "Better get in there and get your breakfast."

We inhaled our French toast at the large oval table while Mr. Keller shouted out a minute-by-minute countdown. Thomas repeated Mr. Keller several times, his voice like a little robot's.

"Ten minutes till the van leaves. Ten minutes, girls," Thomas said over and over as he picked off all the dark parts of his toast and set them aside on a little napkin.

At the three-minute warning, Thomas jumped down from his chair and came up to me, his face inches from mine. "Three minutes till the van leaves. Three minutes, Emerson. You better go." He looked terrified even though he wasn't making eye contact. Brandon and Daniel sat quietly on the other side of the table. Their shaggy hair and transfixed gazes as they watched Thomas melt down made the twins look like they were in one of those "big eyes" paintings. Two little ragamuffins with giant alien-like saucers for eyes.

Daniel blurted out, "He does that because he doesn't like it when people are late."

"It's okay," I said, and then I lifted Thomas's chin so that his eyes were more level with mine. "Thomas?"

"Yeah." He still wouldn't let his eyes meet mine. They were darting from the ceiling to the floor to the walls around me.

"Will you look at me?" He did, but he looked extremely uncomfortable when he did it. "Everything is going to be okay. Sophia and I are going to make it to school on time." I smiled.

A brief look of serenity flashed in his eyes. He smiled back and then looked at the floor and muttered, "Okay, but now you only have two minutes. You better go."

We all laughed except for Thomas, who went back to picking at his toast.

At the one-minute mark, Sophia and I were walking out to the Sprinter van in the driveway. "Have a good day at school, girls," Mrs. Keller called from the doorway.

Mr. Keller was already in the driver's seat. He didn't say anything until we were pulling into the driveway at New Clayton High. "You'll go to the office up that path for your schedule, Emerson. Your guidance counselor will walk you through it."

"Okay, great."

He glanced at me in the rearview mirror. "After school you'll walk straight to the library in the center of town to meet Sophia. She gets out after you, so wait on the steps until she gets there. Mrs. Keller will pick you girls up at four p.m. Make sure your homework is done by then."

"Got it, Mr. Keller. Thanks for everything. 'Bye, Sophie."

"'Bye." She leaned over and whispered, "I want to hear about the kissing later. Don't forget."

"I'm sure you'll remind me."

We laughed. I jumped out of the van, and right before I closed the door, Mr. Keller looked back at me and said, "Remember the rules, Emerson."

"I will."

I WAS THROWN into life with the Kellers, a version of foster home Stepford robots, with Daniel and Brandon, the precious, neglected, doe-eyed twins, and autistic Thomas and his pieces of toast, and Sophia—sweet, sweet Sophia. Then there was me, Emerson, the new girl at New Clayton with her new backpack, her new purplish sweater, and her new bruised eye, and a stitched lip to match.

I wasn't even going to try to make friends on my first day at New Clayton High. I didn't know how long I'd be living with the Kellers; on the drive over, Paula had told me they would look for family members who might be able to take me in. I thought that was hysterical, considering my own mother had abandoned me.

As other high schoolers rushed past me, I stood at the top of the walkway on campus and wondered, *Who am I? Will I ever know? Will this shitty-ass life and my shitty-ass parents define who I am? Will I ever feel normal?*

Thankfully, I had been way ahead in my classes at Neeble, so most of what I heard on my first day at New Clayton was review. The day went by in a blur.

After school, I did as I was told and walked to the library to wait for Sophia. As soon as she saw me, she ran from the corner, her heavy backpack swooshing back and forth behind her. When she was about twenty feet away, she called out, "The kissing! You're going to tell me about the kissing!"

"Shhh, Sophia, not so loud."

"What? You can't get into trouble here; we have until four to do whatever we want."

"That's only about an hour."

"Well, I got my homework done at lunch, so we can talk and look for books and you can tell me about kissing Jackson."

I huffed. "Well, if you want to know the truth, Jackson and I only really kissed a couple of times."

This did not deter her. "What was it like? Tell me, tell me!"

I closed my eyes and thought about our kiss. Tingles ran through my body. "Well, it's like this. He closes his eyes and tilts his head, and I do the same, and our lips touch, and, well . . . that's all you need to know at your age."

She looked up to the sky, enchanted. "Wow. I totally want to kiss a boy."

"When I was your age, I thought boys were gross. I even thought Jackson was gross."

"You knew him when you were eight?"

"Yeah, I've known him my whole life."

"So he's like your brother?"

"No! That's disgusting. He was the boy next door, then he became my friend, and then we became more when we got older."

It occurred to me then that I might be able to use the hour after school to call Jackson or meet with him. I brightened at the thought. "So does Mrs. Keller pick us up at four every day?"

"Yep, like clockwork. It's so we have a quiet place to study. The boys get antsy and loud in the afternoon."

Sophia and I went into the library and checked out some books. I finished up a few geometry problems, and then we waited on the steps until the Sprinter van pulled up with Mrs. Keller at the helm and the three boys in their booster seats across the first backseat bench.

"Mrs. Keller, can I sit in front?" Sophia asked.

"Sure."

I slid into the far backseat. It felt like I was riding the school bus again, but Jax wasn't there to hold my hand. Mrs. Keller and Sophia talked about school. Although I think the Kellers tried very hard to maintain a sense of reserve and formality, I could sense a bond between Mrs. Keller and Sophia. It made me happy for her. She deserved it.

Later that night, Sophia told me more about the Kellers.

"They have a son, Liam. He's a hotshot lawyer in New York. I guess Mrs. Keller tried to have another baby for a long time but couldn't. That's why she does this."

"Does Liam ever come to visit?"

"On holidays and stuff, but he doesn't really hang out with the foster kids."

"What about money?"

"What about it?"

I was thinking about how I could get money to call Jackson after school. "Do the Kellers give you an allowance?"

She laughed. "Yeah, right!"

7. Talking

"Go! Go! Go, baby!!" Trevor yelled at the TV and then leapt to his feet. "Woohoo!" He did a ridiculous touchdown dance while screaming at the top of his lungs. I looked up from my book and sniffled.

Cara peeked her head out of her room. "Keep it down, you big oaf!"

"Hey, Avril Lavigne, why don't you go find an open mic night somewhere?" I looked up from my book and marveled at how casually he teased Cara. Why didn't Trevor and I have that same kind of playful dynamic? In fact, why didn't I have that with anyone? The last person I'd been that close to was Jase.

Cara came up to the back of the couch and leaned over to look at me, smiling. "I never get his insults." She paused. "Wait a minute, are you crying?"

"No," I squeaked.

"Trevor, your woman is sitting here bawling her head off and you're over there dancing around like a fool?"

I laughed through my tears. "I'm crying because of the dancing."

In a low voice, Cara said, "Seriously, are you okay? Come talk to me." Then she shook her head at Trevor and walked away.

Trevor came toward me with a look of faint concern. "Why are you crying—for real, Emi?"

I sat up and he sat down next to me. "I was just thinking about this little girl and these three little boys I was in foster care with."

"You were in foster care? I thought your aunt adopted you when your parents died."

I took a breath. "My mom and dad aren't dead, Trevor. At least, my dad isn't."

He looked shocked. Of course he would be. I had been lying to him. "Where are they now? Why'd you go to live with Cyndi if your parents are alive?"

I took a deep breath. "My mom took off when I was ten. I don't know where she is. And my dad's in jail, I think. At least, he used to be."

Trevor looked stunned. "For what?"

"Felony child abuse and neglect," I said, trying hard not to make eye contact. If I saw pity on Trevor's face, I would lose it.

"Wow, Emi. So he really beat you up?"

"He did the last time. Jase too, kind of." I took another deep breath. "You know what? Maybe it's not such a bad idea for you to read the book when I'm done. It's fictionalized, but it'll give you a good idea of what I went through as a kid."

Trevor sank down next to me and wrapped his arms

around my shoulders. "I'm really sorry, Emi. I wish you'd felt like you could have told me this a long time ago. You never talked about your past, and I didn't want to push. I figured your parents were good people and that you were an orphan, not abused and neglected."

I rested my head against his shoulder. "I'm sorry I lied to you. You really didn't deserve that." And I meant it. It was despicable that I had lied to him. "When we met, I was telling everyone they were dead. It was just easier that way. It's hard for me to relive what I went through, but as I read Jase's book, I'm forced to face it all again. It's not easy." I set the book down on the floor. "I think I've had enough for tonight."

He squeezed my shoulder. "You know what'll take your mind off that book?"

"What?" I asked hopefully.

"A Cal victory." He jerked a thumb toward the TV. "Wanna watch with me?"

My heart sank for a moment. Trevor always took what I said at face value; he wasn't the type to wade into emotional territory if he didn't have to. Just one of the many reasons why it had been so easy to lie to him all those years ago.

I gave him a weak smile. "Sure."

HOURS LATER, AFTER Cal won, we jumped up from the couch and ran through Cara's door shouting, "Go Bears!" She sat at her desk, watching us with a smile.

I was trying so hard to be in the moment, but as we jumped up and down, I felt like I was outside of my body, watching some girl I barely recognized jumping with joy next to her perfect boyfriend and her perfect friend in her perfect apartment. But it wasn't really me. Jase's book had reminded me who I really was.

My smile faded as my mind went exactly where I didn't want it to go. *Why didn't he look for me? Do I even want to be found?*

"What happened, Emi?" Trevor asked.

I took a deep breath and realized I had stopped cheering. "I'm just tired."

Cara watched me with concern. "Trevor, I think Emi and I need a girls' night." She arched her eyebrows at me.

I took his hand in mine and turned to face him. "That actually sounds nice. I could use some ice cream and John Hughes movies."

"I get it, I get it." He smiled, pecked me on the lips, and then called over his shoulder, "Have fun, ladies."

The second we heard the front door close behind him, I turned toward Cara. "Thank you so much."

"You just want to get back to that book, don't you?"

"Yeah, I guess."

Cara smirked. "Then you're totally going with me to his book event tomorrow to meet him. It's in San Diego— lucky us."

My heart started racing. "Um, I can't."

"What? Why not? What do you have to do tomorrow?" She watched me cautiously from her desk as I slowly lowered myself to the edge of her bed. "Why are you acting so weird?"

"Because . . ." I sighed. I couldn't hide it any longer. "Because I know him," I said under my breath. My heart started beating even faster.

"You know who?"

"The author. J. Colby."

"What? Are you fucking kidding me?" She stood up from her desk chair, almost knocking it over in the process. "What do you mean you *know* him? You didn't even know about this book until a few days ago."

"I *know* him, Cara." I widened my eyes for emphasis.

"Like, in the biblical sense?"

"That's not exactly was I was implying, but . . . yeah. I know him that way too."

I could see the wheels turning as she tried to put it all together. "You're from Ohio . . . and he's from Ohio." She stared ahead blankly, like a zombie, then went into the kitchen, grabbed the bottle of tequila, and returned. She took a swig and handed the bottle over to me. "Talk," she demanded.

"I don't have to. You've just read everything you need to know about me."

Her eyes widened. "So it's you? *You're* Emerson?"

I nodded. "It's all true. He glosses over some things, but yeah . . . it all happened."

"Jesus. You haven't finished yet, I take it?"

"No, I'm at the part when Emerson goes to the Kellers'. So far it's all true, except maybe the part about Jax's six-pack." I rolled my eyes.

She was silent for a minute and then she began laughing hysterically, almost psychotically, until I started laughing too. She buckled over, in tears. "This is insane, Emi. In. Sane. This guy wrote a whole book about you and you didn't even know it until you started reading it?" She laughed even harder and then stopped abruptly. "So wait . . . does that mean you were in a foster home with four other kids?"

My own laughter died down. "Yeah, but not for very long."

"Do you have any contact with the little girl?"

I shook my head no. I wished I'd stayed in touch with her. I owed it to her. But like everything else remotely relating to Ohio, I had compartmentalized her away, too afraid to indulge in any memories. "I guess she'd be in college by now." My eyes welled up again.

"Was it true what happened to her? What you did?"

"You mean before I left?"

"Yeah."

"I haven't gotten that far yet, but so far everything that I've read really happened."

Cara stood up and hugged me. "I'm so glad I know you, Emi." I started crying immediately, giving in to the emotional roller-coaster ride. She pulled me closer toward her. "None of it was your fault. You know that, right?"

Years of therapy had tried to convince me of the same thing.

"Fine, let's avoid the hard stuff. Tell me more about the guy. Is he as hot as I'm imagining him to be? Was every girl in love with him in high school?"

I laughed through my tears. "His name is Jase Colbertson. He and I used to finish each other's sentences. He knew me inside and out. We spent so many years together, playing and talking. We wrote hundreds of short stories and spent pretty much every moment together. Up until I went to live with Cyndi and Sharon, he was the only person who ever truly cared about me."

"He obviously thought very highly of you," Cara said soothingly as she rubbed my back.

"I mean, maybe in fiction. In real life, he hasn't reached out to me in twelve years." I was still heartbroken that he had never looked for me. After I went to college, I had looked for him a few times online, but never got any hits. As more time passed, I figured he had gotten over us and moved on. I could see now that I was right. Jase was living his life in California the way he had dreamed he would, but I wasn't a part of it.

When we were kids he'd say, *I'm gonna publish a book by the time I'm thirty.* And he had done it. He had a bestselling novel and a book tour set up by a publisher, and he'd done it all without me. He was gorgeous and talented and had everything he wanted. Why would he ever come looking for me? That bastard.

Cara pulled back and looked me in the eyes. "You should finish the book and go with me to see him tomorrow."

I sniffled. "I don't know. Maybe." I thought about all those deleted messages I hadn't sent through his website. A part of me still wanted to give him a piece of my mind. "I might be a little curious to see him, but I need to finish the book first."

She nodded. "Okay, I think you should."

I nodded. A short while later, after Cara had turned in for the night, I made a pot of coffee and prepared myself to dive back into the past.

From *All the Roads Between*

On the fifth night at the Kellers', I snuck down to the kitchen and grabbed the phone again to call Jax.

"Hello?" He sounded groggy.

"What's wrong?"

"It's one a.m. I have to get up early tomorrow."

His dismissive tone bothered me, leaving me vulnerable. "Why?"

"'Cause they just canceled the bus route down here."

"What? Really? What do you mean?"

"It means I have to fucking walk, Em."

My stomach sank. "To where?"

"To Carter's. Cal Junior just started giving me a ride to the bus stop on Fifth."

I visualized the route in my head. Jax would have to walk two miles each way every day just to get to Carter's, probably before it was even light out. *And* he had to hitch a ride with Cal Junior, the thirty-year-old son of Cal Carter, the owner of the egg ranch. Cal Junior was strange and creepy, and there was a story about how he had once exposed himself to two kids who had been riding their bikes past the ranch. We stayed away from him as much as possible.

"Oh my god, Jax, I'm so sorry. What happened to Ms. Beels?"

"They won't let her come down this far for one kid."

It's all my fault. "Why on earth are you getting a ride from Junior?"

"Do I have a choice? My mom arranged it. I guess he was hanging around her work last night and she told him about our problem. He offered, and I caught a ride with him this morning."

"Did he talk to you?"

"No, he just smoked cigarettes the whole way into town. I smelled like an ashtray by the time I got to school."

"Isn't there any other way?"

"I don't know." Jackson sounded empty, shattered, and distant.

"You sound depressed."

"I'm fine. Listen, I'm tired. Can we talk later in the week?"

"Sure. Okay, love you," I said, feeling awful that we were getting off the phone without exchanging at least a few nice words.

"Good night."

"I said I love you, Jackson."

"Love you too, Em." After we hung up, I stared at the phone, wondering why Jackson seemed distant.

Over the next few weeks, Jax answered only about half of the time, and each time he sounded more and more depressed. He would ask if I was okay and then he'd rush off the phone. Thankfully, I never got caught, and if Mr. and Mrs. Keller knew, they didn't say anything.

When Jax's birthday arrived, I called him to see if he had gotten his driver's license.

"Hello?"

"Happy birthday! So . . . did you get it?"

"Yep."

"Congratulations, stud! Who took you to the DMV?"

"Cal Junior."

"Really? Weird."

"Yeah, well, beggars can't be choosers."

"Okay, so . . . now what?"

"I guess I'm gonna work at the ranch every day until I have enough money to get a car."

"I'm proud of you, Jax. Even if you don't get a car, I'll be proud of you."

"Yeah?" He sounded down, even though he should have been celebrating.

"Yeah. I miss you," I added.

"Thanks."

"I said I miss you."

"I miss you too," he said quietly.

"Will you come and see me?" My voice was shaking. His steely tone and short answers were making me feel sick. I was twirling my hair into a giant dreadlock at the side of my head out of sheer nervousness. I wondered if he was falling out of love with me, or if life was just getting worse and worse for him and he was afraid to burden me with his problems.

"How am I supposed to do that?"

"After school, I go to the library in town. Mrs. Keller doesn't pick me up until four. I can skip my last class and meet you in the town if you can borrow Junior's truck or your mom's car."

"I don't know, Em. That sounds impossible."

"I just want to see you. I want to put my arms around you and wish you a happy birthday in person . . . and give you a birthday kiss."

He laughed, but there was a hollow quality to it. "Yeah, that would be nice."

"What is it, Jackson? Are you seeing someone at school or something?"

"No. I don't have time for that. I don't have a fucking life, Emerson, okay? Just stop fucking nagging me about this. I have no control over anything. I can't just take my mom's car when she has to work, and Junior's a freak. I'm not asking to borrow his truck."

"Jesus! Okay. I'm sorry." My voice broke, and tears fell from my eyes. "I just miss you."

"Don't cry. Please don't cry. I will fucking die, Emerson. Please just enjoy your three square meals a day and your warm bed. The only thing that's keeping me going is knowing that you're living in peace, finally."

But I wasn't. I would have taken the whiskey monster, the violent rages, and the empty refrigerator just to be able to spend time with Jax. I couldn't be selfish, though; I had to let him think there was hope so he could believe it for himself too.

"Thank you. You're the best person I know, Jackson Fisher."

He laughed again, a sarcastic huff that made my stomach flip in a bad way. "Okay, Em, I gotta go."

We hung up without saying good night. I put the phone back in the kitchen and cried myself to sleep.

What felt like five minutes later, I opened my puffy eyes to find Sophia leaning over my bed. "What's wrong with your face?"

"Nothing."

"Were you crying last night?" she asked. She had a look of sympathy in her eyes. "Did Jackson break up with you?"

"No, I just miss him."

"You'll see each other again soon."

I rolled out of bed and patted the top of her blonde mop. "Little optimist, aren't you?"

She smiled back at me. "It's called faith, Emmy."

LATER, AS I was walking out of fifth period toward my last class, I turned the corner and my eyes immediately shot to a stunning figure leaning against a tree just off the path.

"Jax!" I screamed. I ran toward him, jumped into his arms, and straddled his waist. His lips were on mine in a second. He held me to his chest as he kissed me deeply before burying his face in my neck. He sighed, a deep rumbling sound from his chest that gave me goose bumps. I shivered, but my skin was burning like I had a fever. His nose was cold against my cheek.

"Fuck, I missed you. You smell so fucking good."

He set me down. We took each other in. I could have sworn he had gotten taller. "What are you doing here?"

"Junior let me borrow his truck. I parked it on the road. There's a fence up there we can climb to get out of here so you don't have to walk out the front gate."

"Okay. But, shit, they'll mark me absent in sixth period. I want to go with you so badly, but I don't want the Kellers to find out . . ."

He crossed his arms over his chest and looked down at the ground, defeated. "I don't want to get you in trouble, Em. I just needed to see you."

Jackson could slay my heart with just a look. "I'm coming with you. I don't care what happens."

He gave me a huge smile and grabbed my hand. "C'mon."

He helped me over the short fence and before long we were coasting down the road in the cab of Cal Junior's cigarette-stale, beat-up Chevy.

"Where should we go?" He glanced over at me, but I couldn't speak. I was in awe of him, driving along like he had done it all his life, with confidence and grace. "What is it, Em?"

"Nothing. You just seem so grown-up . . . . different."

"It's still me."

"I know, I know. I just . . . I don't know. God . . . I don't know what to say."

He laughed. "I might be able to do this, like, once a week. Then it won't feel so strange."

"Really?" Those words changed everything. Now I had something to look forward to besides chores and homework.

"Yeah, maybe. How about here?" He pointed straight ahead to a parking lot wrapped around New Clayton's fishing pond.

"Perfect." It was a warm day and less humid than usual for late spring. We found a spot on a picnic bench and sat side by side, facing the water. I studied Jackson's jean-clad legs, spread with confidence. He put his hand on my thigh and rubbed it up and down like it was so natural for us to touch each other that way.

"You didn't go to school today, I take it. It takes at least an hour to get here."

"I planned to. On the way into town this morning, I told Junior you were crying last night, and, well . . . he said I could take his truck to come see you." He fixed his gaze on the road behind me.

"That was nice of him."

He huffed. "Yeah, I guess."

I touched my hand to his cheek. "Look at me."

He turned, his eyes full of pain and longing. I leaned in and we kissed each other slowly. I didn't know what Jax was going through, but everything slipped away when we were together. He was far away but close enough to touch.

"Can you just be here with me and forget about everything else for a little while?"

He glanced at my mouth and then up to my eyes. His chest started to pump in and out and then he looked at my mouth again. There was so much heat and tension between us that I could practically hear it pulsing with currents of electricity. He swallowed and then the restraint was gone as he crushed his mouth to mine. He was more frantic than ever before, stronger, holding my body to his, our tongues teasing each other until his mouth was on my neck, then my ear, and then he was pulling me effortlessly onto his lap. I never resisted him because it was perfectly familiar, like home, to be against his big body that way. He was breathing hard and kissing hard. I took his hand, which was gripping the back of my leg, and I pulled it up to cup my breast through my sweater. He was timid at first, but then he groaned and whispered near my ear, "What are you doing to me, Em?"

"I want you, Jackson . . . all of you." Big words for a fifteen-year-old, but I meant every one of them.

He set me down and pulled away, then turned toward the pond, braced his elbows on his knees, and let his head fall into his hands. "What can we do? I mean, we can't be together—we have nowhere to go." His voice got higher. "There's nothing we can do, Em."

I rubbed my hand up and down his back. "It's okay. I just meant I want all of you someday."

"Someday," he echoed. "Hopefully sooner than later. It seems like everyone is always trying to screw things up for us."

"Everyone who? What are you talking about? My dad is going to jail. Your mom is busy with her men, and the Kellers will be fine, as long as I don't get caught. This is enough for me, Jackson. Just being near you is enough for me for now."

He looked up and there were tears in his eyes. "I know,

I'm sorry, I'm being such a grump. It's just that I'm sixteen, you know?" He laughed finally, and I laughed too as a few tears fell from my eyes. I knew what he meant. We were lovesick. We wanted to connect as deeply as we could. For us, the physical part was innocent. We would've done it out of our love for each other, not out of lust or peer pressure. We were more committed and genuinely in love than most married people—at least the ones we knew. We'd had years to develop our love and respect for each other. Fifteen might have been young for sex for other kids, but for us, it just felt right.

"I get it," I said. "I feel the same way."

"I want you so bad, it's all I think about."

"Just focus on the future. Remember when we used to dream about growing up? You said you wanted to be a ninja and I could be your sidekick, except you wouldn't let me use the samurai sword because you thought I was too clumsy."

"I don't think about ninjas anymore, and I don't think you're clumsy either. I think you're perfect. You're going to stick with me, right?" His tone was serious.

"Yes. Of course I am. Always, Jax."

"I can't live without you. It's such fucking hell living with Leila at the end of that dirt road, all alone, with no one else to turn to. She's getting worse. She doesn't even buy food anymore. I've been living on Taco Bell and cereal."

"I'm so sorry, Jax. I wish I could help."

He looked away like he was too embarrassed to look me in the eye. "When I think about you, about us as kids, it's like some fucking movie. When it was just us, everything was fine." He started to get choked up, but he was trying to be tough. He was fighting it.

"I know—it's the same for me."

"Now you're gone and everything is so real and so fucking brutal. She's disgusting. Leila is awful; she's losing her mind. There's a different guy at our house every night now, and I can hear her with them. I want to fucking die every time."

"Don't say that, please. Go to my dad's. There's no one there. You can sleep there."

He looked up, shocked. "They condemned it, Em. The county is tearing it down."

"What? What about my stuff? My clothes, my books, my mom's stuff?"

"It's all gone."

I felt a lump forming in my throat. "What will my dad do?"

"He's going to prison, and then he'll probably go to a half-way house or something. This is it, Em. Everything is changing."

My chest was heaving. "I better get to the library to meet Sophia."

"Yeah." He grabbed my hand and pulled me toward the truck. But before opening the passenger door, he pushed me against it and rubbed his nose along my jawline. Jackson was only sixteen, but he was a man: strong, athletic, and masculine. "I just want to remember the way you taste and smell." He kissed me hard, almost biting down on my lip. The pain felt good.

I stopped him and pulled away, breathing hard. "Don't say 'remember.' You don't need to remember. We'll see each other again soon, right?"

He pulled away, panting. "We have to."

"We will." I touched my hand to his face. We looked at each other for several silent moments, but it wasn't uncomfortable. "We were so young once. Remember us on that bus with stupid Mikey and . . . who was that other kid?"

"Alex Duncan."

"Yeah, Alex. Remember you guys were so mean to me?"

"We were mean to *each other*, Em. We were just kids."

"Look at us now." I laughed. "Would you ever have thought we'd be like this? Grown-up and wanting nothing more than to be with each other every second of the day?"

"I always knew."

I laughed. "You're lying."

He was impassive. "No. I did. I swear to you. I always knew we would be like this one day. I think you always knew too."

"Maybe." My voice shook, and my eyes started to tear up.

He pulled me to his chest and held me.

"Jackson?" I asked.

"Yeah?"

"What's going to happen?"

I could feel his heart beating fast against my chest. "Nobody knows."

"I hate that," I said.

"I know, I hate it too, but I guess it's like reading a good book. The kind where you don't want to skip pages to see what happens at the end. Each moment is a story in itself."

"Would you say every moment is good? What about my father and your mom?" I sniffled, wiping tears from my eyes.

"Our story is great. Maybe not all the other shit, but the story of *us* is perfect, Em."

"Yeah, I like that. You have a way with words, Jackson Fisher."

His chest rumbled. "A regular wordsmith, huh?"

"You better keep writing. You're an awesome writer, and if you stop, I will personally kick your ass."

"All five foot four of you. I'm so scared."

I pulled out of his arms. "Still teasing me?"

"Flirting—it was always flirting. Come on." He opened my door and helped me in.

We didn't speak as he drove through town. At the library, Sophia was already sitting on the steps when we drove up. I watched her eyes grow wide as we approached. From fifteen feet away, I could see her blushing. I looked back at Jackson walking behind me from the parking lot. I smiled. He looked past me to Sophia and smirked his cocky, teenage man-boy smirk. Sophia jumped up and held her hand out to him.

"Sophia Lyle. Pleasure to make your acquaintance."

He shook her hand. "Jackson Fisher. It's nice to meet you as well."

"What a great name. So, um, did you pick Emerson up from school?"

"I did."

"Cool." Sophia was nodding nervously.

"Jax has to get going," I said.

"Okay, well, Jax—you don't mind if I call you that, right?"

"Of course not, Sophie."

I thought she was literally going to faint.

"Okay, well, um, any time you want to see Emerson, I can totally cover for you guys."

"No, Soph," I said. "I'm not going to let you get in trouble with the Kellers."

"Well, I just mean, I won't tell," she said.

"Okay," I told her.

Jackson leaned down and pecked me on the lips. "'Bye, Em."

I grabbed his face and leaned in close to his ear. "Love you."

I'll always have trouble remembering the first time we said,

I love you, because by the time we said it freely, we had been feeling it for years. It was as natural as saying, *See you later.*

"Love you," he said, before turning and leaving a captivated Sophia and a longing Emerson behind on the library steps.

"Oh my god, he's such a dreamboat."

I laughed. "People don't use that expression anymore, Sophie. That was, like, way before your time."

"I know, but I like it and it suits him."

"Yeah, you're right, it does. Come on, let's get some books."

WHEN I REALIZED that no one had noticed I was missing from sixth period, I was relieved but I knew I couldn't let it become a habit. Later in the week, at the breakfast table, I mentioned to Mrs. Keller that the library was open until five thirty on Mondays.

She didn't hesitate. "That's fine. You girls can stay there until closing time."

Sophia looked up from her oatmeal and smiled. I looked away. Before we left for school, Sophia went up to Mrs. Keller as she was doing the dishes. She hugged her from behind like she was thanking her for me, but Mrs. Keller remained rigid and didn't return the gesture; she simply waited for Sophia to let go and then she went back to doing the dishes. When Sophia turned back to face me, she looked as happy as a clam.

I called Jax that night and confirmed that he would borrow Junior's truck the following Monday to come and see me.

I counted down the minutes until then. I couldn't sleep at night, I couldn't focus at school, and at church I fell asleep from exhaustion. Mrs. Keller elbowed me. "Emerson, sit up, girl. What is with you?"

I yawned. "This is boring."

"You might want to strengthen your connection to Jesus. You certainly could use a little divine intervention."

"Why do you say that?"

She put her finger to her mouth. "Shhh. I'll pray for you."

I shrugged it off.

ON MONDAY, JACKSON picked me up after school and we went to the fishing pond. He seemed distant as he drove. When we pulled into the parking lot, he rested his forehead on the steering wheel and took a deep breath. I scooted across the truck bench and put my hand on his thigh.

"You okay?"

"Yeah."

I let my hand roam up his leg until he jerked his head up. "I don't want to touch you in here," he said.

"Why?"

"I just don't. I brought a blanket. We can go sit by the shore."

"Are you okay, Jax?"

"Yeah, I will be."

We got out of the truck and walked close to the water's edge and laid the blanket out. We flopped down and lay on our backs, my head resting on his shoulder. "It's nice today."

"Yeah."

"Hey, why do you seem so faraway?"

"I'm here," he said.

I turned and propped my head on my elbow. I used my free hand to caress his face. "In here, you seem distant."

He cupped my neck and drew my face toward his until our mouths met. We kissed and kissed. His hands went everywhere. I kept looking up to make sure there was no one around.

"It's just us. Let me feel you," he said.

Touching me through my clothes, he gripped my bottom and ran his other hand up and down my waist, lifting my shirt in the process. He kissed and sucked at my neck until he was trailing a path down to my chest. He pulled the top of my T-shirt down and kissed the swells of my breasts. I arched my back. "Ah, Jackson, don't," I said, but I wanted nothing more than for him to keep going.

Through my T-shirt, he circled my nipple with his thumb. "Let me kiss you here." His eyes had that dreamy, lazy look of desire.

"Okay," I said breathlessly.

He undid my bra through my T-shirt and rolled me over onto my back, covering part of my body with his. His hand traveled over my bare skin from the bottom of my shirt, up to my neck, until my breast was in his hand and he was touching me gently. I closed my eyes and whimpered. His hand slipped away, and I sucked in a quick breath when I felt him take my nipple into his mouth. I held his head to my chest as he kissed and sucked and teased me. His hand roamed down the outside of my jeans between my legs. I pulled his head up to kiss my lips again. I could feel him hard on my hip.

His fingers continued stroking and rubbing until I was writhing under his touch. He moved his hand up to the button of my jeans. "No. I'm on my period."

"I don't care," he said, his voice strained.

"I do, Jackson. Stop. Not now, not like this, please."

"Okay, okay." He took a deep breath. "I'm sorry." He pulled my shirt down but continued kissing me, only his kisses were lighter, just gentle little pecks up my neck.

I pressed my hand to the outside of his jeans, and his eyes shot open. "Don't! I'll either die or totally embarrass myself."

We laughed. He lay back on the blanket.

"You okay?" I asked.

"Just let me catch my breath."

I snuggled up into his body. The wind picked up, giving us some reprieve from the humidity. With my head resting on his chest, listening to his heartbeats even out, I watched the breeze ripple the water's surface. Jackson's breaths lulled me to sleep.

Around four thirty, I startled awake.

"Welcome back," Jax said with a wink.

"I can't believe I fell asleep."

"I can't believe what you were saying in your sleep, Em." His smile was teasing.

"Oh my god, what did I say?"

"Just incoherent babbling at first and lots of drooling. Then you went on and on about how much you wanted me."

I sat up and socked him in the chest. "Well, that's no secret, doofus."

He grabbed my hand and pulled me back down on top of him. "Soon," was all he said, and then he kissed me, slowly, sweetly.

"We better go. I need to make sure I get to the library before Mrs. Keller."

We drove toward the library, and even though the day had gone perfectly, I had an unsettled feeling. As we approached the tall brick building, two figures waiting on the steps came into my view. It was Mrs. Keller, standing with her arms crossed over her plump belly, watching us drive past. Our eyes met, and she followed my gaze as we passed, but there was nothing in her expression that I could read. Not anger, not disappointment, and certainly not sadness. And then there was poor, sweet Sophia staring down at her shoes, her shoulders sagging, her body listless.

"Oh shit," I said, and then laughed hysterically. "That was Mrs. Keller."

As Jax pulled into the parking lot of the library, he kept glancing over at me in disbelief. "What are you laughing about?"

"Oh, just how fucked up this is going to get."

"What will she do?"

"I have no idea," I said.

He parked the car. We both looked out the back window to where Sophia and a glaring Mrs. Keller stood.

"Em, if it's gonna get ugly, just come with me. I'll take you back to my house."

"Leila would never go for it."

"You can stay in the fort until we figure things out. Leila is hardly there; it won't be that bad."

Scooting across the truck bench, I took his face in my hands and kissed him. "I have to do this. I can't run. I need a place to live."

"You wouldn't be running. You'd be with me, and I could stop borrowing this stupid truck."

"Oh Jesus, what would I do, Jax? Drop out of school and live in your backyard?"

He squinted and then dropped his head onto the steering wheel. "Should I at least go meet her? Maybe she'll like me."

"I guess it can't hurt." I scanned his attire. He was wearing a blue Radiohead T-shirt, dark jeans, and Vans. His brown eyes were as light as they could be without being green or yellow, making him look like a celestial being in the sunlight. But it was his long hair that worried me. His hair had grown out to his shoulders, but he wore it tucked behind his ears. I stared at him, thinking idly that he would fit in perfectly in California once we got there. But I was also wondering if it was a good idea to introduce him to Mrs. Keller.

While I was looking at him and wishing we could both disappear, he lifted his head, looked me in the eye, and smiled. *Fucking adorable. What woman wouldn't think so?*

"Whatcha lookin' at?"

"You. Now . . . give her a big smile, just like that. Really lay on the charm, okay? I know you can do it—I've seen you in action."

"I'll do my best."

As we made our way to the library steps, Mrs. Keller grabbed Sophia's hand and pulled her along. She didn't stop or make eye contact with me.

"Come along, Emerson. We have some work to do."

"Wait a second. I want you to meet Jackson."

She passed us and didn't look back. "Come along, I said."

Sophia glanced back over her shoulder and jerked her head at me, urging me to follow. I leaned up on my toes and gave Jax a peck on the lips. "I'll call you and let you know what happens."

"Okay." He was staring at Mrs. Keller and Sophia in disbelief. "Are you sure you're gonna be okay? She seems weirded out."

"I think I'll be fine. I mean, what did I really do wrong?"

In the van, on the way home, neither Mrs. Keller nor Sophia spoke. Sophia stared out the passenger window while the boys pinched each other in the second row. As for me, I just waited with bated breath for someone to say something.

It wasn't until after dinner that Mrs. Keller came up to my room, along with Sophia. I was standing near the dresser brushing out my hair. "You girls will need to pack up tonight. Your social workers will be here in the morning."

My stomach dropped. "Wait, what? What are you talking about?"

Sophia looked up at me with wide eyes. "We broke the rules, Emmy. Remember, zero tolerance?"

"No, you're kidding. Wait . . ." Mrs. Keller wouldn't look at me. She turned on her heel and left the room.

"What the fuck?" I yelled.

"Shhh!" Sophia said.

"Who cares about being quiet if we're out of here?! This is insane. What the hell did you do to deserve this?"

"I lied."

"What? What are you talking about?"

Sophia sat on my purple bedspread looking down at her fidgeting hands clasped in her lap. "She asked me where you were, and I said you were studying at school."

"What if I was? I'll tell her Jax gave me a ride so I wouldn't be late. What the hell? Why are *you* getting sent away?"

"That's the thing. She saw you at the fishing pond, kissing him by his truck." She looked up finally with tears in her eyes and a sad smile on her lips.

"Oh my god, Sophia, I'm so sorry." I started to cry. "But what will they do? Where will you go?"

"Another foster home, I guess."

I sat down and took her in my arms as we both sobbed.

"But you've been here practically your whole life. This is insane!"

"It's okay, Emmy. I'll be okay."

"No, I won't have it. I'll do whatever. I'll say whatever, I don't care. They're sending you away for this? I can't believe it."

"You know why, though, right?" She sniffled.

"Why?"

"They don't actually love us. I don't even think they really like us. Trust me, I didn't just discover this information today. I've had seven years to work all this out in my head."

"But you said you wanted to be here!" My mind was racing. Where would I go? Where would Sophia go? Would I ever see Jackson again?

Sophia pulled out of my embrace and wiped her nose on the sleeve of her flannel pajamas. "I do want to stay here. Status quo and all that, you know?" I nodded. "It's comfortable for me, but I can be a big girl about it. They would have found a reason to get rid of me eventually."

People like Sophia and I had to grow up fast. We knew things about people that most adults hadn't even figured out. The thing was that I knew Mrs. Keller was closer to Sophia than either one of them realized. I stood from the bed, wiped my eyes, and squared my shoulders. "Stay here, Soph. I'm gonna go downstairs for a bit."

I found Mr. Keller sitting on the sofa in the living room, reading a book. "Hello, Mr. Keller."

"Hello." He looked up over his bifocals.

"I need to use the phone to call my social worker and my family friend Jackson Fisher, who I've known my whole life." My voice was unemotional, pragmatic.

"Go ahead," he said, and went right back to reading his book.

I walked into the kitchen and dialed Paula first. As the phone rang, I watched the boys as they ate pie and shoved each other. Mrs. Keller was nowhere to be seen or heard. I wondered if she was hiding from me and Sophia. The coward.

"Hello?"

"Paula, I need to talk to you."

"Listen, before you say anything, I actually have some good news. I know things went terribly wrong today, but I have some information that I think will change everything.

For a minute, I forgot about the awful predicament I was in. "What? Tell me."

"Do you know of your aunt Becky?"

"I don't have an aunt Becky. I don't have an aunt anyone."

"Actually, you do have an aunt Becky. Everything has been checked out. She's your father's half sister, ten years his junior."

"I have no idea what you're talking about." To my knowledge, no one from CPS could find my mother, and I had no other living relatives, as far as I knew.

"It's true."

"Did my father know about her?"

"He's the one who gave us her information. We contacted her in San Francisco, where she lives, and asked her if she would take over guardianship."

"What?!" I shouted. The boys went silent, all three of them staring at me as I leaned against the counter. "I'll have to move to San Francisco?"

"Yes."

"No, I can't. I can't leave Jackson. What's going to happen to Sophia? Why didn't my father tell me I had an aunt? I don't even know her. I'll never fit in there. This is going to ruin my life!"

"Slow down."

I started feeling woozy. Mr. Keller came into the kitchen and braced me by the elbow. I swayed. Quietly, he said, "Come on, sit on the couch."

When I sat, he left the room. "They're kicking me out because I spent a few hours with Jackson?"

Paula's voice became low and soothing. "I know you've been through a lot. Please hear me out. Sophia is going to a new foster home nearby. It's a decent place, but they don't take teenagers, and anyway, believe it or not, your aunt Becky sounds like a very intelligent and warm person. She has no children of her own, and get this . . . She's a creative writing professor at Berkeley."

"None of this information is helping. Why didn't my father ever tell me about my aunt?"

"Well, because your aunt is . . . how do I put this? Well, she's the product of an affair that your grandfather had, and they had to keep it all hush-hush to avoid a scandal. But apparently your father knew about her. I don't know if they were ever truly in contact, but he wrote to her from prison, and being a very kind and generous person, she's agreed to let you come and live with her and her partner, Trina."

My mouth was open in disbelief. I couldn't even process what she was telling me. I was going to live with my lesbian aunt in California? No fucking way. I wasn't going to leave Ohio—I didn't care if the president himself gave me a room at the White House.

"How much time do I have to disappear?"

She chuckled. "Don't worry, I have a feeling you'll be very happy in this new arrangement. I'll be there tomorrow at ten a.m. to pick you up."

We said our good-byes, and then I stormed up the stairs to

the second floor and barged through the door of Mrs. Keller's bedroom, where I found her sitting on the edge of the bed, crying.

"How could you do this? I don't care anymore about me, but how could you do this to Sophia? She's been here for seven years. My god, you're like parents to her. What is wrong with you?" She hung her head silently as I continued. "Listen, please. She did nothing wrong. For all she knew, Jax and I were studying. And who cares if she told a little white lie anyway? Please, you'll fuck up that little girl if you send her away. She's so good. She's so innocent."

Mrs. Keller looked up, her eyes swollen and bloodshot. "I have to. She has to learn that her behavior has consequences."

"But your consequences are too extreme. I know you love her. Please don't send her away."

Mr. Keller walked in behind me. "What's going on?"

"Just hear me out. You're all that little girl has. I just discovered I have an aunt, and I'm almost sixteen. I'll figure things out. But Sophia is eight and doesn't have another person in this world she can rely on. She loves you and you love her. You're good people. You have crazy-ass rules, but you're good people. Don't do this to her." I urged, my eyes pleading.

Mr. Keller sat next to Mrs. Keller on the bed. "Emerson, you're excused. Mrs. Keller and I need to discuss some things. Please go up to your room and gather your things. Your social worker will be here in the morning."

Before I went to my room, I ran back downstairs, grabbed the phone, and took two stairs at a time until I was in my bedroom. I dialed Jax.

"Hey."

"They're sending me to San Francisco to live with my aunt."

"What? Really?"

"Yeah, really."

"You're gonna leave?" His voice was empty, shocked. It wasn't a question. He was trying to process what I had just said.

"You have to come get me. I'm not going anywhere."

"Where do the Kellers live?" He sounded preoccupied, like he was trying to figure everything out.

"Two thirty South Primrose."

"I'll be there, Em, I promise. But it probably won't be until around one a.m."

"I'll meet you on the road at one."

I packed up my clothes, left everything the Kellers had given to me in a neat pile on the bed, and waited. Before lights-out, I walked down to Sophia's room. She was reading in a wicker chair near the window. I leaned against the doorjamb.

She looked up and smiled. "Whatever you said worked."

I was stunned. "Really?" I walked toward her.

She stood up and hugged me. "It's true. They're letting me stay. They said I would only get this one chance, though."

"Oh my god, you have no idea how happy this makes me. I know you won't mess up, Soph. Look out for yourself, okay, kid? You don't need to do anything for anyone ever again. Just take care of yourself." I hugged her again.

"Yeah, I guess whatever you said really got to Mrs. Keller. Thanks, friend."

"It wasn't me. They love you, okay? They just have a hard time showing it. Mrs. Keller was crying when I went in to confront her. I promise you, it was nothing I said. They want you to be here with them. They just have too much pride in their rules."

She shrugged. "Maybe. But what about you?"

"I'm San Francisco–bound." I smiled, even though I knew it was a lie. I had to play the part.

"Wow, that's fantastic!"

"Yeah, I have an aunt there and she's some big-time college professor. Probably loaded. I'm sure I'll get a car and stuff."

"That's great, Emmy. We are so lucky."

"We *are* lucky, aren't we?" Sophia was too young to understand the irony. It was better that way.

I said good night to Sophia, and we hugged. I didn't let her know it would be for the last time.

At twelve fifty, I took my small suitcase, left through the back door, and wheeled it a half mile down the road to the main highway. Jackson pulled up in Junior's truck right on time, and I hopped in.

"Hi," I said.

He looked exhausted, but he smiled anyway. "Hi, beautiful."

"Hardly. I feel like I've been run over."

"You're with me. You're okay now. We have to go by Carter's and then Cal Junior will take us home. My mom's working tonight."

"Does she know?"

He pulled up to a stop sign and looked over at me. "No, Em, she can't know. She's crazy. She thinks you're going to ruin my life. Pretty bold coming from her, huh?"

I still remembered the pain we all felt when Brian died. How could Leila think I would do anything to hurt Jax? "How would I ruin your life?" It hurt me to say those words.

"She doesn't want anyone taking her meal ticket from her."

"What does that even mean?"

"She's knows I'll get a scholarship. She knows I'll do something with my life. My grades are perfect. I've already gotten a near-perfect score on the PSAT. She's going to want me to take care of her."

It occurred to me that asking Jax to help me run away could jeopardize everything for him. Maybe Leila wasn't being as selfish as he thought. Maybe she was looking out for him. Maybe I should too.

"Someone will catch on. Paula will go to your house . . ." I told him.

"You really think Paula is gonna go searching past the tree line for you?"

"Why do you say it like that?"

"It's just that teenagers go missing all the time and people stop looking. Remember my brother's girlfriend? She lived in a fucking storm drain." He reached over and grabbed my hand. "Everything is going to be fine."

"I don't want to live in a storm drain, Jackson."

"Not even with me?" He laughed.

"It's not funny, and no, not even with you!"

"You won't, and we won't. Everything will be fine. You are too fucking smart, Em. Hell, *I'm* too fucking smart, and we work too fucking hard for this shitty life. It won't happen."

"Swear to me," My voice was tiny.

"I swear on your life," he said, and I believed him. "But right now I'm kidnapping you in some loser's truck so I can hide you in my backyard. Let's just hope we can get past this part. I don't think colleges will look too fondly at a juvenile record."

I didn't say anything, but the weight of what we were do-ing struck me. There was no way to quantify the impact of our actions at that point. It seemed like if I went to San Francisco I would die without him—literally wilt and turn into dust. But if

I stayed, I could be putting his future on the line, and my own. How could I measure the consequences of choosing love at fifteen?

People call teenage relationships puppy love, but what Jackson and I had was far beyond that. We had a lifetime of moments that were meaningful, spiritual, and transcendent. We refused to reduce our love to some flippant expression based on our age. We were mature enough to know that our actions, in that moment, were selfish. He didn't say it, but the impending doom was palpable for both of us. And he was right: we were smart for our age. We both knew that one of us would have to make a sacrifice.

Jax glanced over at me, as if he knew what I was thinking. He grabbed my hand. "Em, just be here in the moment with me for now, okay?"

I smiled back at him, my eyes already watering. "Don't make me cry, please. We were laughing just two minutes ago."

We rode the rest of the way in silence.

8. Saying Good-bye

I was breathing hard as I lay the book on my chest, right over my throbbing heart. I remembered that moment when everything started crumbling down around us. There was nothing we could do; we were just a couple of powerless, poor kids, so desperate to find a way to be together . . .

It was the middle of the night by that point, and I was too frustrated to keep going. I didn't want to wake Cara, so I took a bath, got back into bed, and texted Trevor, but he was already asleep. I went into Cara's room to see if maybe she was burning the midnight oil on her next story, but she was sound asleep as well. I wasn't ready to go back to the book, so I spent the next three hours lying in bed, thinking.

When I was eighteen, I saw a therapist who convinced me to go back to Ohio to look for Jase and see where we grew up to try to work through some of my issues. Cyndi and Sharon, being the amazing women that they were, dropped everything to take me there. We found the dirt road right at the five-point-five-mile marker, right where it had always been. There were just two lone wooden posts and a memory of the battered mailboxes. We couldn't drive down the road because there was a locked gate and a sign that said NO TRESPASSING, but that didn't stop Cyndi. Sharon had tried to talk her out of it, but Cyndi insisted that we climb the fence and make the half-mile journey down the road to where the two dilapidated houses once stood.

When we arrived at the end of the road, there was nothing. The houses had been torn down. All that was left were two concrete foundations and a couple of wooden beams. I was happy they were gone.

"Say good-bye, Emiline," Sharon said. "Say good-bye to the horrible things that happened here."

I cried and cried in Cyndi's arms. Echoes of Jase were everywhere. I could see a twelve-year-old Jase as he stood on a rock with his arms in the air. *Look at me, Em, I'm the king of the world!* And there I was, a skinny mess of a kid with my arms crossed, laughing. *Well, you're no Leonardo DiCaprio, that's for sure.*

I laughed through my tears as Cyndi asked, "Are you having a good memory or a bad one?"

I smiled. "This one's a good one."

We walked past the gravel toward the tree line and spotted the small structure still standing in the distance. It was the toolshed-turned-fort that Jase and I had made our own.

"Is this it?" Sharon asked. I only nodded.

We tried to pry open the plywood door, but it was so weathered and warped that it was jammed shut. Sharon, a fairly petite woman, came at it with the broad end of a thick wooden stump.

"Watch out!" she yelled as she pummeled the door, busting it open.

After the dust settled, Cyndi patted my back. "You go. We'll be right here if you need us."

I stepped in, legs shaking, heart pounding. It was empty except for a few twigs and a lot of dust. On the back of the door, I could still make out the fading orange paint where Jase had written the rules of the fort when we were eleven.

NO PARENTS
NO HOMEWORK
NO FIGHTING

Somehow, those three rules had meant heaven. I looked around, remembering our last night there. Beyond the window, I could see the tree line, more sparse than I remembered it. I could almost make out the little dock on the creek, where we used to swing ourselves off and into the water. An image of Jason's brother, Jeff's floating body popped into my head uninvited. That's when I knew it was time to go.

Managing to hold it together, I found Cyndi and Sharon outside and said, "I've had enough, I'm ready."

We left Ohio and never spoke of my childhood again. Jase was long gone. I didn't know where to look, and he hadn't left me any clues, so I filed him away, like everything else. I thought I had gone back there to say good-bye to my mother and father and to find Jase, but none of those things happened. Instead, I said good-bye to Jase that day because he hadn't come to find me like he said he would. It was the hardest thing I had ever done.

IT FELT LIKE ten minutes later, but it was morning when Cara shook me awake. "Did you finish the book?"

I yawned dramatically. "No, not even close." Every page was sending me on a long emotional journey that felt both painful and necessary.

"Well, what are you waiting for? I want to take it to have him sign it."

I grumbled, "Um, why?"

"Because I just want to," she whined. "And I want you to go with me."

"What time is the signing?"

Her face lit up. "Are you gonna go?"

"No. I just want to be able to give you the damn book so you can have it signed."

"Come on."

"I don't think I'm going. If he wanted to see me, he would have contacted me by now," I said.

"You. Read that." She pointed to the book. "I'm going to play tennis. I'll be back in an hour. The signing's at three." She looked at her watch. "You need to speed-read, but I'm pretty sure you can finish it in four hours."

"Whatever, you can take it if I'm not done."

"You guys grew up together and you obviously went through a lot. I'm not going to pretend I understand everything, Emi, but don't you at least want to say hello?"

"We did go through a lot," I said absently as I wondered again, for the hundredth time, why he hadn't tried to get in touch with me.

"What part are you at?" she asked.

"When he comes to pick me up from the foster home."

"It's so weird to hear you say it like that."

"Imagine how I feel reading my own thoughts that I didn't write."

"I could see how that would be strange. You must have shared a lot with him."

"Everything." It was true. In real life, we talked for hours at night while I was hiding up in that attic room of the foster home. I'd told him every detail like I was reading him a story.

"Well, get back to it," Cara said, interrupting my thoughts.

Her ponytail bounced as she walked away. I knew it was my own issue, but her perkiness irritated me. I wasn't ready to get back to the book, so I did the other thing I needed to do: I called Cyndi.

"Hello?"

"Hi, Aunt Cyndi."

"How's my girl?"

"I'm okay. So, um, I hate to spring this on you out of the blue, but . . . Jase wrote a book," I said, coming down hard on that final consonant.

"Oh my goodness! Are you serious?" she said excitedly.

"Yeah. He wrote a freakin' book about our childhood and got it published. And it's a huge bestseller."

"Oh dear god." That was Cyndi's expression for something catastrophic — she wasn't even a smidge religious.

"Have you heard of *All the Roads Between* by J. Colby?"

"*That* book. Wow!" She cleared her throat. "I mean, yes, I've heard of it. It's been criticized by some." She always tried extremely hard to make me feel better in every situation. It was just one of the many things I loved about her.

"Oh, don't give me that. Don't think I haven't googled every single article about this book. It got one bad national review. Otherwise, it's a critical darling."

I could hear Cyndi cover the mouthpiece and whisper-shout Sharon's name. She came back on the line. "Okay, Emi, we'll figure this out."

I shook my head. "Hi, Sharon. I know you're on the line."

There was a pause, and then a "Hiiiii, sweetie. I'm so sorry you're going through this, but try to think of it as a cathartic experience that you can use in your writing." This was classic, sensible Sharon. "Have you read the book yet?"

"I'm reading it now. It's basically a roman à clef, except that he wrote it from my point of view. Can you believe the nerve?"

I could hear them both sucking air through their teeth, and then there was more off-phone whispering. Cyndi came back on the line. "We're taking tomorrow off. We'll be in the car, on our way to you, in less than an hour. Expect us in the early evening. Our girl needs us."

"No, you guys don't have to come down for this."

"You bet your ass we're coming down, and we will all work through this together."

I sighed—partially from resignation, partially from pure relief. "Thank you so much you guys." I felt pathetic after I hung up, but there was no use fighting the combined forces of Cyndi and Sharon.

Five seconds later, Cara walked by my room on her way to the kitchen and yelled, "Keep reading!"

I looked at the book on my bed, grabbed it, and headed for the living room. I didn't want to be alone for what I knew was coming next.

From *All the Roads Between*

We pulled into Carter's egg ranch just after two a.m. Cal Junior was sitting on a wooden bench propped against one of the chicken barns, waiting for us.

"Don't talk to him, okay?" Jackson said as he parked the truck.

"Why?"

"Just don't. He's a fucking bully."

Cal Junior walked over to the passenger door and opened it. He brushed his greasy hair from his eyes and smiled a crooked-toothed grin. "Scoot to the middle, princess. We'll let Jax here drive so we can get reacquainted with each other."

Jax held up his hand to stop Cal from getting in. "No, you're not gonna touch her."

"Calm down. I ain't gonna bite." He scooted in next to me, stinking like cigarettes and manure.

"Like I'd let him?" I said.

"I told you, don't talk," Jax barked.

I swallowed and then nervously moved over as close to Jackson as I could get. He put his right arm over my legs for the rest of the trip. It was only two miles to our road, but it felt like forever. Occasionally, Cal Junior burst into laughter at nothing at all, like a lunatic.

We drove down to the end of El Monte Road. I looked over and saw caution tape and yellow signs nailed to the outside of my father's dark, desolate house.

Cal Junior got out and walked around to the driver's side. As Jackson stepped out of the truck, Cal slapped him hard on the back. "See you tomorrow, kid! You owe me."

Jackson took my hand and pulled me through his house to

the back door, through the weeds, to the fort. Our fort. When he lit the camping lamp, I noticed that he had added blankets and pillows to the cot and laid out some bottled water and snacks on the bedside table, as well as a stack of books I hadn't read before.

"Leila's shift is over in two hours. You can leave your bag here and take a shower in the house." We were standing near the wooden door. I realized Jax looked like a giant inside of our fort.

"Will you sit with me for a sec?" I asked.

He hesitated and then sat on the cot. I sat next to him and rubbed my hand down his thigh.

"Have you been working extra hours at the egg ranch? Is that why Junior lets you drive his truck?"

He swallowed and then nodded.

"Jackson?"

He leaned forward, bracing his elbows on his knees and dropped his head into his hands.

"Look at me, Jackson."

When he turned his neck to look up at me, I could see tears in his eyes. I put my hand on his back and rubbed up and down. "What have you been doing for Cal Junior? When he said you owed him, what did he mean?" My voice was getting higher, almost frantic, and my heart was beating out of my chest with a sense of dread.

His face was back in his hands. He made a sound that fell somewhere between a sob and groan. "Em . . . . I . . ."

I pulled him toward me and took him in my arms. "Tell me. I won't judge you."

He shook his head no.

"Tell me."

He pushed me away, sat up, and wiped his hands down his face, as if to erase the sadness and anger. He was impassive now, sitting perfectly upright and staring at the door when he finally spoke. "I sell weed for him at school." His voice was phlegmatic. "He wants me to sell other stuff, like meth . . . to kids." He looked in my eyes, expecting disappointment in my own, like I would think less of him . . . but I could never.

"You won't do it anymore, Jackson. You don't have to." I knew the drug thing tore him apart because of its impact on his mother and the still-painful rumors about his brother's death. Jackson hated drugs. I wanted to say that I was sorry. It was all my fault that Jackson felt like he had to do something as unconscionable as selling drugs to kids. I rubbed his back and tried desperately to soothe him.

Through tears, he fumbled over his words. "I feel like such a hypocrite. Junior started talking about Carter's and how it was going under. He said he and his dad had been making meth for years. It's how they kept the family business going. It's so fucked up. That money we earned growing up was drug money. Tainted."

I took his face in my hands and forced him to look at me. His eyes were fixed on the wall behind me. "Look at me now, Jackson. We were just kids, collecting eggs. We earned that money and we didn't know any better. And what choice did we really have in a town like this? Look at us. We're stuck now. I don't want to be stuck anymore, and I don't want you selling drugs so you can pay some asshole to use his truck. You will not go back there—I won't let you." I was crying too now.

"What if he tells people?"

"Jackson, you are smarter than this. Junior will never tell

because he'll go to jail. They're making the drugs, not you. You could put him away yourself, you know."

"I don't know, Em."

"If you don't, I will."

He looked panic-stricken. "No! You can't. They'll send you away."

"Don't you care what he and his father are doing to this town?"

"This town?" He squinted at me.

"To you, to us, Jax. Don't let our circumstances affect your integrity. Even if you stop selling drugs, Junior will just find someone else to do it. I know who you are. You're not going to let that happen."

He leaned in slowly. I saw a faint smile tugging at his lips. He kissed me and then pulled away and took a deep breath. "I don't deserve you, Em."

I laughed and it lightened the mood a bit. "Well, that's true, but at least you appreciate that fact. I better get in there and take a shower. Are you gonna be okay?"

"Yeah. I'll be here when you get back. Don't leave any evidence."

"I know."

Jackson's house hadn't changed over the years—same stained couch, dingy carpet, and cigarette stink. In the bathroom, the frosted shower door had a rusted track and mildew caked on the tub lining. I undressed quickly and jumped under the cold water, shivering until it warmed up.

I cried for Jax. I couldn't hold on anymore. Face-to-face, I could be strong for him—he needed that—but once I was alone, I cursed the whole goddamn universe. I cursed Leila, the whiskey monster, that asshole Cal Junior, the Kellers and their stupid rules, and I even cursed dead Brian for leaving us. Then, when all I could taste was the salt from my tears, I sank to my knees under the scalding water and cursed my mother.

Flush it all away. Neeble and the monsters who live here, the stench of death, the drugs, the abuse, the blood and the bodies floating in the river, and all of the unloved children. Just flush it all away, god.

I cried and cried, and soon the water turned cold again. My arms were wrapped around my legs and my head was resting on my knees when the shower door opened and the water was shut off.

"Stand up, Em," came Jackson's soothing voice.

He instantly wrapped a towel around me and held me to his big body as my sobs turned into sporadic hiccups. I reached for my clothes and felt a trickle of blood run down my leg. I held the towel to my body, took a step back, and looked down. I had forgotten to ask god to flush away the whole period thing. I looked up at Jackson through my puffy eyes and smiled. "Being a woman sucks."

He laughed. "You used to brag about it."

"Not anymore," I said.

"I'll give you a minute. Just hurry. My mom will be home in an hour."

"Okay."

I cleaned up all traces of Emerson in the house and bathroom, and by the time I made it out to the fort, the sun was coming up. Jackson was asleep on the cot. I curled up next to him and he instinctively opened his arms so I could rest my head on his chest.

That night I slept more soundly than I ever had in my life.

SOMETIME THE NEXT day, when I woke up, he was gone. My period was over, thank god, and Jax had left me a bowl of dry Cheerios and a note.

Morning, Em. Sorry for the dry Cheerios. Mother of the Year hasn't gone to the store in a few weeks. I took her car to school. She's inside the house with some dude, so keep a low profile. Sorry about last night, too. I shouldn't have put that on you. Junior is not your problem, he's mine. I'm done with the drug thing. I should be home by three thirty. I love you.

I looked at the stack of books on the small table and then beyond it to the black leather-bound journal sitting under a brass candleholder. My hand shook as I reached for it. I picked it up and held it to my chest. My fifteen-year-old brain wanted to open it so badly, but my heart wouldn't let me disrespect Jackson that way. Holding it to my chest, I stared out of the small shed window to the tree line and thought about our life so far. I tried to predict how the story would end, or even what would happen to us after that day, but I couldn't figure it out. We were just kids.

There were footsteps coming toward the shed, and then I heard Jackson whistling. I opened the thin, wooden door. "Welcome home, honey."

Jax was wearing a cocky grin. He held up a piece of paper with a big A-plus in red ink. "Boom! Aced my World History test."

I wrapped my arms around him. "How'd you get so smart?"

"History Channel."

"That's right, you had cable," I whispered near his ear.

"You make that sound sexy."

"It *is* sexy to a ten-year-old nerd."

"We're not ten anymore."

"I can tell," I said, and then we were kissing. I reached for the bottom of his T-shirt and pulled it over his head.

He kicked off his shoes while his hands roamed underneath my sweater from my sides to my back. He led me toward the cot, sat down, and then pulled me on top to straddle him. "Take this off," he said, tugging at my sweater dress. I took it off and his mouth was on me instantly, kissing a trail from my neck to the tops of my breasts. He smoothly unclasped my bra. I dropped my arms and let it fall to the ground.

"God, Em." He was kissing me all over. "You're . . ."

"What?"

"You're so . . . God . . . I want you . . . You're so beautiful."

Lying back, he pulled me on top of him and rolled us over so that we were on our sides. He slipped his hand easily inside of the front of my panties but froze. I was gripping his neck and holding his mouth to mine. He pulled away, breathing hard.

Our chests were heaving in and out. His eyes were darting everywhere, from my mouth to my eyes. "What is it, Jax?"

"Is this okay?" He lowered his hand.

"Yes. Just kiss me."

I got lost in all of the feelings, and before long we were completely naked under a thin sheet, Jackson's fingers were inside of me, and his mouth was on my neck, kissing me senseless.

Suddenly, his hand was gone, and I whimpered. "No, don't stop," I said. He shifted onto his hands and held himself over me. I opened my legs for him and reached down to touch him. "No, don't, Em."

When I pulled away, he thrust his hips once. I felt him hard against my thigh. I reached down again, but he quickly moved away from me and sat back on his knees. "Shit, we can't do this."

"What? Why?"

"We need protection." A bead of sweat rolled down the side of his face.

It looked like he was in pain, but I didn't know if it was mental or physical. "We can do . . . it . . . just once."

"No! No, that would be so dumb of us."

I had never seen Jackson completely naked like that. He was beautiful, even at sixteen. "We can do other stuff," I said.

He swallowed and then nodded before collapsing into my arms.

It could have been hours or days or years that we spent like that, exploring each other, tangled in each other. He made me a million promises that our first time would be perfect and magical, and we would know exactly what to do because everything felt so right when we were together.

AFTER SUNDOWN, WE heard Leila yelling for Jax from the house, but we were still tangled up in the sheets, lying in each other's arms.

"What should we do?" I asked him.

Jax froze. "Get dressed." Her voice got closer and closer to the shed as we scurried around, trying to find our clothes. "Don't make a sound. I have to go. When she leaves for work, I'll come back out."

I pulled on my pants and shirt. "Okay."

Before he left, he reached down and turned off the lamp. "I'm sorry, I have to."

"It's fine; just go. Hurry."

I curled up under a musty blanket and closed my eyes. In the distance, I could hear Jackson talking to his mom, but I couldn't tell what they were saying, and then their voices got farther and farther away. The shed felt even darker and lonelier. I tried to sleep, but I had been sleeping for most of the day while Jax was at school, so I didn't feel tired. You couldn't have much of a life while you were hiding out in a shed.

My stomach was rumbling with hunger as I lay there. There was a sliver of moonlight coming through the tree line and streaming through the window. I stared at it and tried to count the dust particles dancing in the moonbeams. I was thinking mindlessly about kissing Jackson when I heard him yelling outside.

"No!" He was screaming. I could tell that he was running toward the shed. "Em!"

I stood up and bolted out of the door. Flashlights illuminated him from behind, silhouetting him as he ran toward me.

My heart was racing. "Run, Em!" he screamed.

Without another thought, I turned and started running toward the creek. Jackson and I both knew there was nothing for miles. I ran out of fear that we would be torn apart again, of our entire lives changing in the blink of an eye.

The only sounds were of our feet crunching against twigs and leaves and our heaving breaths. When the light faded behind us, we slowed.

"I have to stop, Jax." I turned to face him. There was just enough moonlight to see him bent over, bracing his knees.

He was breathing hard and his voice was strained. "Fuck! Fuck! That fucking bitch!"

"What happened?"

"She reported me."

"What do you mean? She's the last person who wants to see you in trouble," I said.

He was trying to catch his breath. "Not my mom. Your social worker came here looking for you this morning. My mom didn't tell her anything at first because she didn't know. Then Junior came to the house wondering why I hadn't shown up in the morning. He was pissed, and when my mom started defending me, he told her that I had taken his truck to get you."

My heart was pounding. *Shit, shit, shit.* "So how the hell does Paula know I'm here?"

Jax straightened and looked away. "She called Paula because she said she didn't want you dragging me down and getting me into trouble."

I winced. It was painful to hear Jackson say those words because part of me knew it was true. I was confused, but I knew this much: I was standing on a precipice. I could jump off with Jax, but was it fair to take him down when he had so much going for him?

"Paula reported the whole thing to the police?" I asked.

He nodded.

"Those were police officers chasing us?"

"Yes," he said.

I nodded and walked toward him. "We have to go back." I was surprised to hear that my voice was strong. Resolute.

"No, Em. I can't live without you. We can't go back."

"Jackson, I want to be with you so badly, but we can't stay this way. I want to see the world with you, but how can we? Like this? Running? Or trapped in Neeble? If we stay here, we'll just be digging this hole deeper and deeper. We deserve better."

"But it won't get better. I'll still be stuck here on this road with Leila. Can't we leave together? I know we can do it, Em . . . You and me . . . we can do anything. We just have to get out of here."

The flashlights were coming toward us again, and we could hear a man calling our names in the distance. "I'm sorry," I said, leaning up to peck him on the lips. But it wasn't true. I wasn't sorry. I knew what I had to do. "We're here!" I yelled as I stepped away from Jax. "We're right here!"

"No," he whispered. "Please, Em, don't do this to me."

He tried to run, but I held him as hard as I could. "Please let me go," he cried. "Why are you doing this to me?"

"Because it's what's best for us," I told him, but I knew he wouldn't understand.

"You're killing me, Em. Please let me go."

He finally escaped my grip but was standing face-to-face with two police officers, one holding a nightstick in the air. "Don't move, son. Turn around slowly and put your arms behind your back."

"You're handcuffing me?"

"You're under arrest for kidnapping and fleeing law enforcement."

The second officer grabbed me and pulled my arm in the other direction. I looked at Jackson and saw the desperation in his eyes.

"I love you," I called out as the second officer led me away, but Jax didn't respond. I was overwhelmed with guilt and sadness, but I couldn't continue dragging him down. Because I did love him. I loved him too much to ruin his life.

When we got to the house, I saw that Paula was waiting for me, and that my things had already been removed from the shed and piled up in the backseat of her car. I could hardly look at Paula, but when I finally did, I didn't see anger and judgment in her face. Instead, I saw sympathy.

I couldn't breathe, let alone speak, but on the way to the airport, Paula said one thing that stayed with me. "You did the right thing. For him, and for yourself."

I stared out the window and wondered if he would ever forgive me . . . if he would ever understand.

9. This Is Us

Throwing the book down on the floor of the living room, I let out a frustrated, painful sigh.

Cara was watching me from the other couch, her eyes as wide as sand dollars. "What? What is it?"

"It's not true. That's not how it happened." I stood up and paced, frantically twirling my hair into a tight knot.

Cara remained silent, watching me as I tried to untangle the mess in my head. Jase had written my life story from my perspective, and up until now, it had been mostly accurate, with a little bit of fictional flair. But he had taken some serious liberties with this last chapter.

Because Jase was the one who'd actually turned us in.

I turned on my heel to face Cara, wild with anger. "Do you think all this critical attention is deserved? I mean, this isn't some great literary novel. It's just a straightforward book about two kids. It doesn't make sense that it would be a bestseller."

Cara shrugged, her eyes sympathetic. "Is this what's really bothering you, Emi?"

I stared at her. I was angry and jealous of his success, but underlying all of that was a deep and endless hurt, which felt fresher than ever now that I was reading Jase's book. But I couldn't focus on that now. I couldn't wrap my heart and mind around why he turned us in all those years ago. So I focused on the jealousy, like a bitter writing instructor who couldn't write herself out of a cardboard box.

"Cyndi and Sharon are coming over, and I just want to forget all about this, okay? I don't want to think about him or that book ever again."

"I think you're being irrational, Emi," Cara said in a soothing voice.

"No, I'm not." I walked toward her, braced her shoulders, and tried my best to compose myself. "I spent years in therapy trying to work through, or at least forget, everything that happened. I just can't read it anymore. Please understand."

"There're, like, ten more chapters, Em. I think you should give it a chance. I think it'll be healing for you."

"*She's* Em, Cara. I'm Emi. We're not the same person. I appreciate you trying so hard, but no, I'm not going to give it a chance. He did his thing, and now I'm doing mine. End of the real story, as far as I'm concerned."

"Okay," she said unconvincingly. I gave her a hug. "You should still go to the book event. He deserves readers who love and support him. He's a fucking bestselling published author, after all. But please don't mention me to him."

She nodded. "I would never."

I went back to my room and crawled under the sheets.

SOMETIME IN THE early afternoon, I woke to a pounding headache and mild nausea. I looked at the clock. It was three. My apartment was eerily quiet, and I remembered that Cara was at the bookstore, waiting in line to see Jase so she could congratulate him on basically telling the entire world the horrors of our childhood and then making me look like the bad guy.

I moped around for twenty minutes until I couldn't take it anymore; I had to text her.

Me: R U there?

Cara: Yes, there's a line around the building

Me: Ur kidding me?

Cara: Lots of giddy women

Me: That fucker.

Cara: glad 2 c ur mood has changed

Me: Where is it?

Cara: Ur coming?

Me: Don't know yet. Where?

Cara: Mysterious Galaxy Bookstore

Me: K

Cara: I'll save you a spot

Me: No, get ur book signed

I stared into my closet for what felt like hours. Finally, I said fuck it and went with jeans, a high-necked sweater, and tennis shoes. I put the most minimal amount of makeup on, just a touch of lip gloss and mascara, and then flat-ironed my hair. I still felt like I was trying too hard, so I slicked my hair back into a ponytail, grabbed my keys, and ran out the door.

Right after grad school, Cyndi and Sharon had bought me an old Honda. Even though they had plenty of money for something nicer, they refused to let me drive around in a rich-kid car, especially since they never made me get a job while I was in school. I felt like I had paid my dues, but I appreciated their efforts and didn't really care about cars anyway.

I sped down the freeway with shaking hands. My mind was spinning. What would I say to him? How would he look?

When I pulled into the parking lot, my mouth fell onto the floor of my Honda. Cara wasn't exaggerating. The line was literally wrapped around the building, and it was mostly women.

I joined the end of the line, and within minutes a woman came over and told me I had just made it. I was the last person that Mr. Colby would have time for before the store closed. I texted Cara.

Me: Where are u?

Cara: Inside. U here? U wanna come
inside? I can say I was saving
ur spot?

Me: No. Can you see him?

Cara: Yes.

Me: And?

Cara: He's gorgeous, Emi. Nice suit.

Me: He's wearing a suit?

Cara: Wearing it well, my friend. He
looks like a model. He has perfect hair
and he's charming the panties off
these women. Can I please flirt
with him?

Me: I'm leaving

Cara: NO!!!!!! I was kidding.
You have to see him

When I got inside, there was a large bookshelf obscuring
my view of where Jase was set up. I stood on my tippy toes to
try and get a better view, but all I could see was the top of his
head. I didn't see Cara in the crowd, but she texted me later
to say she was waiting in the parking lot.

Me: Did he sign your book?

Cara: Yes

Me: What else did he say?

What did he write in it?

Cara: He was really polite. He just said
thanks for reading and for coming out and
then he asked what my favorite part was.

Me: What did you say?

Cara: I said the ending

Me: Wait, how does it end?

Cara: You'll have to read it

Me: I still have a ways to go until I'm
at the front of the line. You don't have to
wait for me. I'll meet you at home.

Cara: You sure? You won't need
moral support?

Me: I'm fine.

Cara: K. See you at home.

When the line moved past the bookshelves, I could finally see the table where Jase was sitting, but his head was
down as he signed books. Every once in a while, he would
look up to the person he was talking to and smile or shake
hands. When he stood to take a picture, he looked taller
than I remembered. There wasn't much of the boy I used
to know in him anymore. He carried his broad shoulders
confidently, and he smiled a lot. He seemed charming and
friendly. It was too bad I wanted to beat up his beautiful face.

With my head down, I continued to move with the line

until the last woman in front of me was standing at his table. I kept my distance and looked at the shelf to my right until I heard him say to the lady, "It's so nice to meet you—thank you for coming."

When I looked up, he was standing, staring right at me, but his face gave nothing away. I took three hesitant steps toward him until we were standing directly across from each other. A beautiful woman dressed in stilettos and a pencil skirt stood behind him, just off to his left. She was staring at me the same way . . . impassive.

He blinked. I blinked. There was silence.

"Jason," I finally said.

"Emiline," he said.

Screw you and your smooth voice.

The woman behind him sauntered up to the table. "Did you want to buy a book, sweetie, and have Mr. Colby sign it for you?"

Without taking his eyes off me, he responded, "I've got this. Can you give me a minute, Andrea?"

She shook her head and then walked away. I couldn't find my voice. He crossed his arms over his chest and rocked back on his heels. His lips were flat, his expression inscrutable, but his eyes were probing mine for something, some clue, some tell.

"Why?" I said.

He grinned.

What the hell? "Don't smile at me," I quipped.

He jerked his head back and scowled. Did he not understand why I would be angry?

"Why . . ." I repeated, but couldn't find the right words to continue.

"Why, what?" Now *he* looked confused.

"Why on earth did you lie?" I said finally.

Something happened in his eyes, and then his expression went back to that same inscrutable look. "It's a work of fiction, Emiline. Did you not read the disclaimer on the copyright page?" He looked past me toward the door, indifferent, like he wanted to leave.

Don't cry, Emiline. It's not your fault he grew up to be an asshole.

"What did you do to us?" My voice broke. "What have you done?"

"Did you read the book?"

"I read enough."

"Why didn't you finish it? That's not like you."

"You don't know me anymore, Jason." He winced. "I haven't seen or heard from you in twelve years," I said.

Andrea called out to Jase as she walked by. "You've got about five minutes, Jay. We have an interview to get to."

"Who is that woman?" I asked.

"My agent."

"Oh, your *agent*? I see. So you're a big shot now?"

He just shook his head. I still couldn't read his expression. "This isn't how I expected . . ."

"Expected what?" I shot back.

There were another several moments of awkward silence. I wanted to peel my skin off, leave it on the floor, and run away. Yet Jase didn't seem the least bit ruffled, and aside from that moment of confusion, he just remained cold and impassive. I looked him up and down, standing in front of an endcap dedicated to his successful book, perfectly composed in his glorious beauty, with his chiseled jaw and perfectly mussed-up, golden-brown hair.

I made a frustrated sound. "Ugh."

He frowned. "What's wrong, Emiline?"

"Stop saying my name." I balled my hands into fists. "I can't . . . I'm just . . . I'm frustrated. I came here to chew you out and you're just standing there like . . . ugh."

He chuckled and uncrossed his arms. "Standing here like what? Chew me out if you have to. Go ahead."

"You're just . . . dammit . . . Why are you so good-looking?" The last part came out like a cry. I wanted to punch the smirk off his face.

"Well, you're beautiful. So there." I froze. "Then again, you always were."

"Oh, don't charm me with your wordy magic."

For a moment, a real smile, not some shit-eating grin, came to his lips. And just like that, in an instant, we were fifteen again.

I held my hand up. "I'm done here. You're free to go to your interview."

I started to turn and walk away, but he grabbed my arm and spun me around. "You didn't come here to tell me I'm good-looking."

That was the damn truth. But as I stood in front of him, I couldn't find the words to say what I wanted to say: *Where have you been? What was your life like? Did you miss me? Did I mean as much to you as you meant to me? Why'd you turn us in?* I couldn't find the courage to make myself vulnerable like that. Not when he had everything I wanted.

"I came here because you lied in the book."

"Call it artistic license. Anyway, I think you should finish it."

"You painted a really nice picture of yourself, didn't you?" My hand was in my hair, twirling it into a massive knot. I could see that he noticed the childhood habit, but I didn't want him to feel like he still knew me. I pulled my hand down and blinked.

"I can tell you still haven't worked through everything," he said. "Why didn't you finish the book?"

"I was mad that you lied."

"Emiline, those details don't matter. I had my reasons for changing it."

"But so much of the rest of it is true. Why change something so crucial?"

"Like I said, I had my reasons."

He was so much more intimidating than I remembered. "Are we gonna talk about what happened, Jase, or just keep beating around the bush?"

He looked behind me when the door jingled. "Em, you had to have known I was gonna write this book someday."

"No." I shook my head. "I didn't."

"I told you I would find you, didn't I?"

Synapses were misfiring in my brain left and right. *This is how he was going to find me? What did he mean?*

Still looking behind me, he said, "Do you know that guy?"

I turned to see Trevor leaning against the door with his hands buried in his pockets. *Shit.* "Um, yeah. He's my boyfriend."

Jase didn't miss a beat. "Do you want to introduce us?"

"Not really."

He threw his hand up and waved Trevor over. "Hey, man. Come on over."

With my back to Trevor, I whispered to Jase, "I'm going to kill you in your sleep."

"Does that mean you're gonna sleep with me first?" he whispered back. "Not a bad way to go."

I was a nervous, fumbling idiot.

Once Trevor got to the table, I awkwardly introduced them. "Jase, this is Trevor. You might recognize him. He was the star quarterback at Berkeley."

"Nice to meet you," Jase said as the two men pleasantly shook hands. "I'm not much of a sports guy, but I remember hearing your name when Cal won the championship a few years back."

Oh Jesus Lord, now he's trying to charm Trevor too?

Gorgeous Agent Andrea walked up and looped her arm through Jase's. They clearly had more than a working relationship. Damn them. "Interview. Remember, Jay?"

He pulled her arm out of his and put some distance between them. "Right, the interview. Well, Emiline, it was nice seeing you. Thank you for coming. Trevor, it was nice to meet you as well." They shook hands. "I have to run." He turned and faced me. "Em . . ." he said, looking right into my eyes and smiling. I felt my knees go weak. "I'm really sorry I can't stay longer and fulfill your desire to berate me in public. Maybe we can do this again some other time." He chuckled and then walked away.

Asshole. I was seeing red.

"Wait!" I shouted. "Why did you write it from my point of view?"

He continued walking but called back, "It's just a book!" But I knew it wasn't. Jase was always deliberate. He took the long view of everything, even at the age of eight.

I started to hear a beeping sound in my mind, like a bomb was about to explode. How could I let him walk away without getting the answers I wanted? The beeping was getting faster and faster as I walked out of the bookstore toward my car.

"I have to get out of here. I swear to god my heart is going to explode," I said as Trevor trailed behind me.

"You're like this in every situation. Ticking time bomb, Emi. Calm down—nothing happened."

When I reached the driver's-side door, I turned around and leaned against it. "Why are you here, Trevor?"

"Cara texted me. She told me what was going on, so I came over. I came here to support you. But once again, you don't appreciate it."

I didn't know whether to be moved or irritated. "I don't need rescuing."

"You're clearly very upset," he said.

"Of course I'm upset! That guy in there wrote a book about my awful, terrible, traumatic childhood, which he must know I can't bear to relive, and he didn't even ask me for permission! He hasn't even tried to talk to me in twelve years! *And* he won! He published a whole novel before I've even figured out how to write a decent short story that my own boyfriend would like. I can't handle any of this."

Trevor looked thoughtful for once. "Do you have feelings for him? Is that why all of this is getting to you? What do you want, Emi? Do you want to be with that guy in there?"

I took three deep, cleansing breaths, and then I knew. I knew there was no point in hiding the truth any longer. Not from myself, and not from Trevor. As much as we'd been struggling lately, he didn't deserve it. I didn't deserve it.

"I do. I'm sorry, but I do. I have feelings for him, feelings that run so strong and so deep. Until this fucking novel came along, I'd kept them buried, and I thought they'd stay buried forever. And I'm scared, I'm really fucking scared. I'm afraid of what will happen. I'm afraid because I just saw my first love for the first time in over a decade, and he just stood there with complete indifference. And I'm scared because you're standing here in front of me, and I'm being honest with you in a way that will definitely destroy our relationship. And I'm scared because I feel like my heart is going to blow up into a million pieces inside of my chest."

Trevor squared his jaw, and I could see the muscles in his face flexing. A born athlete like Trevor really only comes to life when there's a challenge. Up until that point, he had moseyed through our relationship like he was warming up for a game with some jumping jacks. But now he realized he was already in the fourth quarter, there were mere seconds left on the clock, and he was down by three. Would he run the ball and try to get in field goal range? Or would he throw a Hail Mary and try to win it all right here?

"Marry me and forget him," he said with no trace of emotion.

I actually laughed. *Hail Mary it is.* "This is a strange moment to propose, don't you think?"

"It's actually not. This is real life, Emi, not some fantasy. This isn't a novel."

I wanted to say that novels weren't always fantasies. The book Jase had written certainly wasn't.

"I know this is real life, Trevor. I'm the most realistic person you will ever meet. But if you think any woman would be happy with a proposal like this, clearly made in desperation, then you're crazy. It's been seven years. We've never even talked about moving in together."

He threw his hands up. "Is that my fault or yours?"

"I don't want to play the blame game with you." The truth was, it was both of our faults. We weren't right for each other. We were both just going through the motions.

"Do I need to get down on one knee to show you I'm serious? Is that what you're saying?" He rolled his eyes.

I was ready to end the conversation. "Please don't. I have to go, Trevor. I don't feel well. I need to go home and recover from this crazy day."

"Fine." He bent and kissed me on the cheek. "Will you just please meet me for dinner tonight?"

I huffed, and he shook his head. "Don't do that, Emi. Just meet me for dinner. Let's talk when we've calmed down."

"Okay," I said after another long, deep breath. He kissed me again on the shoulder, got into his truck, and drove off, peeling onto the street in the process.

I got into my car and started the engine when a knock on my window startled me. It was the girl who worked at the checkout counter of the bookstore, motioning for me to roll down my window.

"Christ, lady, you scared the crap out of me," I said.

"Sorry. I just wanted to catch you before you left. J. Colby asked me to give this to you." She handed me a note.

"Thank you." I took it, rolled up the window, and unfolded the piece of paper.

We need to talk . . . alone. Meet me on the terrace at George's at ten tonight.

A wave of nausea hit me, and I rested my head on the steering wheel. Tears ran steadily down my cheeks as I tried desperately to regain some control. The smell of a leftover Big Mac on my passenger seat—the forgotten remains of my stress-eating binge from my drive over here—was making everything worse. My skin felt oilier than usual.

I heaved once, jumped out of the car, ran to a small patch of grass near the parking lot entrance, and purged the entire contents of my stomach in one stream of vomit. I put my hands on my knees and tried to catch my breath.

The woman who had given me the note came running over. "Are you okay?"

"Yes," I choked out.

She put her hand on my back. "Let me get you some water."

I looked up at her with tears in my eyes. "Thank you."

"It's okay, sweetie." She ran off and came back moments later.

I had gone back to lean against my Honda. "Is he still in there?" I said as she approached me with a bottle of water.

"No. He went out the back."

"Of course he did," I said, under my breath.

She leaned against the car next to me. "I'm Beth, by the way." She had bright pink hair and a T-shirt with matching pink bows on it that said BOOKWORM.

"I like your shirt. I'm Emiline. I'd shake your hand, but I have McDonald's vomit on mine."

We both laughed and it made everything better for a moment. "So that must have been quite a note he left you. If I got a note from J. Colby, I'd be freaking out too."

"It's just a receipt," I lied.

"Oh," she said, laughing.

"You a big fan?" I asked.

"Probably his number one fan. He's so talented and gorgeous and sweet."

I quirked an eyebrow at her. "You know the book isn't totally true."

"Of course. Why would I think it was? It's a novel."

"I thought maybe you thought he was Jax."

"It did cross my mind in the beginning. I just think it's amazing how well he can write from a girl's perspective. He's so tuned in to women, you know?"

I sighed. "I guess. I'm gonna go, Beth."

"Okay, well, I hope you feel better."

"Thank you." She smiled and walked back toward the store. "Seriously, thank you!" I called out to her.

"No problem," she yelled back.

I got into my car and unfolded the paper again.

It wasn't a request, and he obviously knew where I lived. George's was within walking distance of my house. I wanted answers, but I wasn't sure he deserved a chance to explain himself.

On the drive home, my mind went back to that last night in Ohio.

When the police had come up to us near the creek, I didn't yell out so they could find us. I'd run. I'd run until the bottoms of my bare feet were bleeding. I would have run all the way to fucking Mexico with no shoes on for Jase. He had been the one who had eventually given up.

We had spent that night huddled together in a cornfield, shivering, until he had finally said, "I can't do this."

"Yes, you can. We can. We can do anything together, remember?" I had argued.

I had convinced him to walk a few more miles with me. By the time dawn had arrived, Jase was carrying me on his back. We had found a main road and a convenience store, and he had told me to hide by the Dumpsters while he went in to get us food and to see if they sold at least some cheap plastic flip-flops. I had known he'd only had a few dollars. I had known it was the end. But I had followed his lead anyway.

The police had found me hiding where Jase had told me to wait. My feet had been raw and bloody, and I had been shaking as they led me to the police car. Jase was in the back of a different police cruiser, and when I had walked by, he mouthed the words *I'm sorry* and then started to cry. I had known he had turned us in. I had tried to fight my way out of the cop's hands and run to him and bang on his window and sob so he could see how badly he was hurting me.

As they had pulled me along, I'd screamed, "How could you do this to us?" He had just dropped his head and cried even harder.

That was the last time I saw him. And then I was shipped off to live with Cyndi and Sharon.

All of the therapy I'd had, all the talking about my problems, had somehow minimized the love Jase and I had experienced to a childhood crush—something more manageable for me to deal with. I was so heartbroken after he turned us in, but reframing our relationship allowed me to move on from the nightmare of being neglected by my mother, my father, and then, finally, by Jase.

But reliving what we had gone through within the pages of his book brought everything back . . . both good and bad. And I was feeling it all again. My heart was growing right alongside the pain, and I didn't know what to do with myself. It's impossible to really hate someone if you don't love them at least a little.

I ripped up Jason's note and threw it on the floor of my car.

10. Reading Between the Lines

By the time I got home, I only had a couple of hours before I had to meet Trevor, so I read and read and read. I had only three chapters left when I finally stopped.

Everything after Jax and Emerson were caught was totally made up. Emerson goes on to live with her aunt but has a terrible experience in California, while Jax becomes a distant memory. Emerson struggles to get over her past and ends up marrying a guy right out of high school who turns out to be an abusive alcoholic, just like her father.

I didn't know if I should be relieved it hadn't gone that way, or if I should be even more pissed at Jase for tarnishing the good parts of my story. Those chapters made Jax and Emerson suddenly feel like characters in a book, not fictional embodiments of me and Jase, and it made the dirt road seem far away. Maybe what Jase said at the bookstore was right. Maybe this really was just a book.

I got ready for dinner with Trevor and then rushed past Cara at the breakfast bar. "See ya!"

"Where are you running off to now?"

I paused at her choice of words. "I'm going to dinner with Trevor."

"You're not going to tell me about J. Colby?" she asked, her eyes wide with concern.

"I told him hello, it was nice to see him, and that was the end of it. He found success, so good for him. I just want to move on." In other words: run far, far away from him. "See ya."

"Wait, what?" But before she could continue that train of thought, I zipped right out of the apartment and down the stairs in ten seconds flat.

I met Trevor at a tiny Italian restaurant we went to often. He was sitting at a small two-top table in the middle of the dining room, facing the front door. I walked up and pulled my own chair out and sat down, leaning over the table to kiss him as I shrugged my sweater off. "Hi."

"Hey," he said. "Are you in a better mood?"

"I'm okay." I searched his eyes. "I read some more of the book and realized it's really not about me."

"It's not?"

"Nope." Trevor looked relieved. "I have a couple of chapters to go, but basically it's rounding out to be your run-of-the-mill unrequited love story." I huffed.

"*Romeo and Juliet*, huh?"

"Something like that." *No, nothing like that.*

"Hmm. So, earlier, when you said you had all those deep feelings for him . . ."

I looked away. "I don't know. Seeing him brought up a lot of feelings, but I think it was just my ego getting the best of me. I felt rejected by him, you know? He broke my fifteen-year-old heart."

"Yeah. I'm sorry for that, Emi."

I looked into Trevor's blue eyes, so light you could barely tell what color they were. "I bet you broke some hearts in your day too," I said.

He laughed. "I've been with you most of my adult life."

I swallowed. "Do I hear regret in your tone?"

"No. No regrets." He lifted his linen napkin, revealing a red ring box. I gasped. He stood from the table, came to my side, and dropped down on one knee, revealing a gold band at the same time. "Will you marry me, Emiline?"

Holy crap. Was he really serious with that parking-lot proposal?

Twenty seconds went by as I stared at the ring, stunned.

Trevor swallowed. "I'm on the floor of a restaurant. Are you going to say something?"

"I can't," I blurted out.

"What do you mean? You can't say something?"

"No. I can't . . . . marry you."

He looked wounded. "What? Why?"

Nothing about the moment felt right, but I didn't want to crush him. "Trevor, I'm not saying I won't marry you someday. I'm just saying I can't get engaged to you right now, not after everything that just happened. I wouldn't be saying yes in the right spirit. Please get up and sit."

He closed the box, threw it on the table, and sat down. He was clearly angry. With his arms crossed over his chest, he leaned back and scowled. "I don't understand you."

"I know I've been acting strange lately, but just bear with me," I said.

"Isn't that what I've been doing? Bearing with you?"

I stared at him for several seconds, then I went to stand up.

"Don't run away from me, Emiline. You know I don't deserve that."

I sat back down. "I don't know what to do. I know you don't deserve this, Trevor. But I also don't deserve to be guilted into an engagement."

He nodded. "I agree. I'll give you six months to think about it, to get him out of your system. When you give me your answer, promise me that it won't have anything to do with him. This should just be about us." He pointed out the window, but I knew exactly what he meant.

I nodded in agreement because, right now, I wasn't sure why I was saying no. Yes, it didn't feel right, but what if Trevor was being serious about all of this? If Jase hadn't come back into my life, would I have wanted to marry Trevor? Or would I have run from this proposal no matter what?

We finished dinner in amiable silence, but my mind was adrift. Every few minutes we'd look up at each other. I would make an effort to smile, but Trevor remained serious. When he paid the check, he said, "I'm gonna watch the game at a bar. Do you want to come with me?"

I looked at my phone and saw that Aunt Cyndi had texted me to say she was at my apartment, and that Cara had let her in. "Hold on," I said to Trevor before texting her back.

Me: Make yourself at home. I'll be there in a little bit.

Cyndi: No rush, we're busy reading your journal.

Me: I don't have a journal.

Cyndi: Well, you should, you're a writer.

Me: I'll be home in twenty.

I checked the clock on my phone. It was nine p.m. I had no intention of going to meet Jase, but I couldn't help thinking about him waiting for me at George's in an hour. I snuffed the thought out.

"I need to get home. Cyndi and Sharon are there. You go and watch the game. I'll text you later."

"Okay. You want me to come up with you and say hi?"

"You don't have to." Aunt Cyndi never said so, but I knew she didn't think Trevor and I were right for each other. She spent way too much time trying to set me up with guys in the writing program at Berkeley. She firmly rejected the notion of opposites attract. Plus, Trevor rarely made an effort with her. The obligatory offer to come up and say hi was his usual MO. I wanted Trevor to want to come up and say hi, but I knew he felt out of place.

I left Trevor at the front of the restaurant with a quick peck on the cheek. "I love you," I said.

"You too. I love you too," he said stiffly, as if he were speaking a foreign language.

I WALKED THROUGH the door of my apartment and was greeted instantly by Cyndi and Sharon, who insisted on smothering me every time I was in their presence.

"She's here!" Cyndi said as she and Sharon crushed me between them.

"Can't . . . breathe . . ."

Cyndi and Sharon were in their late forties. If you saw them in a restaurant, you would think they were just friends. Cyndi looked like a less glamorous Julia Roberts, and Sharon resembled her slightly thicker, more stylish sister with blonde hair. They looked and acted like buddies, so when they did partake in public displays of affection, people sort of looked on in shock. I thought it was cute.

"Have you been eating? You're skin and bones," Sharon said as she tugged at the skin on my hip. Needless to say, they loved their parental roles. I never really had parents, and they never really had kids, so it was great for all of us.

I smiled wide. "Actually, I had a Big Mac for lunch, but then I puked it up."

They looked at each other, horrified, and then they scanned me from top to bottom. Cyndi put her hand on her hip and gave me her best concerned face. "Bulimia is no laughing matter."

"I'm not bulimic. I just had a weird day. A horrible day, really."

"Tell us everything," Sharon said, pulling Cyndi onto the couch. "We're certainly not going to read it in any journal of yours." They both stared up at me, gripping each other's hands like they were about to watch a movie about the Holocaust.

"Well, I decided to go see Jase at his book signing here in town and ask him why he lied about what happened between us in his novel. And then I saw him and he looked like a fucking supermodel. And then Trevor showed up and asked me to marry him. And then Jase wrote me a note. And then I read it and threw up. And then I had dinner with

Trevor and ordered an arugula salad, which gave me a stom-achache. And then Trevor asked me to marry him again. And then I said no." I glanced up to see two sets of wide, unblinking eyes. "And then I kissed Trevor good night, and then he acted like it was hard to say I love you, even though he had *just* proposed to me. Twice. And now here I am."

Cyndi shook her head. "Wow. Terrible diction, sweetie. What did they teach you in that writing program of yours?"

"Valid point, honey," Sharon said, "but, Emi, what did the note say?"

I sighed. "He asked me to meet him tonight."

"Well, did you?" they both asked in unison. I swear to god, it was like they shared the same brain sometimes.

"No. He wants to meet at ten, but I'm not going to. I don't care what he has to say; I'm not subjecting myself to all that."

They stared at each other, as if they were communicating telepathically.

"We think you should meet with him," Cyndi said.

"I do too!" came a voice from the other room. Cara peeked her head out of her bedroom and then walked into the living room. "Emi, please tell me you finished the book."

"No, I didn't," I said with a hint of irritation in my voice. "Why?"

"Come, sit," Sharon said, scooting over and making room for me in the middle of the couch. "Cyndi and I read it on the way down here, and we think—"

"It's not about Jase and me," I said bluntly.

"Of course it is. And you should go talk to him," Cara said from the kitchen as she scanned the contents of the refrigerator.

"It's not like us to give away the ending," Cyndi said, "but I think you should finish the book."

"Why is everyone being so cryptic?" I asked.

"Just go meet him! He's so hot!" Cara shouted from across the room.

Without taking her eyes off me, Sharon said, "I like her."

I looked at the clock on the wall. It was almost ten. "Fine."

"Oh goody!" Cyndi exclaimed. "At the very least, he can give you a few pointers on word choice. That young man is a very talented writer."

I rolled my eyes and then hurried into my bedroom, with Sharon, Cyndi, and Cara trailing behind. I gave myself a once-over in the full-length mirror. "Why is everyone so eager for me to go meet him?"

Sharon furrowed her brow. "You can't go like that." I looked at my uncombed hair, sneakers, and pilling sweater. I was a wreck.

Like a flash of light, Cara took off for her room. Ten seconds later, she returned with a black slip dress, a cropped denim jacket, and black booties with a short heel. "Here. You'll look hot, but you won't look like you're trying too hard."

"Again, why is everyone so eager for me to go see him?"

"It'll be good for you. Might give you some closure," Cyndi said noncommittally, though I could sense she wasn't telling me the whole truth.

My clothes went flying in every direction, and then I pulled the new outfit on. As I ran to the door, I applied lip gloss and pulled on my boots at the same time. "Look at her:

she can multitask. She gets that from me," Cyndi said to Sharon as they followed me onto the landing.

"We love you!" they shouted as I jogged down the stairs.

"Love you!" Cara yelled from inside of the apartment.

I waved over my shoulder to them and slowed my pace once I got to the street. I walked the two blocks to George's, past the boutique stores that I normally window-shopped, and tried to focus on putting one foot in front of the other. I patted the pockets of my jacket several times to make sure I had slipped my keys, wallet, and phone into them before rushing out the door, and I nervously smoothed my curly hair as best as I could. I was sweating, but I was too afraid to do a BO check. My bootie heels clicked against the sidewalk in rhythm with the steady beat of my thoughts. *What am I doing, what am I doing, what am I doing?*

When I got to George's, I checked my phone. Ten p.m. I went up to the hostess stand and paused.

"Welcome to George's. Do you have a reservation?" the hostess asked.

"No. I mean, yes. Well, not me. I'm here to see Jase? I mean, Jason Colbertson." Wow, I seriously needed to get my shit together.

She nodded and then led me into the restaurant and then out again to a table at the edge of the terrace, under a heat lamp. Jase looked up as I approached and immediately stood to pull my chair out for me. Before I sat, he put his hand on my hip, leaned in, and kissed my cheek. I sucked in a deep breath and held it when his lips touched my face. In that moment, it felt like my heart stopped. I at least stopped breathing.

"Took you long enough," he whispered near my ear.

"Huh?" My brain was short-circuiting.

"Never mind. Sit," he said, gesturing toward the chair.

I sat with a clumsy thud while he gracefully slid back into his seat. He was wearing the same well-tailored, charcoal-colored suit and white shirt he'd had on earlier, but he had ditched the tie. The top button of his shirt was undone, and for a moment I imagined undoing the whole long row of pearly buttons beneath it.

"I wasn't going to come," I said.

"That's a shame." He blinked impassively.

"Don't you want to know why?"

"No. You're here now." There was nothing left of the timid Jase I once knew. He was in full command here.

I looked out to the ocean. "Quite a view, isn't it?"

His eyes were fixed on me. "Yes. It is."

Our table was so small that I could easily reach across and touch him if I wanted to. Which I did. I just didn't have the courage.

"A bottle of wine, perhaps?" he asked.

I nodded. "Sure, you choose."

"Red okay?"

I nodded again. I was rapidly losing any mastery I had over the English language.

He summoned the server and ordered an expensive bottle of pinot noir, like he had done it a million times.

"So . . ." I said after the server left to get the wine.

"You didn't finish the book this afternoon, I take it?"

"I read some, but I was busy." The server returned with a bottle and two glasses. She poured the wine as Jase continued to pierce me with his gaze.

"Thank you," he said.

I took a sip and smiled. "It's very good."

He sipped from his own glass and looked out to the ocean and then back at me. "God . . . I missed you so much, Em."

My smile faded. I tried to fight the tears sprouting into my eyes. "Don't, please."

He looked away again. "So . . . Trevor, huh? Never pictured you with a jock."

"It's not like he's an abusive alcoholic," I said defensively.

"Is that all it takes?" he said with a wry smile.

"No, I mean . . ."

"I'm just playing with you."

"You're still exasperating, Jase."

"You're still beautiful, Em. Even more so than I remember." His eyes traveled over my shoulders, my breasts, down the length of my black slip dress.

"When did you become such a pig?"

"I was just . . . appreciating how much things have changed," he said, flashing a grin before he took another sip.

"Please." I rolled my eyes. "We're not children anymore."

"We weren't children then. If memory serves, we grew up pretty fast."

"Regardless, I'm still mad at you," I replied.

"I can tell." He smirked.

"Stop fucking smirking at me."

"Okay." His lips flattened, but he couldn't mask his cocksure expression.

A few moments of silence went by as we sat, sipping our wine and enjoying the view. Far from feeling strange, the tension between us seemed to relax.

"I'm so glad to be here with you," he said, finally

sounding earnest. "Crazy, huh?" He looked out at the moon glistening over the ocean. "California, like we always said. Can you believe we're here, together?" I remained silent. "So, tell me, Em, what has your life been like? Because from the outside, it seems like you've got everything figured out."

"Not at all, actually," I mumbled, looking down into my lap.

He looked at my lips and then back up to my eyes. "Trevor is a good guy, I assume?"

I nodded. "Yeah, he is." And I meant it. Trevor, for all his flaws, had been a dedicated and loyal boyfriend for years.

"And you're an adjunct writing professor now?" Jase asked.

"More like an underpaid instructor," I corrected him.

"Well, I know you're so much more than that." The look on his face was like the look I remembered from when we were young. Few people in my life were as truly open-hearted as Jase. Though he could be cocky and stubborn, he could also be intensely sincere.

"Those who can't do . . . you know . . ." I shrugged. "I'm figuring out what to do next. I never really had your writing chops."

"I doubt that's true. You've always been so hard on yourself." He reached across the table and took my hand in his. I instinctively gave in to the moment of intimacy, my urge to run dissolving from moment to moment. "Why did you come here, Em? Why are you so torn?"

I looked up at him. "I came here because I would do anything you asked me to." My voice trembled.

He smiled. "Anything?"

I nodded.

"Then break up with him."

I withdrew my hand. "You ruined me that night, and you're ruining me again with this book."

"I thought I was saving you."

I started to cry.

"Don't cry." He wiped the tears from my face. "You know me, I was trying to be valiant." He laughed. "Guess my plan didn't work."

But it had. He had slain me with his words. I knew what he was trying to do, but so much time had passed. Wasn't it too late? Why had he waited so long? I had spent seven years with Trevor, almost the same amount of time Jase and I had been friends growing up. I squared my shoulders, collected myself, and sat up.

"Are you sleeping with your agent?" I said out of the blue.

"Are you sleeping with Trevor?"

"Are you?"

"No, Emiline, you've been the only woman in my life since I was fifteen." One side of his mouth turned up. The mood felt lighter.

"Don't be a smart-ass."

"Andrea and I are, hmm, how do you say it?" He looked up and cocked his head like he was thinking. "We're fucking. Yeah, basically, we're fucking. Is that okay with you?"

"Do you love her?"

"No."

"Does she know that?"

"Yes, she does."

"Why are you being so blasé?"

"I don't really understand this line of questioning, but if you must know, yes, Andrea and I are colleagues with benefits."

"That's unprofessional."

"We're grown-ups. She was in an eight-year relationship with some dumbass. She's not looking for a boyfriend."

"That's what you think, but you don't see how women view you."

"How do women view me?" he said, taunting me.

I took a sip of wine and rolled my eyes. "I met one of your superfans earlier, and she called you gorgeous and smart and so tuned in to women."

"What do you think?"

"What do I think of you? Right now, you're a bit of an enigma to me, but if I were meeting you for the first time, I would say, arrogant, self-aggrandizing, self-absorbed . . ."

"Ouch," he said, although he didn't look the least bit wounded. "You really think I'm selfish?"

"I spent years in therapy trying to forget all of the shit we went through. Now you've written a book and found success by telling *my* story to the whole world." I waved my hand in his direction. "And then you show up looking like this?" I shook my head. "I wish I weren't so angry with you right now, because I want to hold on to the good memories. Because there were so many good memories."

"I want to hold *you*," he said quickly. "But I can't because I'm too late."

"You can't do this to me after all this time. I have a life now."

"Don't be angry with me, Em." I saw a boyish spark in his eyes as he spoke. "As for the book, read the rest of it if you want. Work it out for yourself—don't do it for anyone else." He shook his head then abruptly looked up and called to the server, "Check, please!"

"Already? That's it? In the book, you made it seem like this was all my doing. But I didn't turn us in—*you* did. You've been too late for a long time now, Jase, and you only have yourself to blame."

"Everything I wrote in the book was for a reason. I hoped that you would understand it . . . understand why I changed how that day ended. I hoped writing it from her point of view would help you get inside of Emerson's head and understand her choices, but it seems like you're still too resentful."

"You're acting as though you wrote it for me," I said.

"I did," he said quietly. "Don't you remember that Vonnegut quote? You're the one who said it to me. When I was writing the story about the ant family . . ."

I shook my head no, but I did remember.

"Something like, 'Write for just one person'?"

The waitress brought the bill and Jase handed her a credit card without looking at it.

"But most of your book wasn't about us at all. Everything that happens after that night is pure invention."

"I didn't say 'about,' I said 'for,' but let's just leave it at that." He scribbled his signature on the receipt, stood, and reached a hand out to me. "I'll walk you home."

"That's not necessary."

He took my hand and gently pulled me along. "Come on."

We walked shoulder to shoulder the two blocks back to my apartment. I knew we were both thinking the same thing: how good and right it felt to be walking beside each other once again.

"How's your mom?" I asked.

"Good. Clean. She lives in Philly. That's where we moved after I turned Nick in."

Nick was Cal Junior in the book. I hadn't known that Jase had actually gone through with it. That explained the demolished house when I had returned to Ohio.

"Good for you, Jase. I'm happy to hear that."

He followed me all the way up the steps and to the door. I turned around and leaned against it and stared at him for a long time. He didn't look away. I didn't know what to do or what to say. I just knew I couldn't let him go again.

"Jason?"

"Yeah?"

"I haven't been able to say it yet, but I'm really proud of you. I'm really proud that the stuff that happened to us didn't hold you back."

"I'm proud of you too. I wish that you could see how amazing you are."

"You think so?" I said, my face flooding with warmth.

"Yes, I do."

In a way, that was all I could ask for.

"I'm angry, but I'm trying to get past it, Jase. I want you in my life—I know that now. But I'm still with Trevor." I looked up at him as he inched closer.

He was staring down at me, wearing a small, tight smile. There was reverence in his expression and something else: resignation.

"Friends?" he whispered.

I nodded. "Will you be in San Diego long?"

"I'm heading home tomorrow and then leaving for a book tour the following day. Twelve cities."

"That's wonderful for you."

"Is it?"

There was so much simmering between us, but not all of it was being said.

My voice dropped. "I was thinking about our day in the shed earlier."

"What were you doing while you were thinking about it?"

"Stop," I said playfully.

"I'm kidding. Isn't it weird that we had nothing at the time . . . but somehow it felt like we had everything?"

"Yes." He took both my hands in his, leaned in slowly with such grace and kissed my lips softly, sweetly, like he had done the very first time. My eyes were closed. I was trying to hang on to the moment, but his lips were gone too soon.

Cyndi swung the door open and shoved her hand out past me. "Hello, Jason, we've heard so much about you."

"Hello. It's nice to finally meet you. Cyndi, I'm guessing?" he said as he shook her hand.

"Yes, that's me, and that's my partner, Sharon." Cyndi was giddy. It was weird. I looked over to Sharon on the couch, who was also smiling wide.

"I saw you in a lecture once, years ago," Jase said.

I jerked my head back to look at him. "Where?"

Cyndi answered for him. "Oh yes, they used to broadcast some of my early lectures on an educational cable channel."

That made sense; Jase was always watching TV or reading.

"Free college, how great is that?" he said. Cyndi and Sharon giggled. Impossibly, Jase's earsplitting grin was charming the panties off my gay aunts.

"Well, ladies, I better get going."

"Hold on." I ran to a kitchen drawer and scribbled my email and phone number on a Post-it. I handed it to him. "Next time you're in San Diego, give me a call."

He took the paper while nodding and slipped it into his pocket. "I will. Have a good night, Em." He kissed my cheek and was gone. I felt like we were fifteen again as I watched him jog down the stairs.

I heard Sharon say, "He called her 'Em.' How sweet is that?"

From behind me, Cyndi said, "We're not saying anything, but I'm pretty sure you know how we feel."

I walked aimlessly around the living room with my head down as they watched me process what had just happened.

"You want to talk, sweetie?" Sharon asked.

"No, I think I'll go to bed." I couldn't wrap my head around it.

In my bed, I thought back to that day in the shed, to what had really happened.

Jase came home from school, tired and weary-eyed but smiling. I was waiting for him all day in the shed, picking at my bowl of Cheerios. When he came in I was sitting at the table, staring out the small window.

"How was your day, honey?"

He fell onto the cot like dead weight. "Longest school day ever. I couldn't wait to get back to you."

"How'd you do on the history exam?"

"Aced it."

"Of course you did."

He kicked off his shoes. "Come lie down with me."

I was wearing a lavender sweater dress that his mom,

Lisa, had given to me. As I walked toward him, he removed his T-shirt. I straddled him and then caressed the muscular grooves of his sides.

He put his hands on my thighs and ran them up, pushing my dress up to my waist in the process. He tugged at the waistband of my flowered panties. "I like these, but I think we should ditch them," he said.

We laughed, making the cot shake and squeak. "This is going to take some finesse."

He gripped my hip with one hand. "Kiss me," he said. When I leaned over, his other hand went between my legs, teasing me from the outside of my panties. We kissed and kissed, our tongues twisting, his hand rubbing and pressing against me, making me writhe against him. Our breaths became heavy. I could feel him hard beneath me. Jase was never frantic, always smooth, even at sixteen. I didn't know it then, how perfectly suited we were for each other, because he was all I knew. But later I would learn that no one could ever come close to replicating how Jase had made me feel.

He tugged at my sweater. "Take this off."

Pulling it over my head, I said, "Don't laugh." I wasn't wearing a bra, so I was on full display to him, sitting atop him in the bright sunlight that was shining through the small window.

His mouth fell open. He just stared and then his hands moved up to cup my breasts. "Why on earth would I laugh? You're the most beautiful thing I've ever seen." He leaned up and kissed my breasts, one and then the other, before moving me onto my side. I wrapped my arms fully around his neck as we lay kissing. His hands were roaming everywhere, and then my panties were off and his fingers were inside of me.

We explored each other, made out, kissed, touched every-thing. And then when I felt like I was going to literally catch on fire, I reached down and undid the button of his jeans. "These have to go too. Fair is fair."

He stood up, removed a condom from his pocket, and threw it on the cot. "I stole that from my mom's drawer. Kind of weird, huh?"

I just laughed. "Gotta do what you gotta do," I said.

"Yeah this might be a little awkward."

"It won't be," I assured him. He removed his jeans and boxers and walked toward me to where I lay on the cot. It was the first time I had seen him like that and he was beautiful. His skin was perfectly smooth and his shoulders broad for a sixteen-year-old. His longish hair was tucked behind his ears and his eyes were searching mine, looking for reassurance. I reached out and touched him.

He closed his eyes and made a strangled sound. "You might not want to do that."

"Did I hurt you?"

"No. Not hurt at all."

He rolled the condom on and kneeled on the bed between my open legs.

"How'd you learn to do that?" I was afraid of what he was going to say.

"I saw it on TV."

"Really?"

"Yeah, cable." He shrugged.

Jase sat back on his heels between my legs, waiting for something. "Come back," I said, but he remained where he was. I didn't feel remotely exposed to him. He knew me. I just wanted him to touch me.

"Are you sure you're ready? It might hurt," he said.

I nodded.

"I love you, Emiline. I loved you before I even knew what it meant."

"I love you too, Jase . . . I'll love you forever."

"Swear to me."

"I swear I want this."

He was staring right into my eyes. "Swear that you love me and trust me," he said.

I knew the feeling like my own name. "Jase . . ." I swallowed and then tears filled my eyes. "I swear to god on your life and my own that I love you and trust you."

And that I'll love you forever.

That was bigger than any promise I had ever made, but I knew it was true, even at fifteen.

"Don't cry, please." He thumbed the tears away, smiled, and kissed the tip of my nose. "You're absolutely positive you want it to be me?"

I sniffled and laughed at the same time. "Jason Dean Colbertson, that is a stupid question. Have you ever done this before?"

"No."

"Are you sure you want it to be me?"

"You're right, that was a dumb question."

He leaned over and kissed me and then a moment later he was inside of me and we were moving together. Neither one of us really knew what to do, but we were patient, and after a little while, we figured it out and it didn't hurt anymore.

Afterward, Jase went back into his house and got more condoms. We spent the rest of the afternoon having fun, awkward, love-filled, responsible teenage sex.

We were in tune with each other so much that I didn't even realize it. I fully expected every sexual experience after that to be just as comfortable, sensual, and sweet, but nothing ever measured up. I remember after I left Ohio, my girlfriends would say sex gets better and how the first time is always terrible, but mine wasn't because Jase and I had spent years and years getting to know each other first.

In bed, in my apartment, I stared up at the ceiling, lit ominously by a streetlight streaming through my curtains. I wished that I had asked him what his life was like when we were apart. And I wondered if he was in some hotel room nearby with Andrea.

11. Head in the Game

When I woke up the next morning, the sun was blasting me in the face. My eyes were caked shut and swollen from crying. I could hear Cyndi, Sharon, and Cara busying themselves in the kitchen. I slithered out of bed and snuck into the bathroom, undetected. Staring into the mirror, I wondered why I was avoiding the book. Maybe I was afraid once I finished it there would be nothing left of Jase and me.

I walked out into the kitchen and was greeted by a smiling Trevor, a derisive Cyndi, and Cara, who was trying to melt into the wall.

"Where's Sharon?"

"She went to the store. You had no food here," Cyndi said.

"Oh." I leaned up and kissed Trevor. "Morning. What are you doing here?"

"I thought maybe we could take Cyndi and Sharon kayaking in the caves," Trevor said.

"Okay." I looked away from Trevor toward Cara and mouthed, *Did you call him?*

She shook her head no.

Sharon came through the door with a bag of groceries. "What's up, kids?"

"We're going kayaking!" I announced.

Cyndi and Sharon's eyes darted between Trevor and me. "Am I missing something?" Trevor said.

"No," I said. "Let's get ready."

Cyndi followed me into the bedroom. "Are you gonna tell him?"

"There's nothing to tell. You've never been pushy with me, so please don't start now." She left the room without saying another word. Cyndi and Sharon always preached honesty in relationships, but she couldn't expect me to blurt out in front of everyone that I had met with Jase the night before and that we had agreed to be friends. It seemed insignificant in that moment when I saw that Trevor was there, making an effort.

An hour later, we walked down to the beach and rented kayaks. The guy working the rental stand explained to us that we needed to paddle hard past the ocean break and then we could cruise south toward the caves where the water was calm. Trevor had done it before, but the rest of us were rookies.

Cyndi and Sharon were fit and strong and always up for adventure, so I knew they could do it. They made it look easy, paddling over the first swell and then turning their kayak to wait for us. I sat in the front of our kayak while Trevor sat in the back.

Just before we were about to make our attempt past the break, Trevor called out, "Remember, I can't paddle, so you're gonna have to work harder."

I turned around and glared at him. "What?"

He was holding the oar across his lap. "My arm. I'm still rehabbing it. I'm not supposed to do stuff like this."

"Then why the hell did you even grab an oar?"

He gestured to the oncoming waves. "Turn around, pay attention."

It was clear and warm that day, but it was winter, so the water was too cold for swimming. The idea was to stay as dry as possible. I realized quickly that I would need to paddle much harder.

"This was your idea, Trevor!" I yelled, out of breath.

Sharon and Cyndi had made it past the break easily before a new set of waves came in, but we weren't as lucky. They were waving to us, yelling, "Come on, hurry!" I almost started to laugh at how ridiculous I must have looked trying to paddle past the waves as Trevor sat back, taking in the sunshine.

"I'm so mad at you, Trevor! I can't paddle your two-hundred-and-twenty-pound ass all the way out there."

"You can do it, Emi. Put a little muscle into it."

I growled and then began paddling fast, left then right, but we were too heavy and it was slow progress. The swells were getting bigger and bigger. The first wave came and I barely made it over before it broke. The kayak smacked down over the swell of the wave, causing water to fly up and splash me full in the face. "Oh god, it's freezing!"

"Push, push, Emi! Hurry!"

"Oh, fuck you, Trevor, I don't need a coach right now. I need you to paddle!"

"I can't. Come on, you can do it." He squeezed my shoulder and I almost hauled off and hit him with the oar.

"Paddle!" I heard Cyndi yell.

"Oh no!" I screamed. A huge wave was coming.

"Straighten out!" Trevor yelled. Our kayak was turning parallel with the wave, and I couldn't stop it.

"Oh shit!" I was paddling as hard as I could but getting nowhere.

"Oh fuck!" Trevor said behind me.

The wave lifted the kayak and flipped it over like a hot dog on a rotisserie, except that it didn't flip back the right way. It just dumped me straight into the freezing water. The heavy plastic kayak was on top of me. I swam out from underneath to where I could stand and found Trevor standing perfectly upright in waist-high water with his arms crossed. He didn't look the least bit disheveled. I, on the other hand, had wet, frizzy hair sticking to my face and burning eyes from the salt water, my sunglasses floating somewhere among the waves.

Peering at him through my one unobscured eye, I tried to catch my breath. "Oh my god, we almost drowned."

He shook his head. "We weren't even out very far."

"How did you get over here so fast?"

"I jumped out before the wave hit us. I could tell you weren't gonna make it." Trevor was completely impatient with people who were not as coordinated as him.

"Were you just gonna leave me trapped underneath that thing?" I yelled.

"What was I supposed to do? You know how to swim."

Unbeknownst to me, the kayak was coming toward me on the white water of a small wave. It smacked me right in the back, forcing me into Trevor's huge body. "Ouch!"

"Jesus, Emi." He hitched one arm around my waist and stopped the kayak with his right arm. "Fuck!"

He spun me around so that I was in shallower water and set me down. I was shivering, so I ran up onto the beach and found our towels. I watched Trevor pull the kayak onto the shore, using his left arm and holding his right to his body like it was broken.

I waved to Cyndi and Sharon. "Just go!" I yelled. They turned and went paddling toward the caves.

Trevor approached me, looking disappointed. I threw a towel at him. He caught it and began drying off. We didn't speak. There was only the sound of the waves hitting the shore and my chattering teeth.

I plopped down onto the sand, wrapped in my towel, and tried to soak up some sun to warm my freezing body.

"Are you a good guy?" I asked, finally.

"What do you mean?" He turned and scowled.

"Why are you so hard on me?"

He threw his hands up defensively. "I'm not, I just thought you could do it."

"Well, I can't . . . You should know me better by now. By the way, in case you haven't noticed, I'm shaking, freezing, and stunned, but you're sitting five feet away from me?"

He scooted toward me and reluctantly draped his arm over my shoulder. "After I left you last night, I went to the Spot to watch the end of the USC game. I stayed and had a couple of beers."

My stomach dropped. I knew where he was going with this. "Okay . . ."

"I saw you walk by with him."

I felt crushed that it appeared to Trevor that I was sneaking around. Had I told him I went to meet Jase last night, it wouldn't have come to this. I'd made something innocent seem deplorable by keeping it from him. "Yeah, I met him for a drink. Nothing happened. We just talked a little bit about the book. He's leaving on a twelve-city book tour. I don't even know how long he's gonna be gone." I was rambling nervously, feeling a twinge of guilt for not being upfront with Trevor. I had gone to meet another man just after he had asked me to marry him. "I'm sorry, but we're just friends. What are you worried about, Trevor?"

"Nothing. As long as I know you're not gonna throw a seven-year relationship away because your childhood crush came back into town."

I wasn't even going to address how he was reducing what Jase and I had had. "Trevor, I feel like the only reason you're trying so hard now is because you feel challenged. I mean, you've never cared to hang out with Cyndi or Sharon. You've never shown up at my house on a Sunday morning to go out and do something when there are a thousand football games on."

He didn't respond. We just sat in silence until Cyndi and Sharon came back. I thought about how Trevor basically treated me like a dude. We'd had sex on the first date, and he had been respectful and charming. He couldn't keep his hands off me . . . in the beginning. Now we were just buddies, but I didn't even know if I could call us that. Yes, we still slept together, but it was purely physical—nothing transcendent about it. Most of the time it was over in five minutes, and usually I did all the work because of Trevor's damn throwing arm. With Jase, it had been the exact opposite. We'd started with friendship and then added layer after layer on top of that.

I hated comparing Trevor to Jase because they were

different. I had to keep reminding myself that Jase had sent me away all those years ago, and Trevor was here with me now.

Once we returned to the apartment, Trevor didn't stick around, and Cyndi and Sharon headed back up to the Bay Area. Cara was out with friends, so I was alone when the book started calling to me . . .

From *All the Roads Between*

The year I turned fifty, my husband, David, died in a car wreck. Suddenly, my unremarkable, ordinary marriage was over, and I was left alone in my unremarkable, ordinary life. I had spent my adult life taking care of a man I wasn't sure I had ever really loved.

Ever since David and I had graduated from high school in the Bay Area, we had moved around from city to city, following David's long career in the military. He was gone a lot, and since we never had children, I was alone a lot. I would think of Jax often—his sweet face and the hope he had in his eyes as he pleaded with me to leave it all behind that night in Ohio. I walked through life with that guilt, wondering if he had ever forgiven me. I prayed he had moved on and that he had found peace out there on the long dirt road.

I couldn't bring myself to call or write to him because I was afraid that he hated me. If I knew he hated me, I wouldn't be able to go on. All I could do was hope he understood that I did what I did for *him* . . . so that he could rise to his potential without me weighing him down.

Later that same year, my father died in jail. The bill I received for his cremation costs was my only notification that the whiskey monster had been laid to rest. I didn't even know what he had died from, and I didn't attempt to find out. I sent a check and breathed a sigh of relief. It's easy to let yourself become the burden of your own life, especially when you were given the label of being a burden by your parents before you could even reject it. I was technically free—of the husband I had settled for, of the father who had sent me down this life path. But I didn't *feel* free. My adult life wasn't tragic, but I could never allow it to be extraordinary either. My self-imposed penance kept me from the bliss that Jax and I dreamed about finding together as we lay in the fields near the creek all those summers ago.

I regretted not looking for my mother, Diana, and making peace with her, but more than anything, I regretted a life without Jax. I would have taken the hardships on the dirt road just to be with him.

Three years after David passed away, I moved back to Ohio, to New Clayton. I didn't have much to retire on, so I had to get a job at a diner in town, waiting tables. I was at the Salvation Army looking for a pair of comfortable shoes to work in when I passed the used books section. There, front and center, almost placed purposefully for me, was a book with a couple embracing on the cover. The title was *First Love Never Dies*. But what really caught my attention was the author's name. Jackson Fisher.

Suddenly, I was fifteen again. It had been thirty-eight years since I'd said his name out loud. "Jackson Fisher," I whispered. My hand shook violently as I reached for the book. It had an old picture of Jackson on the back, maybe in his twenties. It had been published more than twenty-five years ago. I felt gutted—

12. You Might Find the Truth

I slammed the book shut in the middle of the sentence. I was crying hysterically and couldn't bear to read further. Why was there so much regret for Emerson when she had made these choices herself? Hugging the book to my chest, I sobbed and sobbed.

Jase had been saying that he had written it for me, but because the details were different, I hadn't believed him until now. Yet I wasn't totally naïve; I could see the parallels in my and Emerson's circumstances. But there was a scared little girl inside of me who couldn't accept the fact that someone actually loved her enough to write an entire book to help her heal.

Dawn would arrive in a few hours, but instead of going to sleep, I began to put a plan together.

THE NEXT MORNING, I marched through the parking lot at UCSD, full of resolve. I found Professor James in his office, sitting in his high-back leather chair near the window, looking out at the campus. Since he was the department head, I had to come to him first.

"Professor?"

He looked up. "Emiline. Come in."

I walked in and stood across from his desk as he peered up at me over his bifocals. "Can I talk to you?" I asked.

"Sure. Have a seat." He gestured to the chair across from him.

I sat down, clasped my hands together, and stared into my lap. "I want to write something real, I just don't know what it is yet. I need to take a sabbatical."

He chuckled. "You're not a full professor, and you can't take a sabbatical in the middle of the term."

"Honestly, I need to do some soul-searching."

"Famous last words," he said sternly.

"Professor, I don't even know if I'm a writer. I think I might just be a really good reader." I searched his eyes, looking for affirmation.

He held my gaze for a long time. "Emiline, you're absolutely a writer, but you need to know what the hell you're writing about, and who your audience is."

I nodded. "I get it."

"Why don't you start by writing for yourself and see what happens? Just remember, you have to be good before you can be great. And you're not quite there yet." He stroked his beard. "How long would you be away for?"

"Two weeks. Tops."

He chuckled again. "That's hardly a sabbatical, Emiline." Then he looked at me over his bifocals again. "I assume this soul-searching can't be delayed to the summer?"

I shook my head vigorously. "It's very time-sensitive. I

would miss four lectures total, and I could ask Cara to cover for me."

He nodded. "I wouldn't normally approve such a request, but if you can indeed get Cara to cover your class, then I can grant you a two-week personal leave of absence. You'll see to the necessary paperwork?"

"Absolutely, Professor."

"And you'll bring me ten thousand good words?"

I should've known there'd be a catch. "You want me to work on a short story while I'm away?" I said.

He shrugged. "That hardly seems like an unreasonable request. I *am* granting you a leave of absence in the middle of the term, after all."

"Ten thousand *good* words?"

"You have to start somewhere," he said.

"Okay." I stood and shook his hand. "Thank you."

I raced off to find Cara.

Once I was back at my apartment, I packed a small suitcase and then called Cyndi. After a few moments of small talk, I cut to the chase.

"I want to get in touch with my father."

She let out a long breath. "Is this about the book Jase wrote?"

"No, this is about me," I said, and I meant it. "Will you tell me where he is?"

"I've never kept information from you. You know that, right?"

"I know. I just never wanted to know the details, but now I do. Have you heard from him or my mother?"

She sighed. "I only know where your dad is. He's living in Dayton and working as a mechanic. Do you want us to take you out there? We could go in the spring after finals."

"No, I just want his address. I need to do this on my own." There were ten seconds of uncomfortable silence. "Aunt Cyndi, don't take this the wrong way. I love you and I appreciate everything you and Sharon have done for me. You gave me a life I never thought I would have. But I haven't worked through all of this crap, and I won't be able to move on if I don't. I need to do this for myself."

"I'm not entirely sure what you're going to get from your dad, Emiline. I just don't want you to get hurt."

"I know, but I need to see him."

"Are you taking Trevor?"

"Are you worried about my safety?" I asked.

"No. Your dad is sober."

I was completely surprised. Why hadn't she told me? "I'm going alone," I said firmly.

Cyndi finally agreed and gave me the address to my father's apartment and the mechanic's shop where he worked.

I booked the red-eye for that night and found a cheap hotel, texted the details to Cara, and spent the rest of the day packing. By the time Cara got home from class, I was sitting on the couch, waiting with my backpack and suitcase. I had packed only my laptop, Jase's book, and a few outfits.

She looked at my stuff, her brow furrowed in concern. "That's all you're taking for a two-week trip?"

"Yep."

"How are you getting to the airport?"

"I'm gonna call a cab in a minute."

She dropped her stuff on the floor and shook her head. "Nope. You're not a calling a cab. C'mon, I'll take you now."

"You sure?" I asked nervously, though I had been secretly hoping she'd take me.

She laughed. "You think I'm gonna let you have your quarter-life crisis alone? Let's go."

I gave her a grateful smile. "Thanks, Care Bear."

Once we were headed to the airport in Cara's Jeep, I turned to her. "Please don't tell Trevor anything. I have a lot to think about. I told him I was going to Ohio because I needed a break."

"I think he would understand, Emi."

"I really need some time alone," I stressed.

"I get it." She squeezed my hand. "Your secret is safe with me."

Once we got to the airport, Cara hugged me hard. "I hope you find what you're looking for," she whispered. I just nodded, too overwhelmed to say anything.

After we said our good-byes, I walked into the terminal and turned to see Cara waving at me. I waved back until I couldn't see her anymore, like a little kid, then I got my boarding pass and zipped through security in record time — the one benefit of late-night travel.

When I arrived at my gate, I texted Jase.

> Me: Did you watch my aunt's lecture before you came to get me from the foster home?

> Jase: Yes. When you told me you were going to live with her, I looked her up and watched her lecture on resolving conflict in fiction.

Me: Ironic.

Jase: I knew you would be
better off with her in California,
but I wasn't ready to let you go.

Me: So you knew you'd
eventually turn me in?

Jase: I didn't look at it that way.

I stared at his text, unsure how to respond. I wasn't
angry, but I wasn't at peace with the news either. Everything
about that fateful night with Jase had been out of my hands
from the very beginning.

Twenty minutes went by and then he texted me again.

Jase: Did you finish the book?

Me: No. Quit being such an egomaniac.
Don't worry, I'll finish it . . . and I'll tell you
exactly what I think of your sloppy prose.

Jase: I'm shaking in my
proverbial boots.

Me: You should be.

Jase: Ooh, feisty, Em. I like it.
What are you wearing?

Me: Good night, Jase.

Jase: Do you want me to send you
a pic of what I'm wearing? ;) ;)

> **Me: Good night, Jase.**

Jase: Not into sexting?

> **Me: GOOD NIGHT!**

Jase: Night, Em. Kisses.

The word "kisses" made me blush. I looked around at the other travelers, but everyone's eyes were trained on their own smartphones.

I searched for Jase's author website to see which states he would be traveling through. He was hitting major cities on the East and West Coasts, along with Nashville and New Orleans. I looked at past dates and saw that he had already been to Ohio. I didn't know why it mattered. I guess I was just wondering if we were on the same journey.

When my plane touched down at eight in the morning in Dayton, I was wide-awake and full of adrenaline. I'd only gotten a couple of hours of sleep. My mind had been full of Jase, my father, random memories from the past, Trevor, and those ten thousand words I would owe the professor at the end of this trip.

I rented a Hyundai Accent, labeled as a subcompact car, from Avis. It was tiny but got me zipping out of the airport and along the interstate in no time.

By eleven a.m., I was at the check-in desk in the lobby of a Holiday Inn. My room was ready, so I freshened up, texted Cara and my aunts to let them know I had arrived safely, plugged my father's work address into my phone's map app, and headed back out.

Pulling onto a residential road, I spotted the mechanic's

garage at the end of the street, on the corner of a main thoroughfare. I crept down the street in the Accent, trying to stay out of view, like I was casing the place, even though I was driving a bright red jelly bean of a car. I parked down the street, under a tree, and then watched. I didn't know what I expected to see.

After half an hour of staring at nothing at all but a few passing cars and a stray cat eating something out of an aluminum can in the alley next to the shop, I finally worked up the courage to approach.

It was a standard mechanic's garage with two open bays. The sign said, BENNY'S CAR REPAIR. There was an old Toyota sedan in the lifts on one side, and the other side was empty except for Benny. My father.

He was standing there in his blue mechanic's coveralls, trying to rub the grease off his hands with a towel. I wasn't used to seeing his hair cropped close and his face clean-shaven. He rarely looked that way when I was growing up.

He looked up and spotted me, his face impassive at first and then shocked as recognition dawned on him. But he didn't make a move. I could feel another rush of adrenaline through my veins, but there was no turning back now.

"Hello, baby girl." His voice was husky from decades of smoking, and the sound of it triggered sense memories of smoke-filled rooms. I shook my head, desperately wanting to tell him not to call me that, but I couldn't find the words. He seemed weary, apprehensive, as he walked toward me. Throwing the towel off to the side, he looked me up and down. "Look at you, all grown-up and beautiful, like your mom. I'm glad you came. I'm surprised, but so glad you're here."

They were the kindest words I had ever heard him say about my mother to me. "You look good too," I told him.

"I'm a mess right now. Been working all day . . . but I'm sober." He was looking right into my eyes with sincerity. "A hundred percent. Have been for a year and a half."

"Congratulations, that's great." I nodded and smiled stiffly. It felt like we were strangers. In the fifteen years I'd lived with him, I had never really witnessed him sober. He was drinking even when he was working at the paper mill. But the man who stood before me, in front of that garage, was different somehow. I could feel it.

"I told your aunt not to pressure you. She didn't think you were ready when I got cleaned up. I told her that if you ever were . . . ready or willing, I'd like to see you. I'm glad to know she gave you the message. Thank you for coming here." He started to choke up.

"It's okay."

"No, it's not. Listen, there's a diner a half a block down. Let me just wash up and close the shop. I want to do this right for once. Will you let me buy you lunch?"

I nodded.

I waited on the sidewalk, watching him as he rushed around tidying the garage and putting his tools away. He disappeared into the back and then came out wearing regular blue Dickies and a flannel shirt. It was chilly, so I wrapped my scarf around my neck two more times.

"Are you warm enough?" he asked.

"I'm good."

"It's right down here."

We walked down a quiet commercial street and through a jingling door into a small, empty diner. An older waitress poured coffee and spoke over her shoulder without turning around. "Anywhere you'd like."

"Two coffees for us, Pat," my father said, and then he motioned for me to sit down in the booth closest to the door. The booth itself was classic blue vinyl, and the Formica tabletop looked like it had come straight out of the sixties, though it was in pristine condition.

Pat wore a standard diner waitress uniform, a tight gray bun, and glasses on a chain around her neck. "Hi, Benny. Who's this pretty girl?"

"This is my daughter, Emiline." My father's face was alight with pride.

"Oh," she said with a smile. "How nice to meet you."

I didn't doubt for a second that Pat knew our whole life story. My father was obviously a regular here, but I could tell Pat was the type of woman who understood the value of discretion.

"Likewise," I said.

After she left us, I looked over the menu as my father watched me. "Do you know what you want?"

"Yeah."

He called Pat back over. I ordered a grilled cheese and French fries, and he ordered a turkey sandwich.

"I don't know if I'm gonna have much of a stomach after this, but hopefully it will be worth it . . . . for both of us."

"After what, Dad?"

He reached across the table for my hands, and I gave them to him. Staring down at them, as if he still couldn't believe I was here, he said, "After I tell you what I need to tell you."

"Okay."

He sniffled. "Daddies are supposed to protect their little girls. You know that, right?"

I felt a lump rising in my throat already. "Yes."

"Men, daddies, boyfriends, husbands . . . they should never hurt a woman or a child, with their fists, words, or otherwise."

I nodded, too choked up to say a word.

He looked up from our hands right into my eyes. "I'm so, so sorry, Emiline." His face scrunched up. Suddenly, we both collapsed across the table. His body was a shaking mass of sobs—painful, body-jarring sobs that matched my own.

Pat left a stack of napkins next to my elbow and then went into the back, leaving us alone.

"I couldn't forgive myself. I didn't think I deserved your forgiveness," he cried.

We held each other over the table until the tears subsided. "I didn't think so either, but I need to forgive you. I'm ready to forgive you," I told him.

"You don't have to, Emiline. For so long, I made excuses. I blamed your mom and I blamed the paper mill for closing, but it was all my doing. Your mom left because I pushed her away."

"But she left me there with you," I said. He flinched, like my words had hurt him. "I mean, how good could she have been if she abandoned her daughter like that?"

"She's far from perfect, but I don't think she knew how far I would sink after she left."

I nodded. "Do you remember Jase?"

"Of course I do. If I could apologize to him as well, I would."

"Maybe you will someday. He wrote a book about

SWEAR ON THIS LIFE **225**

everything we went through. He's practically famous now. I think the book is helping me work through it all."

"I'm glad to hear it. Tell him thank you from me."

Thank you? That surprised me.

"Jason was always like that . . . driven to help you, driven to protect you. He looked out for you . . . when I should have."

"He did," I agreed. I tried to will my eyes to stop watering, but it was impossible. Just the sheer emotion of being in his presence made my throat ache.

After a few deep breaths, my father nodded to Pat, who was peering out from the back room. She returned with our plates, and we eased into our meal. He'd look up every couple of bites to shoot me a subtle smile, like he was making sure I was still okay.

"I spoke to your mother about a month ago," he said, breaking the surprisingly companionable silence between us.

I choked on a piece of grilled cheese. "What? I had no idea you even knew where she was."

"Emiline, I said a lot of bad things about her when you were growing up. It might be hard for you to believe, but some of them were true. Not all of them, but some."

"What do you mean?"

"When I said I drove her away, I meant I drove her into someone else's arms. She was always looking for a hero. She's on her fourth husband now." He arched his eyebrows. "That poor schmuck."

I laughed bitterly, and my smile faded quickly. "How could she just leave her daughter, though?"

"It's hard to understand because you're not like her, thank god. You never were."

Hearing those words felt like a hug from God. When your own mother, the woman who conceived you and gave birth to you, is heartless enough to abandon you on a dirt road in some rural town in Ohio with a mean alcoholic, you're always a little concerned that those awful genes will come to life within you at some point.

"Why did you speak to her, then?" I asked.

"I had to talk to her about the property."

"The property on the road?"

"The very same."

"I thought the bank took it and tore the house down?" I had just assumed that my father had lost the property. I couldn't imagine how he would have paid for it from jail.

"The house was torn down, but I didn't lose the property. The rent from Lisa covered the bank payments until I got out of prison."

"You owned the house they lived in?"

"Yes, both houses. A lot of bad memories there, but they're gone now. They were termite-infested, and both had water and flood damage beyond repair. But the land's still there, and it's good land."

It's strange when you learn something wasn't as it seemed when you were a child.

"So you spoke with my mom about the property?" I clarified.

"Yes, she agreed to sign a quit-claim deed so that I could gift it to you."

I jerked my head back. "Me? Why in the world would I want that property?"

"Remember when you were about four or five and I taught you how to swim in the water hole, back when it was fuller? You used to get on my back like a little monkey and I would swim around . . ." He looked to the ceiling, trying to blink away tears. "You'd shout, 'Again, Daddy, again!' and I'd dive back under the water just for a second and then come back up." By that point, I was getting choked up again too. "I remember the feeling of your little arms wrapped around my neck and your fluttering giggle each time we'd come to the surface for a breath. I think about that all the time. I remember those moments."

"I remember now too," I whispered. He called it our little slice of heaven then.

"It's yours. The property is yours to do with what you want. It's just a place, and it can be beautiful. I made it ugly because I was a mean drunk, but it doesn't have to be that way. I also have a little nest egg I've been saving for you since I opened the shop."

I was stunned and speechless. *Why is he doing this?* "You don't have to buy me back."

He reached for one of my hands. "Listen, Emiline, remember what I said about daddies protecting their little girls?"

"I'm not a little girl anymore."

"You're not, but I'll always be your dad. I screwed up so many things. This is the only way I can try to repair some of the damage."

I had never thought of my father as an emotional, empathetic, or even articulate man, but he was showing sides to me I'd never seen. My mind was racing. I knew I had to accept what he was offering me, even though I had no clue what to do with the land.

As I stared past him, trying to visualize what I would

do, he said, "Sell it. I don't care what you do with it. But it's yours."

"Okay."

"So you'll accept it?"

"On one condition."

"I'm all ears," he said.

"I want my mother's address." I was determined to confront her, and I wanted to know if she had abandoned any other poor kids out there.

"Emiline . . . ." His voice took on a warning tone. "She's not going to change. I'm afraid you're gonna be real disappointed."

"There's something I need to do. I need to see her. Please."

I knew he understood. I didn't have to spell it out for him. "I will. I'll give you her address. You're stronger than I was, Emiline. Promise me that no matter what she says or does, you know in your heart that you are good and smart and beautiful. She has her own demons, and if she rejects you, it'll have nothing to do with who you are."

"Thank you. I appreciate that."

"We can't go backward. There are too many regrets. Please just move forward with me?"

I took his hand across the table. "I will."

After lunch, we walked back to the shop and he wrote her address down on a piece of paper.

"She lives in Nashville."

"How far of a drive is that from here?" I asked.

"'Bout six hours." He handed me an envelope with cash in it. "There's three thousand in there. You should deposit that as soon as you can. Actually, let's go now. I'll follow you in my car to the bank."

It does seem a little behind the curve to wait until your daughter is approaching thirty years old before you learn how to be a father, but I was in forgiveness mode. I had held on to the anger for too long. My father and I weren't going to start palling around all of a sudden, but I certainly wasn't going to harbor any ill will toward him when he had clearly spent the intervening years trying to change.

After we deposited the money, I hugged him in the parking lot of the bank.

"I'll send the property deed as soon I get it," he told me.

"Thank you," I said.

"Thank Jason for me. He might not know it, but I think he's the reason you're here with me now, and I'm grateful."

I was surprised that my father was okay with all the dirty secrets being exposed in Jase's book, but I realized that my father had learned something in his recovery that I still hadn't totally grasped: the past would only fester and eat away at us if we tried to hold on to it too tightly.

13. Which Path?

Back at the Holiday Inn, as I planned my trip for Nashville, I found myself staring once again at Jase's website. In four days, he would be at his Nashville signing.

I was leaving tomorrow. I made the decision to bide my time while I was there.

Even though I knew I was slowly waking up to my life, there were still things, questions that I didn't have answers to.

I dialed Jase and got him on the first ring.

"Hi."

"Hi," I said, and then felt my jaw freeze up. There was commotion in the background, like he was in a bar or restaurant.

"How are you?"

"Fine." Before he could say anything, I quickly added, "I haven't finished the book yet, but I wanted to talk to you. Are you busy?"

I had been avoiding the book. Somewhere deep in my mind, I was afraid to finish it out of fear that it would act as some kind of predictor for how things would go. Based on where I had left off, I knew the ending couldn't be anything but sad.

"Just give me a sec. I'm gonna step outside." I could hear shuffling. "Fuck, it's freezing out here!"

"Where are you?"

"Philly."

"Oh," I said, though I already knew. "It's not really important, I can talk to you about it later."

"No, what's up? Talk to me."

"Did you have a lot of girlfriends in college?" I blurted out.

"That's what you want to know . . . right now?"

"I'm curious. I just want to know what your life was like while we were apart."

"I wouldn't call them girlfriends, per se. Hey, why haven't you finished the book?" I could hear his teeth chattering.

I was not to be deterred. "Do you mean that you slept with a lot of girls?"

"What's 'a lot'?" I could tell that he was getting a little annoyed by this line of questioning.

"I'm not getting anywhere with these nonanswers," I said.

"Emiline, I didn't have any girlfriends. I dated and slept with more women than I'd like to admit. But no, I didn't really have serious girlfriends."

"So you never fell in love?"

"No," he said firmly.

"Why?"

"Because none of them were you."

Silence. I swallowed. I wanted to scream, *I love you*, at the top of my lungs.

"Jase . . ."

"I have to go back inside."

"Okay," I said reluctantly.

"Night, Em. Hope you got what you were looking for."

"I did. Night."

A part of me still wasn't sure what Jase's intentions were for us, but now I knew. *None of them were me.*

After I hung up, I pulled *All the Roads Between* out of my backpack and ran my hand over the cover. I promised myself that I would finish it, but I needed to see my mom first.

I MADE IT to Nashville late the next day. I found a hotel and then went to a nearby bookstore and bought a leather-bound journal like the one Jase had had when we were kids.

THE NEXT MORNING, I drove the red jelly bean to my mother's address. As I pulled up, I could see that it was a modest postwar house with an overgrown front yard. In the driveway, there was a mobile dog-grooming van with the words DIRTY DOGS painted in bright red across the side, along with a picture of a mud-covered schnauzer.

I was less nervous to see her than I had been to see my dad because, the truth was, I hardly remembered her. She had been a part of my life for such a short time, her absence looming larger over my life than her presence. I wanted closure, but I knew, even if I got it, it wouldn't be as cathartic as what I had experienced over a grilled cheese with my dad.

The second I rang the doorbell, I heard a symphony of barks on the other side and the sounds of a pack of tiny lap dogs racing toward me.

She swung open the door as she kicked and shooed the dogs away, her eyes not quite landing on me yet. Her hair was short, her dye job a cheap-looking shade of red from the drugstore. She seemed much smaller than I remembered, but then again, I was just a little kid the last time I had seen her. She was round, pudgy, a little unhealthy-looking, or maybe just worn-out. If her looks were any indication, life hadn't been easy for her.

"Can I help you?" she asked.

"I forgive you," I said instantly.

She stared at me hard, and then a look of realization poured over her features. Her eyes looked far from sad, though—they looked scared. "What are you doing here?"

"I just came to tell you I forgive you."

She blocked the door like I was going to burglarize her house. "Great," she said, with zero emotion.

"You're not going to invite your own daughter into your house?"

She stared at me for several long, uncomfortable moments, and then she stepped out of the way hesitantly. "Sure. Come in."

I followed her through a warren of boxes and piles of stuff strewn everywhere and into the kitchen, where there was even more clutter. She was clearly an incipient hoarder of things and dogs. There were at least eight small dogs of all different breeds, jumping and nipping at her feet like hungry rats.

"Sit." She pointed to a bar stool behind the counter. I pulled it out and dusted some powdery white stuff off of it. The house was filthy. I tried to remember if ours was like that when I was little.

"You want some juice or something?" she asked.

"No, thank you."

I didn't know why I was staying.

"I have an appointment that I need to get to." She stood on the other side of the dirty counter and appraised me.

"Are you a dog groomer?"

"It pays the bills," she shot back.

"I wasn't judging you."

"Aren't you, though? Isn't that why you're here, Emiline? To judge me?"

"No, I told you why I was here. To forgive you."

"For what?"

"For abandoning me with him." *Did she really think she was innocent?*

"Well, I wouldn't say 'abandoned.' You were always a daddy's girl."

What? "As if that's an excuse," I snapped. "He went to jail for child abuse and neglect."

"You want to blame me 'cause your daddy couldn't lay off the bottle?"

I could feel my face flushing with anger. *Why am I here?* It was like she had no emotions at all.

"You're selfish," I told her.

She looked at the clock on the microwave. "It's time to go."

"Where's your husband?"

"At work." She glared at me.

"Do you have any other kids you've abandoned?"

"Sure don't."

I stood from the bar stool and headed for the door, then I whirled around and placed my hands on my hips. "He said I was nothing like you. And you know what's sad? I'm super relieved." I started to get choked up. "I don't understand. Why do you hate me? What did I do to you?"

"I don't hate you at all. I did my best. End of story."

"Is it?" I said. I stood there, refusing to cry, and shook my head. "How could you be so remorseless? You almost ruined my life."

She blinked back at me. If there was something going on behind those dead eyes, I couldn't see it.

I turned, opened the door, and slammed it shut.

As I drove back to the hotel, I thought back to how miserable my father had been after she left. Until now, I was always afraid that I was capable of what she had done, like one day a switch would flip inside of me and I'd walk out on the people who loved me. But now I remembered: her indifference had always been there. She was just a cold fish. I had never even seen her cry. The asshole in her wasn't hiding under a sweet façade. It was always there, right on the outside. I remembered her indifference even when I was a small child. There were no hugs, no special bedtime stories, no cute names for my owies or boo-boos. She had been heartless and cold then, and she was the same now. It was my responsibility to let her go, and not to expect her to wake up to her maternal instincts.

I SPENT THE next couple of days in my hotel room, writing. On the day of Jase's event, I looked at his website. He was having a meet and greet in a bar after a reading at a bookstore. I wanted to stay away, to figure things out, but it was as if I could feel him nearby. Call it fate or serendipity, but this mission to tie up the loose ends of my past had led me directly to Nashville. Once again, Jase and I were in the same city. It all felt a bit on the nose, but then again, I had come to him. I had put myself in his electromagnetic field, and now I was being pulled forward, inch by inch. What mysterious forces tore people apart and brought them back together again? Was it all just gravitational waves, or was there something else at work here?

I ate dinner alone and then kicked a rock a couple of blocks down the street while I tried to talk myself out of going to the bar.

But for all my wanderings that night, I ended up right in front of the bar. Of course. Jackson's Bar and Bistro. How apropos.

The small, casual restaurant was packed. Across the room, at the bar, I could see Jase surrounded by women, talking animatedly. At the other end, Andrea stood looking on, seemingly bored.

The vibe was rowdy. There were lots of people talking, and I heard the occasional shriek from a female fan. It made me mildly nauseous. Jase looked a bit disheveled. From where I stood, it was hard to tell, but it looked like one of the women had her hands in his hair. He had the kind of hair that begged you to touch it, and it always looked perfectly mussed. He was wearing suit pants and a button-down shirt, sans tie, but the top three buttons were open. I wondered who had unbuttoned them for him.

I watched for a few moments. Jase was laughing drunkenly

as he attempted to stand on one of the metal bar stools. Andrea looked a bit horrified. His fans helped him up and held him as he addressed the crowd.

He threw his arms out to his sides, "Thank you, all. I love you! You're all amazing and beautiful, every single one of you! I want to take all of you home with me." They screamed in delight at that. I gagged. Andrea stared straight ahead like she had seen it all before. He lost his balance and yelled, "Whoa!"

The women righted him, and that's when he spotted me. I was grinning by that point. "You!" He pointed at me accusingly from the other side of the room. "Did you finish it, dammit?"

I shook my head and then he really did fall. It wasn't pretty. Making my way over to him was no easy task either. I had to push rows of lust-crazed women aside. They were all kneeling around him like he was a wounded animal.

"Oh Jesus, move, people. Give the man some space."

He was lying flat on the floor, looking up at me. "What you doing here, gorgeous?"

"Don't even try it." I held my hand out to help him up and then I shouted, "Back it up! Out of the way." The women gave us some space as I dusted him off. His eyes were lazy little slits, but he was still smiling.

"Your hair is flying everywhere," I said.

He bent his head toward me. "Fix it."

"Ask nicely."

"Please?"

I tried to straighten it out but decided it looked better messy.

Andrea appeared. "We better get this guy back to the hotel before he passes out on us."

With Andrea on one side and me on the other, we draped his arms over our shoulders and made our way outside. He kept looking over at me and smiling.

"Just walk, Romeo."

Neither of us attempted conversation after that.

He was staying at a much nicer boutique hotel than mine. His room was a gorgeously decorated large suite with a separate living area. Once inside, Andrea broke away and headed for the balcony.

"I need to make a call," she said. "You got this?"

"Yeah." I walked him into the room where he collapsed onto the bed.

He was about to pass out, but he was fighting it as I removed his shoes. "Why are you here?" he slurred.

"I came to see my mom. She lives in Nashville."

"Really?" He seemed surprised.

"I just wanted to see who she was. Now I have, and now I need to go back home. I came by because I figured, since we're in the same city, I should say hello."

"Hello." He grinned. I reached for his belt, unbuckled it, and pulled it through the loops in one fell swoop. "Wow, you're good at that." His face scrunched up. "I don't want to know why."

"You can totally undress yourself, huh?"

"Yeah, probably, but you're doing such a great job."

"Well." I walked to the head of the bed. "I should get going."

He reached for my hand. "Stay, please," he said with sweet, drunk puppy-dog eyes.

"What, with you and Andrea?"

"She's not staying in here with me."

"I still have a boyfriend."

"Bummer. Ditch that guy, would ya?" His eyes started to close. I wanted to undress him and curl up beside him.

"You're fading," I said.

He opened his eyes wide and shook his head. "I'm still here."

I leaned over to kiss him on the cheek. He braced the back of my head, holding me down near him. He took a deep breath in. "You smell good."

"You smell like whiskey. Why'd you get so drunk tonight?" I pulled out of his embrace and stared at him. There was humor in his expression. "What?" I said.

"Remember when you had that crazy hair when we were kids?"

"How could I forget? I was made fun of constantly."

"You're so pretty, Em. Your hair's so straight now." He looked confused.

"I have to flat-iron the crap out of it, thank you very much."

"Ohhh," he said lazily.

"I like that you focused on my poor hair throughout the book, but you decided to give yourself a nice little six-pack."

"Hey, I did have a six-pack. Anyway, It's just fiction . . ."

He had a dreamy look on his face. "It has to be . . . You swore on my life . . . I got drunk because you are the slowest reader on this planet, and . . ." Two seconds later, he passed out.

I took a deep breath and sat down next to him on the bed. To those crazed fans at the bar, he was the enigmatic J. Colby. But to me, he was still the same Jase. As I caressed his face, he became an innocent ten-year-old boy again, sleeping peacefully. I left him fully dressed but covered him with the comforter, kissed him on the forehead, and walked out of the room.

Andrea walked in from the balcony. She had kicked off her shoes, but she was still wearing her black dress pants and white silk blouse with a plunging neckline. She was sexy and sophisticated. She looked like she belonged with Jase.

"Is he out?" she asked.

"Yeah."

"So you're her? From the book?"

I nodded. "Listen, can we talk?" I said.

"Sure." She walked to a table with an open bottle of wine. She held it up. "Would you like a glass?"

I shook my head.

She poured herself one and then sat on the arm of the couch while I stood near the door. "What do you want to talk about?"

I hesitated. "Does he drink like that a lot?"

"No, I've never seen him do that. He rarely has more than a glass of wine or two."

"Okay . . ."

"Why, are you worried about him becoming . . ." Her face softened. I realized, as Jase's agent, she probably knew the book intimately.

"I guess. I feel really strange talking to you about this. Jase told me you two have a . . . relationship." I waved my hand around like I was trying to look for the right word.

"It's over." She smiled. "Listen, I love the story. That's why I was dying to rep him and sell this book. Our relationship started with business and will continue with the business, but that's it. It's impossible not to sound crass here, so I'll just say it. Jase and I were just using each other. That's it."

"But you have to have feelings for him. I mean, he's amazing."

"Emiline, I've been around the block a few times. I have no interest in being in a relationship with a man who's in love with someone else."

"Oh." The word left my lips like a breath. "I have to get back to California. You and Jase will be in New Orleans next week, right?"

"Right. What are your plans?" she asked. "I mean with Jase? What will you do?"

I thought her line of questioning was nosy, but then again, she basically knew every personal detail about Jase and me.

"I don't know. It took me many years to figure out how to let him go."

"I bet."

"Now I have him back. I think I just want to keep him safe, right here, with a little bit of distance."

"The two of you are a lot alike. It's no surprise that you grew up together. You both have a lot of fear, but I understand what you're saying." She smiled. "I think it's important to recognize the risks he's taken."

I nodded. "Of course I do." I was a hundred percent sure what she was talking about. I was still afraid that if Jase and I finally gave in to the force driving us together, we would crash into each other so hard that we'd break apart into a million pieces, impossible to put back together. My plan would keep us safe.

"I'm heading back to Ohio tomorrow for one last thing,

so I'll be there for at least another night before I fly home to California."

"I'll let him know. Which hotel will you be in?"

"The DoubleTree in New Clayton. Why?"

"In case the charming J. Colby wants to send flowers for your help tonight," she said, with a laugh and a wink.

"Thanks, Andrea."

"You're welcome, sweetie."

I left the room and walked back to my hotel in the cool night air. When I got back to my room, I finally dug the book out of my backpack and settled into bed.

From *All the Roads Between*

I felt gutted to know Jackson had written a book all those years ago that I had never known about.

"Ma'am, are you okay?" the young woman who worked behind the counter asked.

"How . . . how much is this book?" I asked, out of breath.

Taking it from my hands, she said, "Well, let's see what it says." She opened the front cover. "It's a dollar twenty-five."

"Okay, I want it."

"Sure, ma'am. Do you want me to bring it to the front for you?"

"Yes, but I also need to pick out some shoes." The book would leave me with eight dollars and seventy-five cents. I found some black sneakers that had the slip-resistant soles I needed for waitressing. The price tag said nine fifty.

"Oh dammit."

"What is it, ma'am?" the girl asked from the counter.

"I'm seventy-five cents short."

She looked behind her to make sure no one was watching and then turned back to me and shrugged. "Don't worry about it. I'll cover it. Come on."

She took my ten dollars and handed over a bag for the book and shoes. "Thank you. I appreciate it."

"You're welcome. Enjoy the book. I think my mom read that one. Yeah, as a matter of fact, I know she did. She said it was sweet."

"I'm definitely going to read it."

And that I did. I read it in one sitting as I sat in the empty living room of my apartment.

The first ten chapters were about me and Jax on the dirt

road, though he used different names, of course. John and Allie. They went through all the hard parts, just like we did, but unlike Jax and me, they were never torn apart. They just lived like two lovesick kids their entire lives. They traveled the world, had children, and through all of their adventures, they had no regrets.

It made for a short book, and it was kind of boring. But I cried when I finished it.

Looking in the mirror, I studied my old face and the wrinkles worn like reminders of the hardships I'd gone through. Was the book Jax's way of living out his dream for us? Just a big *what if*? What if I hadn't led the police to us? What if I hadn't married David? What would have happened to us? Would we have ended up like Johnny and Allie?

My life was so full of regret that I didn't know if I could go on.

14. Learning Curve

I tossed and turned the entire night and finally fell asleep at four a.m. I couldn't get the story out of my mind. There was one chapter left. I wondered if Emerson was going to end her life. Was that why Cara thought it was so sad? Or was it because Emerson had so many regrets? Why was everyone calling it a tragedy? I wanted to know, but I was too scared to read on.

I slept for two hours and woke up to Trevor's ringtone. "Hello," I said groggily.

"Why didn't you call me last night?"

"I'm sorry, I got caught up. I went to see my father and my mother."

"And . . ."

"I've just had a rough couple of days, and I'm still trying to figure things out."

"Just stay in touch, okay, Emi? Just so I know you're all right."

"Okay, I will."

After I got ready and packed up, I drove seven hours to New Clayton, where Jessie and the Bonners lived, otherwise known as Sophia and the Kellers.

The house was exactly the same: a perfectly pristine yellow Victorian with white trim. Mrs. Bonner opened the door and perked up when she realized it was me. "Well, hello, Emiline! It's been a very long time. You look well. Come in, come in!"

"Thank you, ma'am." Some habits were hard to break. "I just wanted to stop by for a visit and see how everyone is doing. Sorry I haven't kept in touch."

"Don't worry yourself," she said as I trailed her toward the kitchen. "The door is always open for you. Even if it has been over a decade. Would you like some tea?"

"That would be great. I also came by to see about Jessie too."

She turned to hand me a mug. "She should be home any minute. She just ran to the library."

My face broke into a wide smile. "How's she doing?"

"She's excellent. Really well. She goes to college nearby."

"I knew she would," I said as I took a seat at the table.

"You didn't have to stay away, Emiline. I really thought it all worked out for the best, don't you? I've raised so many foster children, and it's so rare for them to get taken in by their families."

I nodded. "That's not why I stayed away, Mrs. Bonner. I've just had a lot to figure out."

She smiled. "Did I hear from your aunt that you got your master's in creative writing and you're teaching college courses now?"

"It's true." I didn't know that my aunt had contact with

her, or that Mrs. Bonner had cared enough to keep tabs on me. I guessed it was just me who had been shutting the world out.

"We're proud of you." I couldn't tell if it was an obligatory statement.

I heard the door open and close, and then a moment later, a still-angelic Jessie came into the kitchen. "Oh my god, Emi!" She screamed. I stood and she was in my arms a moment later.

"You're so tall! Wow, look at you." She was at least five seven, and several inches taller than me.

We hugged for a long time. However short-lived my time there was, I had gained something so precious: a little sister.

"I haven't been good about keeping in touch," I told her. "But that's gonna change."

"Emi, oh my gosh, you have to see my book collection." She pulled me upstairs to the bedroom that used to be mine on the third floor. One entire wall was covered in bookshelves filled with books.

"This is amazing," I said.

"I know, right?"

She began telling me about all of her favorite stories, and she talked about the characters like they were real.

"Jessie, this is wonderful. You're a true bookworm."

She laughed. "I know, Mom's always telling me that."

I felt my throat tighten. It made me emotional to know that Jessie had gotten to that place with the Bonners. I knew I had made the right choice pleading for Jessie to stay.

"They adopted me, didn't you know? Like, officially." She paused and looked closely at my face. "Are you crying, Emi? Why?"

"I'm just happy for you, I guess. What happened to the boys?"

"They're still here too. Almost out of high school now. Things changed a lot after you left. Mom warmed up and stopped taking in new kids. She adopted all of us. I think she regretted not adopting you." I could tell Jessie genuinely believed that, though I didn't think it was true.

"My time here was important, but it was good for me to be with my aunts."

I plopped down on her bed and looked out the window. The room felt the same, and not much had changed. She sat next to me and took my hand in hers. "Whatever happened to Jase?"

"Jessie, Jessie, Jessie, you were always so curious. I like that about you." I swayed into her, knocking my shoulder against hers playfully. "I'm with someone else now. A man named Trevor, but Jase is well." That might have been a lie. I mean, he was doing well, but could I really say he was well after the stunt he had pulled the night before?

"Guess what? I have a boyfriend now." Her face flushed.

"That's great, Jessie!"

"Mom wouldn't let me date in high school, but she's lightened up a lot since then. I mean, I'm in college now— she kind of has to." She shrugged. "So tell me, Emi, what is Trevor like? I bet he's handsome! Tell me about him."

"He's tall, good-looking, muscular . . . ." I made a silly face.

"What's he like, though?" She was always wise beyond her years.

I struggled to describe him. "He's nice . . . . caring."

"Is he funny and smart like Jase?"

"Yes," I lied. Trevor could be a lot of fun, but he wasn't clever. He had qualities that other women would kill for . . . just not me. How could I have known that all along and still have stayed with him?

"So, how long are you staying in Ohio?" she asked.

"Just until tomorrow, or the next day, and then it's back to California. I still have a lot to do." I stood up. "I have to get going soon."

She hugged me. "Well, I'm glad you came by. Let's keep in touch, Emi."

"I will," I said, and I meant it.

I CHECKED INTO a room at the DoubleTree in New Clayton. It was a surprisingly clean, newly renovated standard room with one king-sized bed and a flat-screen TV. I called Trevor.

"Hello!" he yelled over loud crowd noise in the background.

"Hey!" I yelled back cheerily.

"The game's on, babe!"

"You told me to keep in touch."

"What?!"

"I said, you told me to call you!"

"You're breaking up, can I call you after the game?"

"Okay," I said, and then hung up.

I texted Jase.

> Me: How are you feeling?

> Jase: Like I got hit by a truck. You?

> Me: I'm okay. I have a chapter
> left of the book. It's really good,
> Jase. Sad, though. I just went to
> see Jessie and the Bonners.

Jase: That's great.

I thought that was an interesting response. Seconds
went by.

Jase: How do you feel about it?

> Me: Relieved.

Jase: I'm happy for you.

> Me: Did you know?

Jase: Know what?

> Me: That I needed this?

Jase: Haven't you learned
anything about authorial
intention, Miss MFA?

> Me: So it *was* intentional?

Jase: It always is.

> Me: But how did you know
> I would read it?

Jase: Maybe I nudged destiny's
arm a little. Would you be mad?

I didn't answer. Instead, I called Cara. "Hello."

"Cara . . ."

"Hey, Emi! How's your trip?"

"Good. I have a question for you. How did you hear about Jase's book?"

"Hmm. Well, I had heard of it since it was already a bestseller, then I think I read a review in that literary magazine that came in the mail. Or maybe it was in my box at work? I can't remember."

"I remember that part. I think the magazine is on my nightstand, actually. Will you do me a favor and go look and see who it's addressed to?"

"Hold on."

A moment later, she was back. "I couldn't find the label. It was definitely in my box, now that I think about it."

"Okay, thanks for checking." He had known it would get to me that way. Man, he was patient.

I hung up with Cara and attempted to write in my journal, but nothing came to me. I worked on my story, outlining and jotting down notes.

I knew I had to address things with Trevor, so I tried dialing him again, but he didn't answer. I dozed off, exhausted, and was startled awake by the sound of forceful knocking on the door. I pulled back the blackout curtains and realized it was the next day. Almost noon.

"Hold on!"

I ran around the dark room, flipping on lights while I looked for my sweatshirt. I had been wearing yoga pants and a T-shirt with no bra, so I needed something to throw on. I dressed quickly and sloppily and then opened the door.

"Sleeping the day away, Princess?" Jase said, his voice low and smooth.

I blinked him into focus. He was wearing jeans, lime-green Wayfarer sunglasses, and Chucks with a black T-shirt. It was the way I remembered him: pre-suit Jase, pre-author Jase.

Through a yawn, I said, "I don't know what happened. I zonked out."

"Are you gonna invite me in?" He moved his sunglasses to the top of his head.

"Come in." I crossed my arms over my braless chest and scanned the room for anything that could cause embarrassment. There was a half-eaten turkey sandwich and French fries sitting on the small table near the TV. Jase didn't bat an eye at it. The room smelled like stale food and bad breath.

He plopped down on the bed. "What have you been doing?"

"Do you mind if I go freshen up for a sec?"

"Go ahead." At that moment he spotted his book on the floor next to my backpack. He arched his eyebrows. "Well?"

I shook my head.

"Seriously, when did you become such a slow reader? You would have breezed through it when you were twelve."

"Yeah, but I'm reading every word," I said as I went into the bathroom. "I'll be right out."

I threw on a bra, brushed my teeth, and tried to spin my massive mane into a cute bun on the top of my head.

When I walked out of the bathroom toward the bed, Jase carelessly tossed the book aside, wrapped his arm around the backs of my legs, and pulled me onto his lap.

"Jase!" I shouted.

Our faces were inches apart. He smelled like mint and men's body wash.

"Why didn't you stay the other night? Why'd you make me drive all the way to New Clayton to see you?" he asked.

"You were wasted, I have a boyfriend, and I had my own hotel room in Nashville that night. Plus, I didn't make you come here." I rolled my eyes at him and he pinched my butt. "Ouch!"

"Answer me. Why didn't you stay? We're just friends, remember?" My heart was speeding up. "Don't tell me it's just because of Taylor."

"Trevor."

"Whatever."

"Why did you want me to stay?" I said. "You basically passed out while I was taking your clothes off."

"I would never!" He opened his eyes really wide.

"You did, it's true!" I said accusingly.

He smiled and then his hand moved up to the back of my neck and then over my shoulder and up to my mouth, where he ran his thumb over my bottom lip. His eyes were fixed on my mouth. "I loved kissing you. I haven't forgotten what it feels like."

I sucked in breath. "Jase . . ."

He stood abruptly and gently set me on the floor. "Get your shoes on. I want to take you somewhere."

"Okay."

Once we were in the parking lot, he opened the passenger door to a black Mercedes SUV. "It's a rental," he answered my unspoken question.

"That's *my* rental." I pointed to the jelly bean.

"Really?" he scowled. "That doesn't look safe."

"It's fine. Where are we going?"

"You'll see."

We drove out of New Clayton. After a while, I realized we were headed toward Neeble, and I wondered if he was taking me to the road.

In the town center, he made a turn in the opposite direction. He was quiet and then he reached over and took my hand in his and held it over the console between us.

"Em, do you remember how badly we wanted to go to the Neeble pool?"

"Yes, I do."

"Remember how I promised I would take you?"

I got excited. "Yes," I squeaked.

We pulled into the parking lot of the Neeble community pool, which had been closed down since we had moved away. I felt sad for a moment, but I was happy just to be able to see what we had always dreamed of.

Jase jiggled a lock from the gate of the surrounding fence and then pulled me onto the property. There was nothing, just a few puddles of dirty water covered in leaves. A few rusted pool chairs and a dilapidated lifeguard booth that framed the near-empty hole.

"See? It's just a hole in the ground, and now it doesn't even have water in it."

"Why'd you bring me here?"

"Because I swore that I would."

"Thank you, I guess." I walked toward him to hug him, but he reached out and braced the back of my neck and kissed me. It was sweeter than it was passionate.

I didn't push him away. How could I? "What are you

trying to show me with all this? You're going to fill me with guilt and get me in trouble with my boyfriend."

"Boyfriend, shmoyfriend. You'll figure it out."

"No more kissing, okay, Jase?" I poked him in the chest.

"You liked it," he teased.

I did. That was the problem. "Can we go to the road now?" I asked.

He nodded for a few seconds, like he couldn't say no to me but wasn't really sure it was a good idea. I wondered if the pain from losing his brother there was too much for him to bear.

"We don't have to go to the creek. I just want to see the road while I'm here."

"Okay."

We pulled onto El Monte, and I watched the mile markers pass like I had every day growing up. On the radio, "Human Qualities" by Explosions in the Sky played as we drove toward the weeds, the dust, and the sun setting on the horizon. Neither of us spoke a word. The music told the sad story of the two kids on the dirt road with nothing but their books and each other.

As we sailed past the old egg ranch, long since abandoned, Jase turned his head, like he couldn't take his eyes off of it. His chest rose and fell to the sound of the heartbeats through the speakers. I wanted to say something, but the silence between us was powerful. He grabbed my hand and held on tight.

Jase parked at the end of the long dirt road where the mailboxes used to be. There was nothing, just dust and the tree line in the far distance that marked the creek. "Let's walk," he said.

Walking hand in hand, I thought back to the bus ride and every day we spent on that road. "Whatever happened to the bus driver?"

"No clue," he said. "She probably retired. She was a nice lady."

"I know. I used to wish she would adopt us."

He turned to me with a huge smile on his face. "Me too! I wanted to take all the seats out of the bus and live in it like it was a camper."

"It would have been amazing."

"Amazingly strange. We wanted the bus driver to adopt us so we could live in the bus with her." He laughed. "How sad is that?"

I started laughing too.

We approached where our houses once stood, though now it was just a couple of concrete slabs, infiltrated by weeds. We walked around quietly for an hour. I let all the memories, good and bad, dance in and out of my thoughts.

Jase stood on a wood post. "I'm the king of the world!" he shouted.

King of my *world*, I thought.

"You're still a dork," I said.

"A lovable dork?"

"That remains to be seen."

"You want to go look at the creek?" he asked.

"Isn't that hard for you?"

"It wasn't hard for me when I was fifteen. Why would it be hard for me now? I love it down there."

"You do?"

"Yeah, it's beautiful."

"But your brother . . ."

He grabbed my hand and pulled me along. "Yeah, my brother died there, but I choose to think about all the awesome things we did there together instead of giving false power to the site of his death."

I'd had no idea how well adjusted Jase was about his brother's death. Maybe, during all those years, I had made things bigger in my mind in order to avoid other issues.

We sat on the little wood dock, shoulder to shoulder, swinging our legs.

"The water's low," I said.

"It's almost frozen," he added.

"I feel like I'm supposed to say something." I didn't look at him, but I could see out of the corner of my eye that he was looking directly at me.

"You don't have to say anything." He shook his head. "I wasn't doing this for me . . ."

"Then why?"

"I just want to spend some time with you. I want you to figure out what *you* want," he said.

"That's selfless of you, Jase, like all sacrifices you've made. You're a saint. But honestly, what's all of this for? What are you trying to prove by bringing me here, and with the book?"

"I know you so well. I know what you're doing right now. You're trying to push me away."

"No, I'm not," I said.

He pulled his hand out of mine and then stood up and walked down the dock, leaving me alone. When he reached the road, he called back, "You still don't get it."

"What don't I get?" I got up and hurried after him.

He turned around. "All of those things I said about Jax

RENÉE CARLINO

in the book, did you seriously think I was talking about me? When I said, 'Despite his life, he kept getting sweeter and sweeter . . .' Em, I was talking about you. All of the good things were about you. I just switched it around because I needed you to remember. I'm still mesmerized by how good you are, Emiline, but completely saddened by the fact that you're so terrible to yourself. You're not just Emerson, you're Jackson too. I wrote this book for you so you could see that, and I wrote this book for me so I could heal."

"You are good, Jase. You've always been good," I choked out.

We walked back down the road in silence. He took my hand and led me toward the car and opened my door. The sun had set, and the moon was full in the sky. It was one of those rare, clear nights when the moonlight was bright enough to light the road ahead. Jax and I held hands all the way back to New Clayton.

When we pulled into the parking lot of my hotel, I turned to him. "You can stay with me, but I'm still with Trevor . . ."

"I know, and you're going to do the right thing," he said unbitterly.

"You didn't expect that? You just told me how good I was. I thought you knew me so well, Jase, MD, psychologist/ author extraordinaire." He grinned, and I poked him in the chest. "Yeah, I said author extraordinaire, not that your head needs any more inflating."

"I like feisty, Em."

All the heaviness from before seemed to slip away as he followed me out of the car and up the steps to street level. "Look." I pointed to the 7-Eleven on the corner.

"Dinner?" he said, eyes twinkling.

"Dude, it's on."

We rushed down the street and skipped over to the convenience store. "Remember what we used to do?"

"Yeah, you pick out something, I pick out something, and we share?"

"Yeah, let's do five things each."

We were in and out in minutes. We didn't peek at what the other person got, we just jogged back to the hotel with our bags full of junk food.

I sat on the bed and crossed my legs. Jase sat next to me. "You go first," I said.

"Okay, are you ready for this?" He reached in and pulled out a package of pink Sno Balls.

"Seriously? I got the same thing." I pulled mine out and set them next to his.

"Copycat."

"I didn't know," I whined.

"All right," Jase said. "The next thing is a very special delicacy, an American tradition. These babies are undeniably good and equally disgusting."

"Wait, can I guess?"

"You can try."

"Donut Gems."

"No, but I have those too." He pulled out powdered Donut Gems and set them next to our Sno Balls.

I pulled crumb Donut Gems from my bag and set them down. "Ha! Smart minds think alike. But what's this delicacy you speak of? Did you get one of those rotisserie hot dogs?"

"No." His face was serious.

"Giant pickle?"

"Come on, Em, you're disappointing me. This is so easy."

"Slim Jim?"

"Finally. I thought it would take you forever." He set the Slim Jim next to our stuff. "Whaddya got?"

"Ta-dah!" I held up a package of Fun Dip.

He stared at the Fun Dip. I thought he was going to cry, but he laughed instead. "We're gonna have stomachaches."

"Let's just taste everything. What else you got?"

"Hot Cheetos and M&M's, you?"

"Doritos and a Honey Bun," I said, throwing it all out on the bed. "We're also gonna have really nice breath."

"Who cares?" he said as he tore open the Slim Jim and took a bite. "Not as good as I remember." He held it out to me.

We took off our shoes. I put on my flannel pajama pants and a T-shirt while Jase found a movie to watch. We propped ourselves up on pillows against the headboard and proceeded to devour our score.

"Donut Gem?"

I took a powdered donut from Jase's hand. "What is this movie?"

"*My Girl*. You've never seen it?"

"No. I didn't have cable, remember?"

"That's right." He reached out and wiped powdered sugar from the side of my mouth.

"Thanks."

"You're welcome."

By the time Macaulay Culkin got stung by all the bees, I was hyperventilating. And when they found the mood ring, *that* was it for me. "This is the saddest movie I've ever seen in my entire life," I cried. Jase laughed. "It's not funny."

He rubbed my back. "Ah, Em, I'm sorry. This was probably a bad choice."

I looked up at him, at his sincere expression, as I took a huge bite of Honey Bun. "When did you cut your hair?" I asked him with a full mouth of food.

"A long time ago."

"How come?" Jase's hair was about to his shoulders when I left Ohio, and now he wore it short on the sides and longer and messy on top. He also had a few days' growth on his face, and it was hard for me not to imagine rubbing my cheek against it. His look was effortless; it always had been, but now it was effortless in a sexy-man way.

"Remember, I was trying to grow it out for California?"

I laughed. "Yeah, such a dork." I stopped chewing when I realized he wasn't smiling. I swallowed. "What did I say?"

"Nothing. It's just, after you left, I got pretty bummed out, so I cut it all off. Kinda lost hope in California."

"Oh." My voice was low. "I'm sorry."

"Well, it wasn't your fault," he said.

I reached up and ran my hand over his jaw. He closed his eyes. "Jason Dean Colbertson, how'd you get so great?"

There was silence. He kept his eyes closed and said, "You made me this way, Em."

I should have taken the compliment, but it was such a big statement. "I don't think so at all. I was a mess. Do you know how much therapy I needed?"

Staring at my mouth, he ran his thumb over my bottom lip. "You're not a mess now."

"How did you deal with everything after I left?"

"Like I told you, I wrote the book. It got me through." He leaned in slightly, our bodies just centimeters apart. It looked like he was going to kiss me.

"And all the women?" I said.

"Yeah, there was that." His lips turned up into a tight smile. "I'm not proud of it. I was always looking for you in those women."

"I'm one of a kind." I laughed.

"Tell me about it." He was serious.

"I have to figure things out with Trevor," I said.

"I know." He looked down at his hands.

"I shouldn't be with you, even right now," I said.

"Is that what you really think, Em?"

"Out of respect for him. He's a good person."

"Okay, fine. I understand." He started to move, but I pulled him back.

"But it's weird, I don't really feel like I'm betraying him when I'm with you."

"We're friends and you haven't done anything wrong, so why would you?"

"We kissed," I said.

"I kissed you." He was staring at my mouth.

It was hard for me to find the right words. My emotions were all over the place. "The thing is . . . you see, when I'm with him . . . it's weird, but it feels like I'm betraying *you*." He searched my eyes and then grabbed my hand and held it. "I felt that way before you even came back into my life. That's what you did to me," I told him.

Jase had planted himself inside of my heart so deeply that when we parted he kept growing there. We weren't together, but he was always there, like a part of my soul. I tried desperately to deny it and to forget, but no number of therapy sessions could take him out of me. We were a part of each other.

"God, I want to kiss you right now."

"I smell like Doritos, and I told you no more kissing."

"I don't care," he said, and then his lips were on mine. We kissed and kissed and then sank down onto the bed and fell asleep as the closing credits of *My Girl* ran. I instinctively curled up into his side and felt more content than I had in over a decade.

15. What About Us?

In the morning, I heard Jase shuffling around. I knew he was gathering his things. I wasn't ready to go back to reality yet, so I kept my eyes shut for a while. It's easy to look from the outside and say, *This is a no-brainer; what is she thinking?* But I still loved Trevor in some way. I wanted them both. I wanted Trevor because he wasn't a reminder of anything. I was Emi with him—he didn't associate me with thoughts of pain or abuse. I knew it wasn't fair to either of them, but that's how I felt.

Jase had been wearing a persona too. I saw glimpses of the vulnerable, sweet boy I once knew, but he was also this fancy author, a cocky, brilliant ladies' man. He was as familiar to me as myself, yet we'd spent over a decade apart, changing in subtle ways. I'd seen Jase several times now, but we weren't in the context of our normal lives. Where did he live? What did he do during a normal day? What did he eat for breakfast? I didn't know any of the basic details of his life.

When he came toward me, I closed my eyes and feigned sleep.

Don't go. Don't go.

He sat down on the edge of the bed and rubbed his hands up and down my arms a few times. "I know you're awake, faker."

I started laughing with my eyes closed. "No, I'm sound asleep."

"Your breath smells really nice."

I opened my eyes, covered my mouth, and mumbled through my fingers, "Jerk! Move so I can go brush my teeth."

"I have to go, Em."

"Not yet." Tears sprouted from my eyes. I just shook my head as I felt my throat tighten.

"I have to catch a flight and get to my next event. Emiline, will you promise me something? Two things, actually?"

"Okay," I said, my voice raspy.

"Whatever you decide, wherever life takes you, promise me you'll finish the book and promise me that you and I will not let this much time go by without seeing each other again." He wiped tears from my cheeks.

"I promise. You're still my best friend," I said.

He smiled. "Swear on your life?"

"I swear on *your* life," I told him.

We stared at each other for a few seconds, our faces serious. "I have some things to figure out, but we definitely need to see each other more," I said.

"Naked, I think," he added.

I pushed his arm. "Go, get outta here, Romeo."

He bent and kissed me on the cheek. "Call me. I'll be in New Orleans tonight."

"Okay."

My eyes followed him as he left the room. I went to the window and watched him walk out to the parking lot. Before he got in his car, he looked up at me, kissed his hand, and waved. I did the same, and then he was gone.

I was rushing around my hotel, trying to get my things together before my one p.m. flight that I had booked yesterday, when I finally checked my phone and saw that Trevor had called me three times the night before.

"Shit!" I hit CALL BACK immediately.

He answered on the first ring. "What the fuck, Emi?"

"Trevor, I'm sorry, I fell asleep early and . . ." *First lie.*

"Are you with him right now?"

"No."

He took a deep breath. "When does your plane get in?"

"Eight."

"I'll pick you up," he said flatly.

"Okay," I said, and then he hung up.

I GOT TO the airport early to return my car. In the airport bookstore, there was a display of *All the Roads Between.* I stared at it until an elderly woman approached me and said, "Sad book."

"So I shouldn't read it?"

"Not unless you like being depressed."

"What's it about?" I said.

"It's about two people who fight fate and lose. You're always gonna lose when you go against the big guy." She pursed her lips.

"Is that what you think?"

"It's what I believe."

I used to kind of ignore old people. It's terrible, really, but then I learned that they can offer some really priceless life hacks if you're willing to listen.

"Yeah, but what if those two people weren't sure what their fate was, or what exactly they were supposed to do?"

"Oh, they knew, trust me."

"So God has a plan? And we all know what it is?"

"God, Buddha, the universe, whatever you want to call it. I'm a forward thinker, missy. I don't know if it's that black-and-white. I kinda think it's like magnets. Put them close enough and they'll come together, but turn them around and they'll repel each other. When you feel the pull, you gotta give in to it. These two . . ." She pointed to the cover of the book.

"Don't tell me! Please, I have a copy. I haven't finished it yet."

"Okay, well, when you're done with it, look up the author's photo. He's a handsome one, my goodness." She gave me a little wave.

I couldn't wait to tell Jase the story.

WHEN I GOT to the bottom of the escalator at the San Diego airport, Trevor was there waiting for me. It was hard not to feel nervous around him. I kept thinking he knew everything that had happened while I was away, though of course, he didn't. I used to be annoyed that he took everything at face value and didn't ask questions, but this was one instance where it worked in my favor.

"How was your trip?" he asked as we walked to the parking lot.

I told him about meeting my dad and my mom, and he nodded along beside me.

When we got to his truck, my nose had started running, so I opened the center console to look for a tissue.

"No!" He slammed it back down.

"What's in there?"

"Nothing. My medication." He was pulling out of the parking lot, trying to focus on the road, his right hand still holding the lid closed.

"Let me see." I brushed his hand aside as he made a turn and forced the console open to reveal several bottles of prescription pills. "What are all these for, Trevor?"

He looked straight ahead as we merged onto the interstate. "They're just painkillers and anti-inflammatories. Nothing unusual."

I reached in and started taking the bottles out, and Trevor shook his head. The first two were Vicodin and ibuprofen. I pulled out another bottle that was a muscle relaxer, and then some kind of steroid, and then OxyContin. "How much of this are you taking at any given time?"

"Just what they prescribe."

"They don't prescribe all of these together, Trevor. Be honest with me."

"Goddammit!" He slammed the steering wheel and pulled onto the shoulder, killed the engine, and turned toward me. "What the hell do you want to know?"

"I want to know if you're addicted to all of this shit."

"Well, I want to know if you saw and fucked that writer guy in Ohio."

I stared at him evenly. "I did see him, but I didn't have

sex with him. I kissed him. I lost my virginity to him when we were fifteen, and we have a really complicated history." It shocked me that I hadn't told Trevor that. "He was the only person I had when I was growing up. We took care of each other. I made a mistake kissing him, and I'm sorry. I promise it won't happen again."

"Are you in love with him?"

"I love him, but I love you too. I'm trying to figure everything out."

He closed his eyes and swallowed. The truck was silent except for the sound of Trevor breathing fast and deep through his nose. "I can't get off the pills."

I shook my head. I couldn't understand how Trevor had been able to keep all of this hidden from me. I wondered if maybe I was the one who wasn't being present in our relationship. I guess it's hard to be present when you're busy denying who you are and shutting out the world. All this time, he was falling deeper and deeper into his addiction to pain meds. It explained a lot about his behavior—his mood swings, his air of indifference.

As I sat there in his truck, I realized I had an easy way out. The decision was made for me. I could leave Trevor because he was a drug addict. But when I looked into his pleading eyes, I realized I cared too much for him. I couldn't leave him like that.

"You need help; you can't do it by yourself. Your parents will help. I know they will."

"I can't tell them," he said.

"You have to."

He lowered his head into his hands, so I reached over

and rubbed his back. "Trevor, you were an amazing athlete, but that's not all you are, and you certainly aren't a drug addict. Don't let this become your identity, please."

He started to cry. Trevor never cried. Not once in our entire relationship.

"Let me drive," I told him. "We'll call your parents when we get to my apartment."

When he looked up into my eyes, I thought I was going to cry too. He looked helpless and lost. "You're not gonna leave me over this, are you? You won't leave me for him?"

"No." I shook my head. "I'll stick by you."

AT MY APARTMENT that night, Trevor called his parents and told them. They were completely supportive, insisting that they pay all the costs for rehab. His mother got on the internet and found a place that would take him in a week. He stayed the night and slept in my bed, but we only just kissed each other good night.

I spent the next several days helping Trevor get ready to leave for the month he'd be in rehab. He was distant, but I think it was the drugs and his looming fear of the struggle ahead of him.

I talked to Jase every night after I'd leave Trevor's. We basically just laughed at all of his book tour adventures and the growing number of women who were trying to throw themselves at him on a daily basis. I told him Trevor was going to rehab, and instead of reminding me of the parallels to his book, he just said, "Well, at least he's getting it taken care of."

My copy of *All the Roads Between* sat on my dresser and

taunted me all those days. I promised myself that I would wait to read it until Trevor left, when I would be all alone to think about the book and my life and what I wanted to do. I also knew I owed Professor James ten thousand words before I could show my face at work.

I drove Trevor to the rehab facility, which wasn't too far from my apartment, and sat with him until he was all checked in. When it was time for him to go, he kissed me on the cheek. "I hope that we're both thinking more clearly by the time I get out," he said.

"Me too."

"I love you, Emi." It was the first time he had said it while looking me in the eye.

"I love you too." There are so many ways to love. My foster family, my aunts, Cara, Trevor, and Jase had all taught me that.

I went home and opened *All the Roads Between.*

From *All the Roads Between*

"Emerson, can you wipe down tables one last time before you leave?"

"Sure," I said to Cathy, the night manager at the diner where I worked. I had been working graveyard shifts there for over a month, so I had gotten used to the weird hours. Twenty-four-hour diners can attract some interesting people in the wee hours of the morning, but I didn't mind—it was a job.

I'd leave the diner around six a.m., when the sun was coming up beyond the cornfield horizon. Sometimes I'd stand there, watching the sun rise, thinking about Neeble. I hadn't driven out there since I had returned to New Clayton. I just couldn't bring myself to go back. But that morning, as I stood there in the parking lot, I realized it was my birthday.

After finding Jackson's book a month ago, I had thought about our adventures on the old dirt road. I'd thought about all the pain Jackson had endured too, losing his brother and losing me. I hadn't celebrated my birthday in years, but that morning, as I pulled onto the highway headed toward Neeble, I made a pact with myself that I would face my fears. And if I saw Cal Junior, I'd run him over with my car, even though he was probably almost eighty years old by now.

I pulled onto El Monte Road as the sun crept higher in the sky. Each time I passed a mile marker, I called the number out loud. Right where old Carter's egg ranch used to be was a pile of wood scraps next to the skeletal remains of the big chicken house. Beyond that were just miles of dirt and weeds until I got to the five-point-five-mile marker.

I gasped when I saw that there was still a mailbox there. I thought, *Who in their right mind would want to live here?* I pulled onto the dirt road, which had bumps in almost the same exact places it did thirty years before. When I got to the end and saw that the house Jax grew up in was still there, I almost peed my pants. There were two cars parked in front. I pulled off to the side, still about a hundred yards from the house. After turning the engine off and rolling down my window, I sat back and listened. I could hear the trickling sound of the creek, the loud buzzing of cicadas, and nothing else.

Closing my eyes, I thought about Jax and me playing explorers in the field. I could almost hear the triumphant voice of ten-year-old Jax joyously shouting at me as we chased each other around. I looked in the mirror at my pale eyes framed in heavy lines. I wished they were laugh lines, but they were only reminders of the sadness I had endured.

When I finally had the courage to get out of the car, I walked first to the empty, crumbling slab where my father's house sat and then past it to the field, then past the tree line, and down the short embankment to the creek, where our now-dilapidated dock still stood. I ran my hand over our initials. J & E FOREVER.

On my way back toward the road, I was startled by two figures standing near the old shed. It was a woman in her fifties, and behind her, several feet away, stood a much older woman, maybe in her eighties. The younger of the two said, "Can I help you, ma'am?" She was wearing an apron. Her long, gray hair was braided down her back, and her hands were on her hips.

"Um, I was just wondering if you knew of a Jackson Fisher? If maybe he still lived here?"

"He does," she said unemotionally.

"Are you his wife?" I asked.

"Who wants to know?" came a raspy voice from the old woman, who was scrutinizing me.

"My name is Emerson, and I grew up here, in the house that used to be next door." I pointed.

The older woman put her hand over her mouth and gasped.

"I'm not his wife. I'm his caretaker, Alicia," said the younger woman.

The old woman came closer to me, bent, and looked right into my eyes. "It *is* you."

In that moment, I recognized her too. "Don't take this the wrong way, Leila, but I'm actually surprised you made it this long."

"Me too." Her voice and expression softened. She leaned in closer.

"Why does Jax need a caretaker?" I asked.

"Because he's sick, darling."

I felt a searing ache deep in my chest. "Sick with what?"

"Lung cancer," Alicia's voice came from behind.

I didn't take my eyes off Leila. "But you were the smoker."

"Ironic, isn't it?" she said.

"It should have been you." I used the line she'd used on Jax after Brian had drowned. I was so angry and so sad for Jax that I could feel a part of me dying with him already, and I hadn't even seen him yet.

She looked down at the ground. "You're right. I deserve that, but look at me. I'm an old woman full of regrets."

"Me too," I told her as I fought back tears.

I traveled there to see a place I thought had long since been abandoned, but he was still there. *What was he waiting for?* I wondered. "I saw his book. Did he ever write anything else?"

"No, just the one book," Leila said. "After the book failed, he got a job at the glass factory and worked there until he got sick earlier this year."

"Does he have a family?"

"Just me."

I became extremely emotional. Tears were running down my face, and I was having a hard time breathing. Pulling my sunglasses on, I said, "How long does he have?"

Alicia came up next to me and said, "The doctors say it could be months. Could be weeks. Could be any day now. Basically, they don't know."

I fell to my knees, dropped my head into my hands, and cried. Leila, as old as she was, knelt down next to me and held me. Why did he have to be sick? Why couldn't Jackson have gone on and made a beautiful life for himself? I thought I was saving him when I called out to the police that night. I thought loving someone meant letting go, but by the time I learned that loving someone means fighting for them too, it was too late.

For years, I'd fantasized that Jackson had gone on to be rich in life and love and family. I'd dreamed that the old house I was facing on my knees would be demolished, along with all of our past pain, but it wasn't. It was still there waiting for me.

"Can I see him?"

16. About Life?

My eyes were swollen, and my throat ached from being on the verge of tears the entire time I was reading.

Lying in bed, I thought about Trevor and how in the beginning of our relationship he was all passion and flowers and gifts. Even though he wasn't always willing to share his feelings verbally, I knew I meant a lot to him. When I would call, he came. I thought, maybe after rehab, he would go back to that wonderful guy he was when I first met him.

I thought about Jase and our history, and I wondered if it would always be there, lingering, like a creaking wood slat in the floor, to remind us of what we had endured. I texted him late that night.

Me: You up?

Jase: Yes

Me: Can I call you?

Two seconds later, my phone rang. "Hello," I said.

"Hi."

"When I saw my father, he told me to tell you thank you and that he was sorry." I got choked up. "He's sober now, and he was kind."

"How are you so strong, Emiline?"

"Maybe you taught me." I sighed. "Trevor checked into rehab today."

"That's good. You did the right thing by calling him out on it. I'm sure he'll be grateful to you when he's clean. Sometimes people who love us make us do hard things because it's what's right."

"I'm almost done with the book."

"What, are you reading, like, five words an hour?" he teased.

"I'm savoring it, jerk." There was silence, and then I heard him try to stifle a yawn. "You sound tired. Is Andrea there?"

"No, she has her own room, silly. It's late here, but I don't want to get off the phone with you."

"Go to bed, Jase. I'll talk to you soon."

"Okay. Night, Em. Hey, you know what this reminds me of?" he said.

"When I was in foster care and we used to talk late at night?"

"Yeah, exactly . . . I miss you."

"I miss you too. Night, Jase."

He didn't ask if I had made a decision about Trevor. When I thought about it, Jase hadn't even said anything about a relationship between him and me. It seemed obvious, but was I really going to throw away seven years with

Trevor to see if Jase could even handle a real, adult relationship?

IN THE MORNING, Cara was sitting at the breakfast bar, eating cereal and reading a magazine. "I can't believe you're home," she said. "I haven't see you in forever."

"I know. I was helping Trevor."

She stopped eating. "Kinda sad that he went from, like, superstar to super addicted."

"He's not a bad person. He's a little lost, but he's not a loser."

She gave me a sympathetic look. "I know, Emi. So, have you thought more about what you're going to do?"

"Yeah." I sat down next to her. "I'm torn."

"You'll figure it out." She continued eating.

"That's what I've been told."

"Did you write the piece for Professor James yet?" she asked through a mouthful of Cap'n Crunch.

"No, but I will." I hadn't asked Cara anything about her life lately, and I realized I wasn't being a good friend. "What's new with you?"

She stopped chewing and swallowed. Her eyes darted around the room. "Don't hate me, okay?"

"What?" My stomach started turning.

"I got an agent, and one of my stories is being published in the *New Yorker* next month." She made a face like she had eaten a sour grape.

"That's fantastic! Cara, you are so talented. You deserve every bit of it." I hugged her.

"You seem different, Em." Cara had never called me "Em" before she read the book. "You just seem more confident or something."

"Maybe you see me differently now that you know me."

She scowled. "I thought I already knew you."

"No, now that you *really* know me."

"Hmm." She nodded. "Do you think Trevor knows the real you?"

"Probably not. If you really think about it, Trevor and I really don't know each other at all." I walked into the kitchen and poured a glass of wine. "We've kept a lot from one another. He's a good guy, he really is, but I think we've just never gotten to know what makes the other person tick."

"So what are you going to do?"

"I'm going to stand by him. I'm doing the right thing. We'll figure it out."

THE NEXT DAY, I tried to visit Trevor in rehab, but they told me it wasn't family and friends day and that he was in that crucial period of detoxing.

Later in the afternoon, he was able to call me.

"Hello," I said.

"Hi, hello, how are you?"

I barely recognized his voice. "You okay, Trevor?"

"Not really. My shoulder is fucking killing me. The food here is disgusting, and the people are assholes."

"I'm really sorry," I said genuinely.

"No, you're not. If you were sorry you would have

helped before calling my parents, but you just wanted to get rid of me so you could go back to your precious Jase, even though I've been the one by your side listening to you whine about your terrible writing all these years."

Be strong, Em.

"Okay, Trevor, that's enough." I knew he was sick and being irrational.

"I can't believe I wasted all these years with you." He was getting progressively meaner. Growing up around my dad had taught me how to react to addicts, but the words still hurt, even if I didn't show it.

"I love you and you love me."

"No, Emi, you're wrong. I nothing you."

I hung up and reminded myself once again that it was the drugs talking.

My second conversation with him wasn't any better. But by the third time we talked, almost ten days after he started rehab, his tone had changed. He seemed tired, but I could tell he was coming around.

"Hello?" I said.

"Hi." His voice was low, soft, and distant.

"How are you feeling?" I asked.

"I'm tired. I've had a hard time sleeping, and my arm hurts pretty bad." He took a deep breath. "They're bringing in a physical therapy specialist to try to help me get it straightened out without drugs."

"Oh, Trevor, I'm so glad to hear that. I want nothing more than for you to feel strong again."

"Thanks, Emi. Can I call you in a couple of days when I have more energy?"

"Sure. Love you."

"Love you too."

By the end of Trevor's third week in rehab, I had written twenty thousand words basically chronicling my discovery of *All the Roads Between*, and how I'd found Jase at the bookstore. I had turned in ten thousand words to Professor James earlier in the month, and I was finally walking to his office to meet with him.

"Hello, sir."

He grinned. "Well, well, well, if it isn't our resident memoirist."

I swallowed. "That's not what I had planned."

"Have a seat."

"I never really thought of it as a memoir," I said as I sat down.

"You don't need to hide behind anything, Emiline. You've got it all here. Have you settled back into work?"

"Yes. Thanks again for letting me take that time off. I really needed it."

He leaned back in his leather chair and scratched his beard. "Finish this up. Once you're ready, I can help you make the contacts you need to get this published."

"Thank you, Professor. Do you really think it's worthy?"

He answered slowly. "That remains to be seen. For now, just finish it."

"I can't thank you enough." I stood and took the pages from him.

I wasn't writing a true memoir—more like a roman à clef about a girl who discovers a book about a woman who discovers a book about what could have been, which sounded damn confusing, but it wasn't. The catch was that I *was* her. I was all of those people. I was every possibility; I just had to decide how my story would end.

BY THE FOURTH week of rehab, I finally went to visit Trevor in person. It was time. I drove to the New Beginnings Facility by the Beach and waited to be checked in. There was a long hallway that led to the back pool and patio, which sat high on cliffs overlooking La Jolla.

One of the receptionists told me to go ahead and head toward the pool, where Trevor would be waiting, but as soon as I turned around, I saw him walking in my direction. He looked so different. He was thinner but looked strong, and his hair was cropped short. But the best part was that he was smiling his warm, proud Trevor smile. I ran to him. He held his arms out and caught me. I was hesitant about his throwing arm, but he held me so tight to his body that I actually whimpered.

"Oh fuck, I missed you," he said.

I stepped back and scanned him. "Let me look at you. God, you look amazing, Trevor."

"Thank you. I feel so much better. Let's go hang out by the pool. Hey, do you want to stay and watch my therapy session today? It's pretty cool. I'm using my arm a lot more."

"Yeah, I would love to."

He led me outside. We sat in lounge chairs and talked about his recovery and how well he was doing. He said he had talked to his old coach from Cal about an assistant coaching position for the next season, and it looked promising. We watched the ocean, and after a while, my mind wandered to Jase. To my left, there was a couple standing in a gazebo kissing. I realized Trevor and I hadn't kissed yet.

I glanced over at him. He was smiling and tapping his foot to the soft jazz music they were pumping from the outdoor speakers. "How about you, Emi? How are you doing?"

"I'm good. I started writing again."

"Oh." His expression fell. "About what I said on the phone, I didn't mean it at all. I hope you know that I think you're a great writer."

"You don't have to apologize."

"Actually, I do—it's part of the deal here." He took my hand and looked me in the eye. "I'm sorry."

I smiled. "I forgive you." And I did.

"Thank you. It means a lot to me." He leaned back. "So, have you talked to Jase?"

"I have. We're friends. We have a strange past with each other, and it's kind of connected us all these years, but I made a promise to you. And I love you."

He nodded and then looked down at his feet and frowned. "Do you have the time?" he said quietly.

I looked at my phone. "It's three."

"Okay, let's head over to the gym for my therapy." We didn't say much as I followed him down a few long hallways. We entered a large room with weights and pads and several people bustling through, doing their workouts. A tall woman in her late twenties, with long blonde braided hair, came walking toward us. She bounced a little as she walked, and I could tell from her body that she was fit, even in her ill-fitting khaki pants and regulation polo. I looked at her and thought, *She is a glass-half-full kind of person.* I knew it before she even opened her mouth.

"Emiline, so nice to meet you. I'm Melissa." She stuck her hand out. "Trevor speaks so highly of you." We shook hands.

Smiling, I said, "Nice to meet you too." What I really wanted to say was, *Trevor's never mentioned you*, but she was so nice that I couldn't be rude.

I glanced at Trevor and noticed he hadn't taken his eyes off of Melissa. He wasn't ogling her or staring at her breasts; I could just tell that she simply had his attention.

"Come on, we'll start over here," she said.

Trevor lifted weights and did mobility and range-of-motion exercises with her. Her hands were on him a lot though throughout the session. He seemed really proud of himself and happy.

"You can get to twenty, Trev," she said as he lifted a small dumbbell above his head. When he hit twenty, she shouted, "See, I told you!" I clapped, but she seemed genuinely happy for him. They had accomplished something together. I noticed she wasn't wearing a wedding band, or even a tawdry promise ring.

After the session, they high-fived each other, and I thought that it seemed like the beginning of a nice friendship.

Back outside, near the pool, I said, "Do you like her? Melissa?"

"Yeah, she's great. I wouldn't be able to get through this without her."

"That's not really what I mean."

He swallowed, and his smile faded. "What do you mean? I haven't touched her, if that's what you're getting at. Not only would I not do that, but I'm sure it's highly unacceptable behavior for a therapist to start cavorting with her rehab patients."

"I'm not implying that either. I'm just wondering . . . if she wasn't your physical therapist and you weren't in recovery, would you . . ."

"There's a spark, but that's it."

I stood up. "Can I hug you, Trevor?" He stood instantly and took me in his arms. I knew what was coming, and I knew it would hurt like hell, but I had to do it.

"What is it, Emi?"

I sniffled. "When you're out of here in a week and you're not in recovery and you're not her patient, you should see about the spark."

His arms tightened around me. "What are you talking about?"

"Trevor, I love you. I want to be in your life. I want to see you through this." I stepped out of his embrace and looked up into his sympathetic eyes. "But you know that when you think of a wife, you don't think of me." He looked down at his shoes. "It's okay," I said. "This could be the best thing for us, after it stops being the worst."

Stepping forward, he reached out and pulled me into his arms again and then buried his face in my neck. "I know you're right. I read the book, you know. While you were away. I've never been jealous of him, really. I just didn't want to see you hurt anymore. I care about you."

"But you know we aren't right for each other, right?"

He nodded. "I do."

"Will we be friends?"

"You are my friend. Now. You brought me here and saved me, and I want you in my life too."

He held my hand as he walked me to the front. Near the door, he bent, kissed my cheek, and whispered, "Thank you."

"Stick with it, number seventeen." I socked him in the chest.

"'Bye, Emi."

As I walked to my car, I said good-bye to Emi, the girl who begrudgingly went to frat parties and football games; the girl who pretended like everything was always okay while unenthusiastically teaching Intro to Writing classes; the girl with no past; the girl who wasn't real and didn't exist.

Once I got back to my apartment, I sat down and started writing.

17. How We See Ourselves

Over the next month, I did nothing but work, write, and send updates to Professor James, Cara, and Jase.

One morning, after I finished the full first draft, I got an email from Andrea. She told me that Professor James had reached out to her about my book, and that she wanted to talk. I sped all the way to campus and ran through the halls to the professor's office, where Cara was chatting with him eagerly.

"Hey, girl," she said. "Looking for me?"

I didn't look at her. "Professor," I said, out of breath.

Before I could get anything out, he said, "I knew she was J. Colby's agent and that she'd probably give it a look if you'd let her. You're a better writer today than you were five years ago, and that means my job here is done." He got up.

"Wait," I said.

"Really there's nothing to say. Cara is well on her way out, and you . . . you have a book in its infancy, but a book nonetheless. Go forth and write, my dears. You've got the whole summer ahead of you. If you want to remain here, Emiline, I will gladly keep you on staff, but I have a feeling that won't be happening."

"Thank you, thank you so much!"

"Go, both of you, get out of here." He chuckled a husky, warm laugh from his belly.

Cara looped her arm in mine as we headed toward the parking lot. "See, I told you."

"Thanks for putting up with my shit this year, Cara. You've been a really good friend."

She stopped walking. "What do you think about moving to New York with me? Let's do it, Em. Let's totally live the life and be writers."

I laughed. "It does sound amazing. But you're moving in with Henry, no?"

She shook her head. "I'll be with Henry, but we're not moving in together right away. He's busy becoming a surgeon, and I'll need some time to get myself established there. What do you say? Roomies?"

"I'll definitely think about it." It did sound enticing, the freedom to finally be able to be me.

And I did think about it. I thought about it until there was no other answer.

I was going.

18. Everyone Around You

By July first, Cara and I were the proud renters of a tiny two-bedroom apartment in New York's East Village. We spent the next few weeks unpacking, settling down, and exploring the city together.

Strangely, she and Henry were through almost immediately. She discovered, pretty much right away, that their relationship worked better long-distance, and that Henry didn't have time for a girlfriend. To be fair, she didn't have time for a boyfriend either. Her agent was riding her to put together a collection of short stories, and she spent as much time writing as Henry spent saving people's lives.

One weekend, while we were unpacking, she pointed to a stack of boxes that I had tossed to the side. "Do you want me to take these down to the Dumpster? I think this is the last of it."

"Yeah, but will you make sure I emptied everything out of them?"

"This one still has books in it." She pulled a stack of

three books out of the last box. "It's Jase's book." She looked at the bookmark tucked into the very end. "You never finished it?"

"Not yet. I've been so focused on my own book. Here, hand it over to me." I took it into my bedroom and set it on my nightstand.

A little while later, Cara came back up, but she wasn't alone. She was with a jeans-clad, bearded gentleman wearing suspenders, and both of them were carrying mugs. "Em, this is our neighbor, Kai." She stood behind him and wiggled her eyebrows. "He offered me a cup of coffee, and it's the best-tasting coffee I've ever had in my entire life."

I got up and walked over to shake his hand. "I'm Emiline. Nice to meet you."

"Likewise," he said.

"So what's your secret?" I pointed to his mug.

"Oh, the coffee? Yeah, I just make sure to always heat it to a hundred and sixty-four degrees, and I always use filtered water." Cara had found herself a hipster, and she was glowing because of it. She was staring at him like he was some kind of celestial coffee being sent to her from heaven.

"Well, I'll have to try that little trick, "I said. "So you live right next door?"

"Yeah," Kai said. "Just little old me. I'm a graphic artist and I work from home, so if you ever need anything, let me know."

"Great." I smiled.

"What do you do for fun around here?" Cara asked.

"Well, tonight I'm going into Brooklyn to the Dropzone to see my friend's band play."

"Cara, you should go," I said. "I have a bunch of stuff I still need to do here."

THAT NIGHT WHEN Cara came home, she told me how Kai had introduced her to a husband-and-wife musical duo who also owned the coffee shop on the corner. Cara made friends fast—she always had—and she was excited about New York. I saw her fitting in and living here forever. I, on the other hand, felt lonely and more isolated every minute I stayed.

Over the next several weeks, Cara and Kai became inseparable, and I became more depressed. Cara said writers are supposed to be a little depressed, but I didn't believe that. When I was down, I couldn't write.

I talked to Jase every few days. When I told him how I was feeling, he said it was because I was still fighting it. I knew what he meant, but I didn't let him press it. The old woman in the airport, and her words about fighting fate, were always in the back of my mind.

It was after a strange nightmare I had where I was looking in the mirror examining my old, wrinkled face that I realized it was time to finish the book. I could feel myself crying in the dream, but the old face wasn't moving. I was so scared that would be me, just paralyzed by the fear, paralyzed in one moment of time while the rest of the world was moving on.

We can't always control our circumstances, who our parents are, where we live, or how much money we make, but in those rare moments when we can shape our fate, when we do have the power to make our own happiness, we can't be too scared to do it.

From *All the Roads Between*

Alicia led me into Jax's house and into the living room. The old carpet had been replaced with wood laminate flooring, and there was a hospital bed set up facing the TV. I couldn't see him at first, but I could hear an oxygen machine and the sound of a man's labored breathing.

Leila had wandered down the hall to her bedroom, and Alicia motioned for me to go to him. "Wait," I whispered. "Can I use the restroom?"

"Sure." She pointed down the hallway.

I went into the bathroom. It had been remodeled in recent years, but the setup was the same. I thought about the last time I was in there. I was fifteen years old and Jax had just told me what Cal Junior had done. Jax found me crying in the shower. He held me, and he took care of me, even though he was the one who had been through something horrible.

In the mirror, a face I barely recognized anymore stared back at me. I dug around in my purse for some lip gloss. I applied a thin coat and then finger-combed my hair, trying desperately to tame it. I didn't know what to expect, but even thirty-five years older, I wanted to look nice for him.

I walked slowly down the hall. I peeked into Brian's old room, which Alicia now occupied. She was sitting at a desk, facing me in the doorway. "Go ahead, go see him," she said.

Making my way into the living room, I noticed the TV was still on, but it had been turned down. I went to the side of his bed. His eyes were closed, and he was wearing an oxygen mask.

I took in his appearance. He still had a full head of hair, but he was completely gray. He was thin and sickly, but I could see my Jax in his face. Standing at his bedside I took his hand in mine.

He opened his eyes and squinted and then smiled. Like no time had passed, he smiled at me with perfect recognition and reverence, the way he always had. With his other hand he pulled the oxygen mask away from his face and said, "Took you long enough."

I started to cry and laugh at the same time. "Oh, Jax." I cupped his face and kissed his cheek. "My Jax," I cried. "Why? Why did this happen?"

"Please don't cry, Em." No one had called me that in over thirty years. He started to cough.

"Don't talk. Here," I said as I pulled the oxygen mask back onto his face.

I reached in my purse and took out his book that I had found in the thrift store. "I only just found this recently," I told him. "It wasn't us; it wasn't our story."

He slowly pulled the mask away again. His eyes were sad. "It could have been. I wanted it to be."

"I'm so sorry."

"Please tell me you had a good life, Em."

"I had a good life," I lied. I had to give that to him because he deserved it. If I told him it was horrible, everything we'd done would have been in vain.

"My beautiful girl has come back to me, finally."

"But it's too late." Tears were now running steadily down both our faces.

"Help me sit up," he said. "I have something for you. Will you call Alicia in here?"

Alicia was there as soon as I turned around. "The box, Alicia," Jax said. "The small red box on my desk."

When Alicia returned, she handed him the ring box. "What is that, Jax?" I said.

"What do you think?" He laughed then coughed.

"Slow down," I warned him. Alicia left the room.

"No, listen. I don't know how much time I have. You said we were too young, remember? You said we needed to be apart. It was best for us. I never wrote another book because I needed you. I needed my friend. Now we're here, and we're not too young anymore. I want to write another book, but I need you with me. I need you to help me." He opened the ring box to reveal a gold band.

"Oh, Jax, I've only just walked through your door."

"Jesus, Emerson. Did you hear me? I don't know how much time I have left." He laughed and coughed again. "How much longer are you gonna make me wait?" He took a breath from the mask. "Marry me, dammit. Spend the rest of my short life with me. Do whatever you want after that, but stay here and marry me. We'll sit outside and listen to the creek and we'll make up stories like we always did before."

It was still him, my old friend, my protector, the love of my life. As sick as he looked, he was still sharp as a whip. "I will marry you, Jackson Fisher." I pressed my lips to his. "I will take care of you now. I'm sorry I waited so long," I whispered.

WE DID EXACTLY what we promised each other. I moved back to the long dirt road. A pastor from a local church came to the house and married us, with Alicia and Leila as our witnesses. Every day I would wheel Jax out to the back porch and we'd listen to the cicadas buzzing over the sound of the creek in the distance. He would make up stories and I would write them down. I planted a garden and turned the shed into a little writing hut while Jax watched me from his porch. He still had a sense of humor and told me I was more interesting to look at than the TV. I said that meant a lot coming from him.

Doctors said he was beyond treatment and that we just had to make him as comfortable as possible.

He and I watched every sunset together until he was gone. Five weeks after I first went to see him, he died in my arms.

I don't know much about fate, but I know something brought me back there. Maybe I fought that force for too long, or maybe everything happened exactly the way it was supposed to.

The last words out of Jackson Fisher's mouth as I held him were, "There once was a boy and a girl . . . ."

The end.

For my Em. Don't wait this long. Come let me love you.

19. Until You Know It's Right

Cara was standing in my doorway. "Are you okay? You look pale."

"Pale" was an understatement. I was hyperventilating. "I just finished the book."

"Ohhh." She smiled.

"So. I have to pack my shit. I've got to go." I got up and started running around the room, throwing all my stuff in bags.

"Slow down, Em."

"No, I'm not wasting another minute." I was frantically tossing junk into the garbage and yanking my clothes off the hangers in my closet. "I'll pay rent until you find a roommate."

"Actually." A man's voice came from the hall. Kai peeked his head into the room and looked at Cara. "What do you think?" he said to her. "You want to live with me, Cara?"

"Really?" she screamed. She ran and jumped into his arms. "You're gonna move in with me?"

He twirled her around. "This apartment is way better, and why wait?"

I pointed to them. "Exactly," I said triumphantly. "Why wait if you know it's right?"

They laughed as they watched me dancing around the apartment. "I'm going to write a happy love story," I sang. "About a girl and a boy. But first I have to find the boy!"

I STOOD IN the doorway with a giant suitcase and said good-bye to my very short but eye-opening New York experience. Cara and Kai hugged me and promised they'd have all my stuff shipped to L.A. as soon as I had an address.

At the airport, I paid way too much money for a direct flight, but I didn't care. On the plane, I had a smile on my face until we started taxiing toward the runway. That's when I realized I was terrified. The man next to me asked if I was okay as I gripped the armrest during takeoff.

"Yeah. It's weird, I've never been scared to fly before."

He looked like he was a seasoned flyer, possibly on business. "What are you scared of?"

"Well, crashing, obviously."

He laughed and put his finger to his mouth. "You don't want to say that word too loud around here. I meant, what's changed? What are you scared of now?"

"I have no idea."

I ordered a drink and put my headphones on. When my Bloody Mary came, I downed it, relaxed a little, and then closed my eyes. All I could think about was Jase, being in his arms, laughing with him, talking about books. It was all I could think about.

I pulled my headphones off. "I got it!" I said loudly.

The man next to me looked startled at first, and then he smiled. "Let's hear it."

"I'm in love, like the real kind. I just don't want to miss a second of it, that's why I'm so scared. I'm afraid I won't get to tell him how I feel and . . . and . . . I'm excited about my life. That's why."

He nodded. "Makes sense. Chances are he already knows you love him, but it's always nice to tell someone."

I pulled Jase's book out of my bag. "He wrote a book for me, and then I moved away. He might not know."

He took the book from my hands and stared at it. "This is impressive. I saw this in the bookstore. So it's about you?"

"No, no, it's *for* me."

"Ah, I see. He wrote a book for you and you took off." He chuckled. "I must admit that would be a shot to the ego."

I waved at the air. "Oh, his ego is fine. But I do need to tell him I'm ready now and I don't want to spend one more minute going backward."

"It's quite the honor to have a book dedicated to you, isn't it?"

I laughed. "He wrote the book to help me heal."

"Okay."

I was beginning to think this guy believed I was an author stalker or something.

"Anyway, I'm just excited to get back to him. He's been patient with me."

"Well, you know that saying: if you love something, let it go."

I shook my head. "No, I don't believe that. Jase fought for me. Not with his fists, but with this—his words." I held up the book. "He didn't let me go. He never let me go. He just gave me the right amount of space, and now it's time for me to find him."

He smiled kindly while nodding his head. "He sounds like a good guy."

The plane dipped. "Ahhh!" I screamed. The seat belt lights went on and the flight attendants scurried to their seats.

The man grabbed my hand. "It's turbulence," he said.

"This is bad, bad turbulence." The plane started diving. "Oh my god, we're going down!" My seat was shaking and my heart was beating so hard I could feel it in my ears.

"Shhh, stop that. You're gonna scare the life out of these people. This is normal. The pilots are trying to find some better airspace."

He put his arm around me. I looked up at his nicely coifed gray hair, clean-shaven face, and crystal clear blue eyes. I guessed he was in his fifties but took extremely good care of himself. "Thank you," I whispered.

"It's okay. I have a daughter about your age. She doesn't like flying either." The plane evened out.

"Geez, it's like I finally figure things out and the next thing I know I'm barreling toward the earth in a fireball."

"My daughter is also very dramatic," he said.

I laughed. The nerves were settling. "Is she a writer?"

"No, a painter."

At the same time, we both said, "Artist."

LATER, AS WE were exiting into the jetway, the man waved good-bye and then turned back and said, "I hope it's everything you want it to be."

"What?" I asked.

"The rest of your life."

I thought it was a nice sentiment, but I couldn't help but say, "Well, we won't really know until the very end, will we?"

"Touché," he said.

As I waited in the rental car line, I texted Jase for his address and he sent it to me. I told him to be expecting a delivery in about thirty minutes.

I rented a subcompact car, and to my absolute delight, the Avis guy pulled up in a shiny red jelly bean, just for me.

Jase's beach house was a small cottage at the end of the world, right on the edge, where you can see only ocean and the vast nothingness of empty skies. I jogged to the front door right as he swung it open.

"Jesus, fuck, took you long enough," he said.

"I'm here."

"Man, you read slowly. We have to work on that."

Right there in the doorway, we kissed and kissed and kissed until I pulled away, yanked his stupid book out of my purse, and said, "This isn't us!"

"It could have been, though," he said.

"But it won't be."

Epilogue

We live in that little cottage to this day. We write and we kiss and we do other stuff too. There are no TVs in our house. Jase taught me how to look out at the ocean and imagine whatever I wanted to.

About three months after I moved in, he said, "Do you want to live here with me forever?"

"At least nine months out of the year."

"What will we do for the other three?"

"You can still do math, doofus. I'm impressed."

We were sitting in chairs, watching the sun go down. "Your hair is flying everywhere, Medusa. If I touch it, will it bite me?"

"You never had abs. I still can't believe you wrote that."

He chuckled. "It's fiction, baby. What's on your mind? Why can't we travel more?"

"We can travel during the summers, but during the school year, we'll have to be home."

"I thought you were giving up teaching," he said.

"It's not for me."

"I wouldn't be caught dead in a classroom, you know that." He was laughing. He already knew. Jase always had foresight, and we weren't characters in anyone's book.

"Not for you either," I said.

He leaned in, kissed me, and then put his hand on my belly.

He already knew.

Acknowledgments

Thank you to my devoted readers, some of whom I now call friends. There's nothing I love doing more than writing. I'm so grateful to you for keeping me at it.

To Judith, Jhanteigh, Tory, Jackie, Jin, and the rest of the Atria gang, thank you for getting behind my books and giving me this opportunity.

Christina, you've been here from the beginning and I appreciate your hard work so much. I'm also mind-blown by your vast knowledge of idioms.

And of course, thank you to everyone at Jane Rotrosen for all you do.

To my friends and family, from now on, I'll try to keep it to thirty seconds. That's a promise, but you know how much I love to tell a story. Thank you for loving me and for listening to my meandering tales.

Thank you to Crystal and Dani for making sh@# happen. You're both rock stars. Period.

To Sam and Tony, Mommy isn't crazy. I'm just formulating the next chapter . . . sometimes out loud . . . to myself . . . while I make pancakes. You ARE the joy of my life and the best teachers I'll ever have. I love you.

Finally, to Anthony, it really IS true! You are, were, and will always be the just one person I write for.